Eric Wilson
Canadian Mysteries
VOLUME 1

Books by Eric Wilson

The Tom and Liz Austen Mysteries

Also available by Eric Wilson

Summer of Discovery
The Unmasking of 'Ksan

Eric Wilson
Canadian Mysteries
VOLUME 1

MURDER ON THE CANADIAN

THE CASE OF THE GOLDEN BOY

THE LOST TREASURE OF CASA LOMA

ERIC WILSON

HarperTrophyCanada™
An imprint of HarperCollinsPublishersLtd

As in his other mysteries, Eric Wilson writes here about imaginary people in a real landscape.

Find Eric Wilson at www.ericwilson.com

Eric Wilson Canadian Mysteries, Volume 1
Copyright © 2010 by Eric Wilson Enterprises, Inc.
Murder on The Canadian © 1976, 2003 by Eric Wilson Enterprises, Inc.
The Case of the Golden Boy © 1994, 2003 by Eric Wilson Enterprises, Inc.
The Lost Treasure of Casa Loma © 1979, 2003 by Eric Wilson Enterprises, Inc.
All rights reserved.

Chapter Illustrations for *Murder on the Canadian* and *The Case of the Golden Boy* by Richard Row.
Chapter Illustrations for *The Lost Treasure of Casa Loma* by Susan Tooke.

Published by Harper*Trophy*Canada™, an imprint of
HarperCollins Publishers Ltd

HarperCollins books may be purchased for educational, business, or sales promotional use through our Special Markets Department.

HarperCollins Publishers Ltd
2 Bloor Street East, 20th Floor
Toronto, Ontario, Canada
M4W 1A8

www.harpercollins.ca

Murder on The Canadian. First published in hardcover by Clarke, Irwin & Co. Ltd and The Bodley Head (Canada) Ltd: 1976. First Collins paperback edition: 1983. First HarperCollins Publishers Ltd edition: 1991.
The Case of the Golden Boy. First published in paperback by HarperCollins Publishers Ltd: 1994. Revised HarperCollins Publishers Ltd paperback edition: 1996.
The Lost Treasure of Casa Loma. First published by General Paperbacks: 1982. First HarperCollins Publishers Ltd paperback edition: 2005.
These three books first published in this omnibus edition: 2010.

Library and Archives Canada Cataloguing in Publication information is available upon request.

ISBN 978-1-55468-822-7

Printed in the United States of America
RRD 9 8 7 6 5 4 3 2 1

Conten

Murder on *The (*

The Case of the G

The Lost Treasure o

Murder on
The Canadian

For Mum and Dad
with love

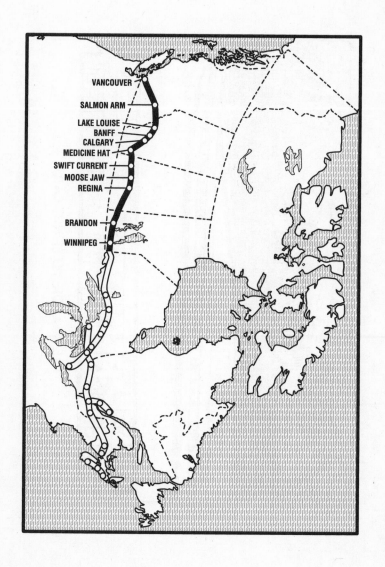

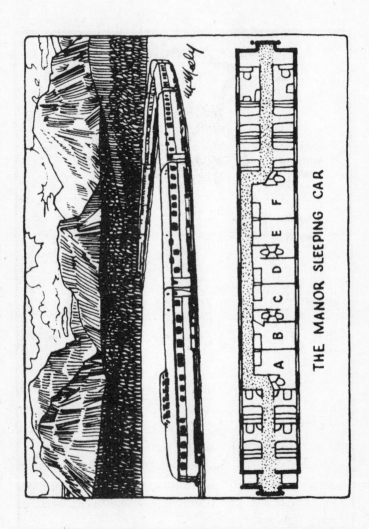

THE MANOR SLEEPING CAR

1

The package was ticking.

A bomb. Yes, Tom was sure it must be a bomb. He studied the plain brown paper, then leaned his head close.

Tick. Tick. Tick.

Frightened, Tom looked around the crowded railway station. What to do? If he yelled "Bomb!" it might cause a panic, a rush to the doors in which women and children would be crushed underfoot.

Again, Tom studied the package which had appeared mysteriously beside his suitcase minutes ago when he'd gone to the washroom. It looked innocent, but the ticking meant it was deadly.

Tom spotted a man in a conductor's uniform across the station. He ran forward, pushing through the crowds of people waiting to board the train, and grabbed the man's arm.

"Please, sir," he said, panting, "please come quickly!"

The man looked down at Tom with huge blue eyes magnified by thick glasses. "What?" he said, cupping a hand around his ear.

"Help!" Tom said, afraid to shout there was a bomb.

The man shook his head. "Can't hear you, sonny. Station too noisy."

The conductor lost interest in Tom and returned to writing on a pad. For a wild second Tom thought he should get out, save his own life, then he snatched the conductor's pad and ran.

"You little devil!" the man shouted.

Faces turned, staring at the flash of Tom's red hair as he darted past, the conductor close behind. The man was a fast runner and had almost caught Tom when he reached his suitcase.

The package was gone.

Impossible. Tom grabbed his suitcase, looking behind it for the missing bomb, and then the conductor grabbed Tom.

"You little brat!" he shouted.

Now everything was confusion. The conductor tore his notepad from Tom's hand; excited people pushed close to watch; a dog began to bark, and Tom found the bomb.

In the hands of Dietmar Oban. Yes, Tom's rival held the package, a wicked grin on his face as he pushed close among the crowd of onlookers.

Tom had been tricked, and now he knew that the ticking "bomb" was really just an old alarm clock.

Feeling stupid, Tom looked up at the angry conductor.

"Please, sir," he said weakly, "I can explain everything."

"I'll have the police on you!"

"Yes, but . . ."

From above, a loudspeaker boomed: "All passengers board the train." The onlookers hesitated, hating to leave the excitement Tom had caused, then turned and shuffled away. The conductor's huge blue eyes stared down at Tom.

"No more trouble, sonny, or you'll end up behind bars."

"Yes, sir," Tom said.

He watched the conductor walk away, then whirled to grab Dietmar, but he was gone. Shaking his head, Tom picked up his suitcase and started toward the platform doors.

Happily, the excitement of the coming trip returned quickly to Tom. Reaching the platform he found a thrilling scene. Redcaps rushed past with piles of luggage, the loudspeaker buzzed with announcements, and porters in white jackets chatted together as passengers hurried by.

But the greatest thrill of all was the train. Huge, hissing steam, its stainless steel body gleaming under the platform lights, *The Canadian* lay like a giant along the tracks, waiting impatiently to hurl itself forward into the coming adventure. Tom shivered with the beauty of the train. He wanted to stand and stare, but the diesel's whistle blasted and he hurried to the nearest car.

"Ticket, please," a porter said, the words whistling

through a gap between his front teeth. Tom studied the old man's face, hoping he would be a friend on the trip.

"I'll take that, sir," the porter said, reaching for Tom's suitcase and leading the way up into the car. They pushed inside through a door marked Sherwood Manor, passed some tiny roomettes, then walked along a corridor with a row of blue doors.

"What's in there?" Tom asked the porter.

"Bedrooms," he answered, "for folks with money."

Around a bend they came to seats facing each other in pairs. The porter shoved Tom's suitcase under a seat.

"This is your place," he said. "When we leave Winnipeg, I'll pull these two seats together and make them into a bed. Have a pleasant journey, Mr. Austen."

Tom smiled at the porter, then looked across the aisle at a man and woman who sat in another pair of seats.

"Hello, young fellow," said the man, whose thumbs were hooked inside wide suspenders, "where you bound?"

"British Columbia. I'm going to spend the summer with my grandparents."

The woman held out a large tin. "Have one of my cookies?" she asked, smiling at Tom.

"Yes, please."

"Your friend ate four."

"My friend?"

"The boy you're travelling with." She pointed under Tom's seat. "There's his suitcase, beside yours."

"Oh no," Tom whispered to himself, afraid to look. He knelt down beside the suitcase, and shuddered when he read the label: Dietmar Oban.

The woman was beaming as Tom stood up. "Such a nice boy," she said. "A bit thin, but my chocolate chip cookies will soon build him up."

What unbelievably bad luck, trapped with Dietmar Oban! A beautiful trip ruined, but at least he could start it by getting Dietmar for that bomb trick. Tom turned to the woman.

"Which way did the dirty rat go?" he demanded.

A frown crossed the woman's face, and she firmly closed the lid of the cookie tin before saying coldly, "To the dome."

"Thanks." Tom didn't know what the dome was, but it was no use asking the woman anything more. Seeing a door in the end of the car, he went through it, crossed a narrow platform, and pushed open a second door. In this car people sat drinking coffee at tiny tables; beyond them, a flight of carpeted stairs led up into darkness.

Up into the dome?

Tom climbed up cautiously, afraid of what the darkness might hold, but he relaxed when he found two long rows of seats surrounded by huge, curved windows. Through these windows, he could see the lights of the station and, straight above, the night sky. Neat!

And there was a bonus: Dietmar Oban was in one of the seats. Tom tiptoed forward, slipped into the seat beside Dietmar, and grabbed his arm.

"You fink," Tom hissed, "I've got you."

Dietmar jumped, and turned to Tom with wide eyes. "Take it easy, Austen, it was just a joke."

"I ought to rub you out," Tom said, squeezing his rival's skinny arm.

"Listen, Austen, I can give you a mystery to solve."

"You're lying, to save your skin."

"I'm not. Let go of my arm, and I'll tell you."

Tom hesitated, gave a final squeeze that made Dietmar wince, then let him go. A mystery was better than revenge any day.

"What is it?" Tom asked. "Shake your news and pour it out."

Dietmar laughed. "You and your detective talk, Austen. You sound nuts."

"Just give me the facts, Oban."

Dietmar pointed to a man sitting across the dome car. "See that guy?"

"Yeah." The man's grey hair and dark business suit looked ordinary enough. "What about him?"

"Go sit beside him, and you'll see the mystery."

Tom got out of his seat, walked along the narrow aisle and sat beside the man. Wanting to avoid suspicion, he yawned and stretched his arms, then pretended to fall asleep. He counted to thirty in his head, then opened his eyes in a narrow slit: there was a handcuff on the man's wrist!

Tom gasped, and the man turned toward him, but Tom pretended to be mumbling in his sleep and began to snore gently. He waited for the man to relax, then opened his eyes again. Yes, a handcuff was attached to the man's wrist, then a short chain ran to a second handcuff, which was locked to the handle of a black attaché case resting on the man's lap. Tom could see a small combination lock on the case, but there was no indication of what might be inside.

Tom pretended to wake up slowly, smacking his lips

and stretching his arms, then he slid out of the seat and returned to Dietmar's side.

"I saw that guy come up here," Dietmar whispered, "and I figured you'd want to investigate him."

Tom looked suspiciously at Dietmar. "You making fun of me?"

"No, I mean it. I know you want to solve crimes when you grow up. What is it you want to be?"

"A gumshoe. That's a detective, like the Hardy Boys."

"Well, gumboot, now you've got a real puzzle on your hands."

Tom shot a dirty look at Dietmar. The most sarcastic kid in Queenston School, and here he was sharing Tom's train trip. Still, he had found a good mystery to solve.

"You know what I figure?" Tom whispered.

"What?"

"That guy's a jewel thief."

Dietmar leaned forward to study the man. "I think you're right. He looks just like a thief I saw on a TV mystery."

"He's got his tools in that attaché case. A skeleton key for opening bedroom doors and a blowtorch to open safes. He's got the case handcuffed to his wrist so no one can open it accidentally and find out he's a thief."

"What are you going to do?"

"Keep him under surveillance. He may be planning to rob some rich people during the trip."

Music had been flowing like thick syrup from a speaker in the front of the dome car. Now it stopped, and a man's voice came out: "Good evening, ladies and gentlemen. *The Canadian* is ready to depart. We hope you enjoy your journey." More music, then the car shook as the big diesel engine started forward.

"Look," Tom said, pointing through a window at the front of the dome, "you can see the whole train."

Both boys stood up to get a better view along the backs of stainless steel cars to the engine, which sent spurts of exhaust smoke into the air as it strained against the tremendous weight of the train. Slowly, slowly, *The Canadian* rolled forward and then began to pick up speed.

Ahead, signal lights flashed from green to red as the engine rumbled past, its steel wheels banging through a series of switches; to each side, rows of boxcars stood in black lines, beyond them the lights of the city. Tom and Dietmar remained on their feet, looking out the big windows, until the train left Winnipeg behind and slipped into the vast darkness of the prairie.

Tom trembled. "It's so black out here," he whispered. "It's creepy."

Dietmar laughed. "The great detective, afraid of the dark."

Tom blushed, and was about to slug Dietmar, when something strange caught his eye. The mysterious man, hearing Dietmar say "detective," had turned in their direction and now his eyes were staring at Tom. Then, suddenly, he swung out of his seat and quickly left the dome, the chain at his wrist clinking softly as he passed the two boys.

2

"You banana," Tom whispered, "now he knows I'm a detective."

"Are you going to tail him?"

"I'd better."

Tom ran quickly down the stairs. Looking through the windows of the connecting doors, he saw the man standing in the sleeping-car, talking to the old porter. As Tom watched, the porter shook his head; the man, looking angry, turned and disappeared in the direction of the corridor with the blue bedroom doors.

Tom hurried into the sleeping-car. "Excuse me, sir," he said to the porter, "where can I find that man you just spoke to?"

"Bedroom A," the porter said, then looked carefully at Tom. "Why?"

"Oh, he, uh, dropped something."

The porter studied Tom's face, then returned to preparing berths for the night. Tom walked on slowly, uncertain how Frank and Joe Hardy would handle this case, then decided to wait around and hope for a break. Perhaps he could catch a glimpse of burglar tools.

Tom saw no sign of the man in the long corridor, but at the far end was the most beautiful woman he had ever seen. Tom stopped, staring, as the woman approached, one arm supporting a man who was very drunk.

Neither seemed to notice Tom as they came slowly forward, being thrown back and forth by the motion of the speeding train. Tom glanced for a moment at the man's bloodshot eyes, then looked with awe at the woman's shining blond hair and violet-coloured eyes. She was marvellous.

Reaching a bedroom door, the woman turned the handle and helped the man inside. The door closed, and again the corridor was empty.

Slowly, Tom walked forward, pausing outside the couple's door when he heard the mutter of voices. Unable to make out the words, he walked on to Bedroom A, but the door was closed. Anyway Tom had lost interest for the moment in the man with the handcuffs. Tom was in love.

He couldn't get the woman out of his mind, the colour of her eyes, the softness of her hair, the creamy smoothness of her skin. Who was she? Returning along the corridor, Tom stopped again outside the couple's door, then rushed to tell Dietmar.

"Guess what?" he said, sitting down. "There's a beautiful woman in our car!"

Dietmar laughed. "That cookie-woman? She's beauti-ful like Godzilla the Hun is beautiful."

"No, a woman in Bedroom C. She's got violet eyes, and she's wearing a gold necklace. I wonder who she is?"

"Cinderella. She turns into a prune at midnight."

Dietmar's sarcasm was spoiling Tom's memory of the woman. He closed his eyes, dreaming of her face, then opened them in surprise when there was a flash of light.

"What was that?"

"Lightning," Dietmar said, pointing out the window. "Over there."

At first Tom could see only blackness, then a streak of pure white ripped across the sky, twisting and ex-ploding in all directions. A delicate pattern of jagged light hung for a moment in the air, then died.

"That's lovely," Tom said.

Dietmar nodded. Together they watched the sky, and were rewarded with another burst of white light. It was followed by a rumble of thunder and the long moan of the diesel's whistle.

"What a creepy sound," Tom said. "Do you know any ghost stories?"

"Nope."

Another streak of lightning trembled across the night sky, bright in Tom's eyes. "Bet you don't know how to kill a werewolf," he said.

"Sure I do. You shove a silver cross in its face."

"That doesn't kill it," Tom said. He glanced up as the cookie-woman came along the aisle and took the seat in front of the boys, then lowered his voice to a whisper, "You drive a stake through its heart."

"A steak? What a waste of good food."

"No, you idiot! You try to catch the werewolf asleep in its coffin, and jab a wooden stake through its heart."

The cookie-woman turned to look at Tom as he lifted his hands to demonstrate the powerful blow needed to kill a werewolf.

"That's a very silly thing to talk about," she said. "Anyway, I'm sure it's long past your bedtime."

"We're on a holiday, having fun," Tom said. "At least, we were until a minute ago."

The cookie-woman looked at Tom with distaste, then turned to face forward.

"So, as I was saying," Tom said after a moment, winking at Dietmar, "I think for fun we should release my snakes tonight while everyone is sleeping."

The cookie-woman shifted uncomfortably in her seat, and Dietmar grinned. "Gosh, Tom," he said innocently, "what if a rattlesnake bites someone, and they die?"

"I didn't bring my rattlers this trip, just the big garter snakes. You know, those long green slimy ones that like to slip into bed and curl up around your feet."

"You sure they won't bite?"

"Not unless someone gets scared. Then they might give the person a nip with their fangs, but the bite only makes your body swell up for a couple of days."

Suddenly, the cookie-woman's head whipped around and she stared fiercely at Tom. There was a long silence while Tom stared back at her, trying to keep a straight face, then he heard Dietmar giggle and burst into laughter.

"I knew you were fooling!" the cookie-woman said, sounding both relieved and angry. Standing up, she shook her finger in Tom's face. "You're a very naughty little boy."

Fighting back his laughter, Tom watched the woman leave the dome, then turned to Dietmar and they both howled. When they had finished laughing, and wiped their eyes, they told each other the story and laughed some more. Then they calmed down and sat watching the thunderstorm light up the prairie until finally Dietmar yawned.

"I'm for bed," he said, stretching his arms.

"Good idea."

Tom led the way to their sleeping-car, where heavy curtains hung along both sides of the narrow corridor. It was dark, the only lights glowing softly at their feet. Dietmar turned to Tom, his face worried.

"Where'd our seats go?" he asked.

"The porter turned them into beds for the night," Tom said. "Haven't you travelled on a train before?"

"Nope."

"Well stick with me, Oban, and I'll show you around." Tom reached for a pair of curtains and began to undo some large buttons. "This is my berth."

Tom threw open the curtains, and there was a shriek. He looked inside, saw the cookie-woman in a nightdress, and jerked the curtains closed. His face on fire, he turned to Dietmar.

"Wrong berth."

Dietmar was grinning. "Wait till I tell the kids at school!"

Tom shook his fist under Dietmar's nose. "Do it, and you'll be eating a knuckle sandwich."

Above their heads, curtains were yanked open and

the cookie-woman's husband looked out. "Pipe down, you kids. Decent people are trying to sleep."

"We can't find our berths," Tom said.

The man pointed at a ladder hidden in the folds of some curtains. "One of you climb up there. The other sleeps below."

"Oh boy!" Tom and Dietmar said together. "A ladder!"

They both made a grab for the ladder, but Dietmar was closer and went up it like a monkey. "See you tomorrow," he said, crawling into the berth.

Annoyed that Dietmar had the best berth, Tom opened the lower curtains. He slipped off his shoes, climbed on to the bed and closed the curtains.

It was like being in a dark cave. Tom found a switch and clicked on a tiny blue lamp, then looked around. A blind covered the window, the upper berth stretched just above his head, and the blue light shone on two soft pillows, white sheets and blankets. Anxious to try the bed, Tom made a pile of his clothes, adjusted the pillows, and crawled between the crisp sheets.

Beautiful. Tom stretched his arms, feeling luxurious, and reached to open the blind. Outside, the night was solid black except for three red lights on a distant radio tower. The train went around a bend, and Tom could see the diesel's powerful headlight slicing a path through the night.

He was falling asleep. What rotten luck, just when he wanted to treasure the feeling of lying in bed with the whole world flying by outside. Tom opened his eyes wide, watched as the train passed a farmhouse with a yellow light shining from a window, and fell sound asleep.

He dreamed of a conductor with huge blue eyes, offering a cookie that turned into a bomb and exploded, filling the air with violet smoke that became violet eyes smiling at Tom as a bedroom door opened and a man wearing a silver cross slipped out, reaching long cold fingers for Tom's throat.

* * *

A whistle shrieked, the bed threw Tom back and forth, and he sat up with sweat on his face. Who was the man? Was he real, or a dream? Again the whistle blew, and Tom looked out the window, realizing it had been a nightmare.

The train was slowing down. Tom could see rows of tracks, a throbbing yard engine, red and green lights on switches, then a long platform with people standing around looking sleepy. Brakes squealing, the train stopped beside a station marked BRANDON.

Quickly, Tom pulled on his clothes, anxious to get off the train and explore. He opened the curtains, stepped into the corridor, and saw Dietmar coming down the ladder.

"Hi," Tom said. "Want to go poke around this station?"

"Where are we?"

"Brandon. Didn't you see the sign from your window?"

"What window? All I've got is a steel wall."

"Gee, that's too bad," Tom said, grinning. "I guess you grabbed the ladder too fast."

Walking through the car, Tom stopped outside Bedroom C when he heard a man's voice shouting angry words. Was that drunk abusing his beautiful wife? Tom looked around, ready to go for help, but he relaxed when he heard the woman laugh.

"Come on!" Dietmar called impatiently from the end of the corridor.

"Okay, okay." Tom looked at the blue bedroom door, memorizing the sound of the woman's silvery laughter, before going reluctantly to join Dietmar.

Outside, the summer night was warm. Tom and Dietmar walked along the platform to the baggage car, where they watched men tossing mailbags into the back of a truck, then continued ahead to the engine. Tom felt small as he stood looking up at its powerful steel body, the huge headlight and curved windscreen.

"I'd love to drive one of those," he said to Dietmar.

"You'd make a good driver."

"Why?" Tom asked, pleased.

"Because you drive me crazy." Dietmar turned and ran, laughing. Tom chased him down the platform, caught him and threatened to throw him under the train. As they wrestled, a hand touched Tom's shoulder.

"Excuse me, young man," an old cracked voice said. "I'd like some help."

Tom let go of Dietmar and looked at an old woman leaning on a cane, a shawl around her stooped shoulders. Without waiting for them to speak, she crooked her finger at the boys.

"Come along," she ordered, turning to hobble across the platform.

"I'll bet she's a retired school teacher," Tom whispered to Dietmar. "Come on, let's give her a hand."

Tom and Dietmar followed the woman to a taxi, where she pointed with her cane at a pile of suitcases.

"These are my bags," she said. "Help the driver with them, and I'll give you both a tip."

The driver, a tall man with a cap stuck on the back of his head, grinned at the boys and winked. He handed them some suitcases, and they walked slowly behind the old lady to the train.

Other passengers were also boarding at Brandon, and Tom was pushed to one side by a short, fat man who arrogantly waved a ticket in the porter's face and climbed quickly aboard. The porter shook his head, muttering, as he took the old lady's ticket.

"I tell you," he said, "some folks make a man tired."

The old lady made a clucking noise with her mouth. "Let me give you some fudge," she said, reaching into her handbag and handing him a sticky brown piece.

The porter put it in his mouth, licked his fingers and helped the old lady up the steps. Tom, Dietmar and the taxi driver struggled along behind with the suitcases, which banged against the narrow walls of the sleeping-car.

The porter had just opened a bedroom door for the old lady when a loud voice was heard swearing. This was followed by silence, then angry shouts. Everyone turned to stare, wondering what was happening behind the door to Bedroom C.

3

The porter was the first to act.

Quickly, he walked to the bedroom door and knocked. The shouting stopped, then a man's voice yelled, "Go away!"

Again the porter knocked, but there was no reply. Down the corridor, the door to Bedroom A opened and the greying man stepped out, the attaché case still linked to his wrist.

"What's going on?" he asked.

"Nothing, sir," the porter replied. "Please go back to sleep."

For the first time, Tom noticed the greying man was still fully clothed, even though it was late at night and other passengers were asleep. As Tom thought about this strange fact, something even stranger happened:

the short, fat man who'd pushed aboard the train a few minutes ago now opened the door of Bedroom B and came out, wearing pyjamas.

How could he have changed so quickly? Puzzled, Tom watched as the two men glanced at each other, seemed about to speak, then went into their bedrooms and closed the doors.

At the same moment, the door to Bedroom C was thrown open. The beautiful woman, dressed in a soft pink robe, looked out angrily at the porter.

"Why are you knocking?" she demanded.

"Excuse me, ma'am," the porter said, "but we heard a fight. We were concerned for your safety."

"Mind your own business," the woman said, closing the door in the porter's face.

Tom was shocked at the woman's rudeness. He looked at the porter's embarrassed face, feeling sorry for the man. The old lady, clucking, reached into her handbag for more fudge.

"Mercy!" she said, passing it to the porter. "I hope this won't be an unpleasant trip."

"No, ma'am," he said. "If necessary, I'll take action against that couple. They won't bother you, don't worry."

Tom put down the suitcases outside the old lady's bedroom and was walking away with Dietmar when she called out, "Just a minute!"

Tom turned, and saw her opening her handbag. She reached inside and took out two nickels.

"Here you are," she said, handing each boy a coin, "thank you for your assistance."

Dietmar stared down at the nickel, unable to hide

his disgust, then looked cheekily at the old lady. "How about some fudge?"

"Certainly not," she said. "It's bad for your teeth."

"So are knuckle sandwiches," Dietmar said. "Maybe I'll treat you to one."

"Goodness gracious!" the old lady said, watching Dietmar walk angrily away. "What a rude little boy. This train is full of hooligans."

Tom smiled at her. "Thanks for the money, ma'am. Have a nice trip."

The old lady beamed. "That's better! Here you are, young man, a little treat."

A piece of fudge was produced, and Tom walked away, chewing happily. He crawled into his bed, watched the activity on the platform for awhile, then fell into a deep sleep.

* * *

Morning came with a *bing bong bing*. Tom felt sunshine on his face, opened his eyes, and again heard the curious sound: *bing bong bing*. It was followed by a man's voice announcing, "Breakfast is served."

The voice died away, and Tom sat up. He looked out the window at fields of young green wheat, swaying gently under a wind that blew toward the horizon. He began to pull on his clothes. He was hungry!

Tom opened his curtains and found Dietmar sitting on the edge of the upper berth, feet dangling.

"Hi," Tom said. "What was that weird sound?"

"A xylophone. Some guy walked by playing it, and hollering 'breakfast.'"

"Wait for me, and I'll go with you." Tom went into the washroom at the end of the corridor, then joined Dietmar and they walked through the train to the dining-car. As they opened the door, the smell of bacon and eggs came to their noses.

"I could eat a horse," Tom said.

"How about an old bat? Like that one who gave us a nickel."

Tom laughed. "She gave me some fudge, too."

"You're lying."

Tom shook his head. He led the way into a room full of sunshine glistening on white tablecloths, on which were silver, glasses and flowers. Waiters hurried back and forth with big trays full of food for the passengers, who chatted together or looked out the windows.

A smiling man approached. "Good morning," he said. "Would you like breakfast?"

"Yes, please," Tom answered.

"This way." The steward led them through the car to a table for four, where he held out a chair for Tom, then the one beside it for Dietmar. He gave them the menu and smiled again. "*Bon appétit.*"

"What did he say?" Dietmar whispered, when the steward was gone.

Tom shrugged. He looked at the silver and china, which tinkled together with the train's motion, then opened the menu. "Oh no!" he said. "It's all in French."

"*Jus de fruits*," Dietmar read, struggling with the words. "Does that mean there's just fruit for break-fast?"

"Here's the English," Tom said, pointing to another

part of the menu. "I'm having Rice Krispies with cream, toast and coffee."

"I hate coffee."

"So do I, actually, but it looks good written on the menu." Tom looked at a pad and pencil which the smiling steward had left on the table. "I think we have to write our order here."

As Tom bent over the order pad, the smell of perfume came to his nose. His heart beating with excitement, he looked up and saw the beautiful woman approaching. Unable to believe his luck, Tom watched the steward lead her straight to his table and hold out a chair; he then put the woman's husband opposite Dietmar, took Tom's order, and walked away.

The woman glanced at Tom, and his face went red. Furious with himself, he looked down and pretended to study the menu.

"*Parlez-vous français?*" the woman's husband said.

Tom looked up. "What?"

The man smiled. "I asked if you speak French. I noticed you reading the French part of the menu."

"Oh," Tom said, his face going redder as he felt the woman's eyes staring. "Oh, French, yes, well, I mean . . . *oui*."

Dietmar laughed. "Austen hasn't even learned to talk English yet. In fact, he still wears diapers."

The woman laughed at the joke, and Tom aimed a kick sideways at Dietmar but missed. The man held out his hand to Tom. "My name is Richard Saks," he said. "This is my wife, Catherine."

Tom shook the man's hand, liking his face now that he wasn't drunk. He looked at his dark-brown hair and moustache, then turned shyly to the woman. "I'm Tom Austen," he said, "and this is Dietmar Oban."

"Oh." The woman yawned, then opened her handbag and took out a gold case and a cigarette holder. Putting in a cigarette, she lifted the long, elegant holder to her lips.

"What will you have, princess?" Richard Saks asked his wife.

"Coffee."

Tom smiled to himself, pleased that he had also ordered coffee. When the woman turned to look out the window he studied the flickering diamonds on her fingers, the string of pearls over her black sweater and the makeup around her lovely eyes.

"Do you know if those are real pearls?" he asked.

Catherine Saks looked at Tom, startled. "What?"

"I can test your pearls by rubbing them against my teeth. If they're phony, they slip; if they're real, they grate." Tom hesitated, feeling foolish under the stare from the violet eyes, then explained, "I read that in a detective handbook."

"Do you think I would wear phony pearls?" Catherine Saks demanded, touching the pearls with her sharp-pointed fingernails.

"No, I . . . I . . ."

"Don't mind old Carrot Top," Dietmar said. "He thinks he's a Hardy Boy."

"I read all their books when I was a kid," Richard Saks said. "They're terrific."

Tom smiled at the man, feeling grateful. A waiter arrived with the Rice Krispies, and Tom poured cream from a silver jug among them, feeling hungry as they crackled.

Not wanting to stare at the beauty of Catherine Saks,

Tom looked out the window at the fields that rolled away toward a distant grain elevator. The train roared past a blue pond, and a cluster of tiny black birds scrambled into the air from an old fence half-buried in the water. Tom felt good, and was trying to find the courage to speak to Catherine Saks when Dietmar looked at her.

"Are you a model?" he asked.

"No," Catherine Saks said, smiling. "Why do you ask?"

"Because you're so beautiful."

Catherine Saks glowed as she looked at Dietmar. "Do you think so? You're very flattering. In fact, I was once in the movies."

"Wow," Dietmar said, "a movie star!"

"Well, not exactly a star. But I had several lines in a movie called *My Little Pussycat*. Have you seen it on TV?"

"Uh, sure," Dietmar said. "You were great!"

Tom looked at Dietmar, knowing he was lying, and hating him for finding it so easy to talk to Catherine Saks.

"Were you in Hollywood?" Tom asked.

"Yes," Catherine Saks answered, still looking at Dietmar. "But I got sick of it, and returned home to Winnipeg with a friend of mine, who'd also been acting in Hollywood."

"They both got jobs in my bank," Richard Saks said, "and it wasn't long before Catherine and I fell in love." He looked at his wife with adoration, but Tom didn't think there was much love in the glance she tossed him in return.

"Do you miss being a star?" Dietmar asked.

"You bet," Catherine Saks answered. She stared off into space for a minute, then said softly, "If I was free again, I'd go straight back to Hollywood."

As she said this, Tom was looking at Richard Saks, and saw a look of pain cross the man's face. No wonder he drank, when he knew his wife wanted to be free of their marriage.

"Where are you going?" Tom asked Richard Saks, trying to change the subject.

"To Victoria," the man answered, his face brightening. "Catherine needs a holiday, she's been under such a strain lately."

"Why?" Tom asked.

"It's nothing," Catherine Saks said, in a tone which indicated it was none of Tom's business.

Richard Saks put his arm around his wife. "Now don't you worry about it, princess," he said, giving her a hug which made her stiffen.

Tom was getting sick of Catherine Saks. He looked down at the coffee which a waiter had brought and lifted the cup, but it tasted bitter. Standing up, he smiled at Richard Saks and left the table. Dietmar and Catherine Saks could spend the whole day gazing at each other for all he cared.

"Your bill, sir," the smiling steward said, holding out his hand.

"Oh, yeah." As Tom took some money from his pocket, he saw the short, fat man cross from another table and speak to Catherine Saks. Smiling at how jealous Dietmar looked, Tom left the dining-car.

4

In the next sleeping-car, one of the bedroom doors was open. Tom looked inside and saw a young porter pulling sheets off the bed.

"Hi," Tom said, "may I see what a bedroom looks like?"

"Certainly," the porter said. He was very tall, and smiled at Tom through glasses with black frames. "I'm Dermot."

Tom gave his own name and shook Dermot's hand, then looked at a picture on the wall of a river bubbling through rapids. There was a sink with a wrap-around mirror and iced-water tap, a speaker for music and a tiny room with a toilet. "Aren't there any chairs?"

"Sure are," Dermot answered, folding the bed into the wall and revealing two squashed chairs. With a quick motion he pulled them up into their proper shape.

"Neat!" Tom said, sitting down. "Are you a university student?"

"That's right. This is my summer job."

"I'd like to do that when I'm older. Is it fun?"

"It certainly is. And you meet some strange people, like that old porter in your car."

"What's strange about him?" Tom asked.

"They say he was a professional boxer, but he was hit so hard in a fight that he was in a coma for months. When he woke up, his mind was unbalanced."

"What do you mean?"

"I hear he has fits of violent temper, when he loses control of himself. Apparently he had a fight with a conductor and threw him out the door of a speeding train."

"Wow," Tom said, feeling his hair stand on end. "That's horrible."

"Well, I don't know if it's true, but I'm always very polite around that fellow." Dermot smiled at Tom. "Well, I'd better get back to work."

"Oh, sure," Tom said, standing up. He went slowly into the corridor, feeling so upset that he forgot to thank Dermot. What if that old man grabbed him in the middle of the night and tossed him off the train? The thought made Tom shudder, and he wondered if he should secretly trade berths with Dietmar so the porter would grab the wrong guy.

Fortunately, the old man wasn't around when Tom got to his sleeping-car. The berths had disappeared, and Tom sat down in the sunshine, letting the warmth ease his worry. Across the aisle, the cookie-woman sniffed and made a big production of putting away her tin of cookies.

Looking out the window, Tom watched the train approach a small group of trees. In their shade a horse was munching grass while its tail flicked away flies. Then a little wooden house appeared and Tom saw a girl sitting on the front steps, the wind blowing her hair. As the train passed, she raised her hand in a wave, and Tom was sure she smiled at him.

Then she was gone. Tom leaned against the glass, trying to see her again, but the little house had disappeared. He sat back in his seat, wondering who the girl was, feeling both sad and happy they had shared that one moment together.

Dietmar was coming. Tom heard his voice in the corridor, talking to Catherine Saks, and decided he didn't feel like being sociable. He closed his eyes, pretending to be asleep, and within a few minutes was no longer pretending.

When Tom woke up, he got out *The Sinister Signpost* and a package of Dubble Bubble. After a good read, he and Dietmar had a cheeseburger in the small restaurant under the dome, then climbed upstairs and chatted happily as they watched the view.

* * *

Getting on and off the train to explore the stations where it stopped gave Tom and Dietmar an appetite and they ate a big dinner of sugar-cured ham steak, then walked to the rear of the train for the evening bingo game.

It was held in the observation car, and everyone Tom knew seemed to be there. The first person he saw was the cookie-woman, who made a point of only saying hello to Dietmar; beside her sat the short, fat man, his shoulders sprinkled with dandruff.

Tom's heart fell when he saw those two people, but he cheered up when he spotted the old lady and she beckoned him to an empty chair at her side. As he walked between the chairs which faced each other across the observation car, Tom saw the man with the attaché case, his eyes studying Tom's face.

Pretending he didn't notice the man's stare, Tom sat down and smiled at the old lady. The evening sun made her white hair look attractive, but Tom didn't much like the powder, rouge and lipstick which she had applied to her face in thick gobs.

"Hi," he said. "I'm Tom Austen."

"And I'm Mrs. Ruggles," the old lady said, smiling.

"Any more fudge?" he asked.

"Naughty boy," the old lady said, wagging a finger. "Mustn't spoil your appetite."

"I've already had dinner," Tom protested.

"Then you'll spoil your breakfast."

Dietmar, who had taken a chair across from them, shook his head. "Cheapskate," he muttered.

Ignoring Dietmar, Mrs. Ruggles opened her handbag and took out a paper bag. She handed a piece of fudge to Tom, then offered the bag to the man with the attaché case, who sat to her left.

"Thank you," he said, reaching in and selecting a large piece.

Mrs. Ruggles got out of her chair and hobbled along

the aisle, offering fudge to everyone, smiling happily as they exclaimed about its qualities. Reaching Dietmar, she held out the bag and he helped himself.

"You don't mind eating a cheapskate's fudge?" Mrs. Ruggles asked.

Dietmar blushed. It was the first time Tom had ever seen Dietmar embarrassed, and it made him feel great. Grinning, he turned to look out the window; as he did, he noticed the man with the attaché case was still staring.

This time Tom returned the stare and the man looked away. What was going on? Puzzled, Tom watched the evening sun drop out of sight, leaving behind a sky beautifully streaked with reds and oranges and yellows.

"Take your cards for bingo," a voice said.

Tom turned and saw Dermot. Smiling, the tall young porter handed bingo cards around and then set up a wire cage containing numbered ping-pong balls. He spun the cage, and removed a ball.

"Under the B, number nine," Dermot announced. "Do we have a winner?"

Everyone laughed. As the porter spun the cage again, there was a commotion from the bar, which was a separate room in the front of the car.

"Under the O, number sixty-five," Dermot said, raising his voice above the noise from the bar.

There was an angry shout, and Tom recognized the voice of Richard Saks. "Get out of here!" the man yelled. "I hate the sight of you!"

Dermot tried to carry on, bravely calling another number, but everyone was staring toward the bar. There was a pause, then the watchers were rewarded with the sight of Catherine Saks stalking down the corridor and out of the car.

"It's that blond hussy," the cookie-woman said to her husband. "I told you she's a troublemaker."

The short, fat man gave her a dirty look. "I think she's lovely," he said.

"I agree," Dietmar said, then looked at the cookie-woman. "Besides, she was a movie star, and I bet you never were."

Before the cookie-woman could express her opinion of movie stars, Mrs. Ruggles looked at Dietmar in surprise. "A movie star? Who said so?"

"She did."

Mrs. Ruggles chuckled, and shook her head. "Some star. She had five lines in one movie."

"At least she's not a cheapskate!" Dietmar jumped up, and threw his bingo card on the floor. "I'm getting out of this dump."

"Mercy!" Mrs. Ruggles said, fanning her face with her card. "Why is everyone so upset tonight? Is there a full moon?"

"I'll tell you what's caused the trouble," the man with the attaché case said. "It's that drunk, Saks. The man is no good."

"How do you know his name?" Tom asked.

The question seemed to surprise the man. "Why, there was an article in the newspaper, on the social page. Saying that Mr. and Mrs. Richard Saks were planning a holiday in Vancouver."

"Victoria," Tom said, watching the man's face closely. "Not Vancouver."

"Oh, well, my mistake."

Dermot spun the wire cage vigorously. "Ladies and gentlemen, can we get back to business? I've many wonderful prizes to give away, like a weekend for two in beautiful Iceburg Inlet."

The short, fat man stood up. "I'm sick of this," he said, putting down his card and leaving the car.

"Excuse me for living," Dermot said, his voice bitter.

"Gracious!" Mrs. Ruggles looked around at the other passengers. "I don't know about you people, but all this tension is hard on my nerves."

"I'm sorry, ma'am," Dermot said, then smiled. "Come on, everyone, let's have fun!"

The game proceeded without further interruption, and Tom was pleased for Mrs. Ruggles when she waved her card in excitement, and called "Bingo!" She accepted a paperback book as her prize, and insisted Dermot take two pieces of fudge in return, then stood up.

"Always quit when you're ahead," she said, reaching for her cane. "Good night, everyone."

Mrs. Ruggles wobbled along the car, the rocking motion of the train adding to her difficulties in walking. Dermot waited politely for her to leave, then announced another game.

Tom moved to Mrs. Ruggles' chair, and looked at the mysterious man. "What's in your attaché case?" he asked.

The man turned to Tom, hesitated, then smiled. "You won't believe this, but there's only paper in my case."

The man was right. Tom didn't believe that story for

one minute. He studied the case, and the silver chain of the handcuffs. "It must be pretty valuable paper."

"It could be worth a million dollars."

Tom nodded his head, pretending to be impressed. He knew the man was lying, but he couldn't think of any more questions that might help to dig out the truth. He had a lot to learn before he could be a pro like Frank and Joe Hardy.

"Under the N, number thirty-eight."

Tom stayed for several games without winning, and his eyes began to feel heavy. Looking out the window at the night made him feel lonely.

Yawning, Tom stood up. He thanked Dermot for the bingo and walked through the car, glancing in to the bar to see if Richard Saks was still there.

The man sat at a small table, face flushed, eyes red. He looked at Tom and lifted a shaky hand. "Hello, little chum," he said, his voice thick.

"Hi," Tom said. "How are you?"

"Not so hot, little chum. How're you?"

"Okay. I lost at bingo."

"Another loser," Richard Saks said, shaking his head. He lifted his glass and drank, but it only seemed to make him sadder. "Take my advice, little chum, and never marry a beautiful woman."

"Yes, sir," Tom said. "Well, good night."

"It won't be for me," Richard Saks said unhappily, looking down at his glass.

Tom walked slowly through the train. The encounter with Richard Saks had deepened his sense of loneliness, and he was glad to reach his car. As he crawled between the clean white sheets of his bed, Tom felt a bit better, but then the whistle moaned out of the black night and he fell into an unhappy sleep.

It was broken by a scream.

Tom sat up in bed, horrified by the sound. It came again, a shriek of terrible anguish. Tom pulled on his jeans and ripped open the curtains of his berth. All was quiet in the corridor, and for a moment he thought he'd had a nightmare, but then the cookie-woman's face appeared between her curtains.

"What was that ghastly sound?" she said, her face white.

"I don't know," Tom answered. "I'll find out."

Again there was a shriek, followed by deep sobs, and Tom ran toward the sound. Rounding the bend into the bedroom corridor, he stopped and stared in horror. Straight ahead was Richard Saks, holding a knife smeared red with blood!

5

Richard Saks was crying.

"My princess," he sobbed. "My princess is dead."

Tears running down his face, Richard Saks looked at the bloody knife and, for a terrible moment, Tom thought he was about to kill himself. But then he dropped the knife and leaned his face against the corridor wall, moaning.

His heart pounding, Tom walked closer. As he did, he saw that the door of Mrs. Ruggles' bedroom was open. Stepping inside, Tom saw her leaning on her cane, face frozen by shock.

"Ma'am?" Tom said. "Are you all right?"

Mrs. Ruggles shuddered. "Thank God help has come," she whispered. "I screamed and screamed. Please, help that poor woman."

Tom nodded. As he did, there was the sound of running feet in the corridor and a confusion of shouting. Tom turned, and saw the old porter grab Richard Saks and wrestle him to the floor. Then the short, fat man leaned over Richard Saks and slapped him across the face.

"You madman!" he yelled. "What have you done?"

The husband of the cookie-woman, wearing a dressing-gown over his long underwear, ran to the door of Bedroom C and looked inside. "My God," he said, his voice shaking, "it's horrible."

Tom tried to get closer, but the man closed the door and looked down at Richard Saks. "You deserve to die!" he shouted. "How could you kill a defenceless woman?"

"No," Richard Saks whispered. His face was grey, with red marks where he had been slapped. "No, no."

By now the corridor was full of passengers, pushing and straining to see what had happened. Realizing that Richard Saks might be trampled, the porter pulled him up to lean against the wall. As he did, Tom spotted the bloody knife.

"Have you got a hankie?" he asked the porter.

The old man nodded, and reached into his pocket. Tom knelt down, studying the strong blade and handle of the hunting knife, then wrapped it carefully in the hankie. He looked up, and saw the face of Richard Saks close by, the sour smell of alcohol on his breath.

"No," Richard Saks said, his eyes desperate. "No, little chum, I didn't do it."

"Liar!" The short, fat man raised his hand, ready to hit Richard Saks again. "I'll make you tell the truth!"

Tom leaned toward Richard Saks, trying to shield him from a blow, but someone grabbed the threatening hand. Tom looked up and saw a big man in a conductor's uniform.

"All right," the conductor said, "what's going on?"

Everyone answered at once, but nothing made sense to the conductor until Tom unwrapped the hankie to display the bloody knife. Then the man went into action, clearing the corridor of spectators before escorting Richard Saks to Bedroom E, which was empty. The porter was ordered inside to guard Richard Saks, then the door was locked and the conductor turned to Tom and the other witnesses.

"Please return to your beds," he said. "I'll radio ahead to the next town, and have the police meet the train. I'm sure they'll want to speak to you all."

It seemed forever to the next town. Tom lay on his bed, unable to forget the first sight of Richard Saks holding the bloody knife, and at last saw a small bubble of light appear ahead in the darkness. Slowly it grew, until Tom could make out streetlights and the colours of neon signs.

The train pulled into the town, whistle blowing and bell clanging as if it wanted to tell everyone of the horrors which had occurred. Tom sat up, and was putting on his shoes when he saw a small station appear. Half the town must have been on the platform, staring, and he saw other people running toward the station as the train ground to a halt.

A police car was parked beside the station, its lights flashing. A Mountie got out and walked to the train; a few seconds later, Tom heard him talking to the conductor as they passed in the corridor. Then all was silence, and Tom turned back to the window.

As time passed the crowd grew larger, gathering in excited clusters under the bare lightbulbs which lit the platform. A man wearing a short-sleeved shirt, hands in the pockets of his trousers, looked up at Tom and said something.

"What?" Tom said, unable to hear through the glass.

The man cupped his hands around his mouth. This time, his words squeezed through the window. "What happened?"

Tom looked down at the hunting knife in his hands. Unable to resist the temptation, he removed it from the hankie and held it up, as if ready to stab someone. The man's eyes bulged, then he shouted something and pointed at Tom. Excitement jumped like electricity through the crowd, and everyone pushed toward Tom's window, fighting for a view of the bloody knife.

Feeling embarrassed and stupid, Tom lowered the knife and pulled down his blind. Now he'd botched it! Some detective, not only showing off to a crowd of strangers, but getting his fingerprints on valuable evidence in the process. Hot with shame, Tom rolled up the knife in the hankie.

A hand was fumbling with Tom's curtains. His heart leaped in terror, but it was only the conductor, who looked in and said: "Would you come with me, please?"

The man led the way to the dome car, where the other witnesses to the tragedy sat at the small restaurant tables. Everyone wore dressing-gowns except the porter.

The Mountie sat at a table, a notebook in his hand. He was very young, with bright blue eyes and blond hair cut short. "Is this the final witness?" he asked the conductor.

"Yes."

The Mountie looked at Tom. "May I have your name?"

"Tom Austen." Trying not to blush, Tom held out the knife. "I'm afraid this may have my fingerprints on it."

"Is that the knife Richard Saks used?"

"I don't know if he actually used it, but when I came into the corridor he was holding it in his hands, then dropped it."

The short, fat man leaned forward in his seat. "He used it all right!" he said angrily. "He murdered his own wife."

"Can you prove it?" Tom asked.

"Of course I can. We all heard them fighting in the bar, and then Saks said he hated the sight of his wife."

"But that's not proof!" Tom said.

"It is to me."

"And to me," the cookie-woman said, drawing her blue dressing-gown tighter around her body. "Don't forget they were fighting last night in their compartment."

"You weren't there," Tom said. "You don't know what happened."

"But I was," the porter said, his eyes jumping nervously between Tom and the conductor.

"So was I," Mrs. Ruggles said. She wore a woolly dressing-gown over a long, white nightdress, and tears had stained her cheeks. "It sounded like a very angry fight."

"Yes, I suppose it was," Tom said quietly. He hated

to think of Richard Saks being a murderer, but all the evidence was against the man. Even worse, Tom suddenly remembered their conversation at the breakfast table. It made things blacker for Richard Saks, but Tom couldn't keep evidence from the police. "There's something else," he said miserably.

"What's that?" the Mountie asked.

"My friend and I had breakfast with Mr. Saks and his wife. She said she wanted to be free again in order to return to Hollywood, and Mr. Saks looked very upset."

The short, fat man slapped his hand against the table. "There's your motive!" he shouted. "He knew he was losing his wife, so he killed her."

"Perhaps," the Mountie said. He looked down at his notebook. "Let me take a moment to reconstruct events."

Despite feeling sorry for Richard Saks, Tom was thrilled to be this close to a murder investigation. He watched the Mountie with fascination as he read from his notes:

"Saks and his wife were heard fighting in their compartment. Yesterday morning, at breakfast, his wife expressed an interest in leaving him. In the evening, they were heard quarrelling in the bar, and she returned alone to her compartment." The Mountie paused, and looked around. "Correct so far?"

Several heads nodded.

"At midnight Richard Saks left the bar, very drunk, and returned to his compartment." The Mountie looked over at the old lady. "Mrs. Ruggles was awakened by the sound of a violent struggle, then heard Catherine

Saks cry out in terror. She raised the alarm, and young Tom Austen was the first to come to her aid."

Tom tried to look modest.

"Tom Austen saw Richard Saks holding a bloody knife, which he then dropped. Seconds later the man was overpowered by the porter, and Catherine Saks was discovered in her bedroom, dead from a number of savage stab wounds."

Tom shivered, glad now that he hadn't seen the inside of Bedroom C. How horrible, to think of that beautiful woman lying in a pool of blood.

"In fairness to Richard Saks," the Mountie went on, "he does deny that he murdered his wife. He says he found her dead, picked up the knife and went into the corridor to seek help. However, he admits to being drunk at the time, and says his memory of events is very foggy."

Tom remembered Richard Saks sitting in the bar, looking down at his drink. If only he had gone to bed when Tom had stopped to say good night. Suddenly, and unhappily, Tom remembered more evidence.

"Excuse me, sir," he said, "but I just thought of something. This evening, when I wished Richard Saks a good night, he looked unhappy and said, 'It won't be for me.'"

The short, fat man looked at the Mountie. "Well?" he demanded, as if addressing an infant. "Now are you going to take my advice, and charge Saks with murder?"

The Mountie gave the man a dirty look, and it was clear who he'd like to put behind bars. "Yes, I'm going to arrest Richard Saks," he said, "on suspicion of murder."

"That's better." The man looked around. "We're all taxpayers, so it's our duty to be sure the police operate efficiently."

The cookie-woman nodded, and stood up. "May we go now?" she asked the Mountie. "You've kept us awake half the night."

"Yes, you may go."

As the people filed out, Tom saw the Mountie shake his head in disgust. No wonder, when he was under attack as he tried to get the facts on a murder. Deeply upset by the events of the night, Tom walked back to his berth. Dietmar's face appeared between his curtains.

"Is Catherine Saks really dead?" he asked.

Tom nodded.

"I hope that guy gets strung up."

"Who?"

"Her husband."

"How do you know he murdered her?"

"It's obvious. He's just like the killers you see on TV."

"Very clever, Dietmar."

Tom climbed into his berth and peeked out the blind at the crowd. He felt like getting out of the train for some fresh air, but what if he was recognized as the boy with the knife?

A disguise would help. Tom got out of his berth and dug in his suitcase for a pair of sunglasses and his blazer. Putting them on, he walked to the far end of the restaurant car so that he could slip quietly out of the train. The door was open, and Tom hurried down the steps.

Every face was turned toward the sleeping-car

where Catherine Saks lay dead, and no one noticed Tom leave the train. Spotting a boy leaning against his bike near the station, Tom walked over.

"Hi," he said, "what's going on?"

"There's been a murder!" the boy answered, his voice thrilled.

"What happened?"

"See that car?" the boy said, pointing to Tom's sleeping-car.

"Yeah."

"Some kid stabbed his mother to death. They locked him in a bedroom until the train reached here, but he escaped and cut up some people who tried to grab him."

Tom stared at the boy, unable to believe his ears.

"You see that window? That's where Hank Sayer saw the kid, waving a big carving knife dripping blood, his eyes rolling around like a madman. Then someone grabbed the kid, but he fought free and now he's hiding somewhere in the train."

The boy stopped talking, breathless with excitement.

"Why don't you go home?" Tom asked. "The kid might sneak off the train, and stab you with his knife."

The boy laughed. "I wouldn't miss this for the world."

"Well, see you around."

"Sure thing."

Tom stuck his hands in the pockets of his blazer and walked along the platform. There was a stir in the crowd, and he saw two men push past carrying a stretcher. Voices buzzed, and people stood on tiptoe to watch as the men climbed into the train. A few minutes later, someone close to the train cried out, "Here they come!"

The men with the stretcher appeared, struggling to get down the steps with their burden. The crowd fell silent, staring at the grey blanket that covered the body of Catherine Saks. Some of the men took off their hats, and Tom saw a woman touch a hankie to her eyes. As the stretcher was carried toward a waiting ambulance, the only sound was the hiss of steam from the train.

All eyes stared at the ambulance as the stretcher was loaded inside, but Tom happened to glance toward the train and saw the Mountie leading Richard Saks down the steps of the sleeping-car.

The two men cut around the back of the crowd and headed for the Mountie's car. Anxious to see Richard Saks a final time, Tom ran quickly to the car and reached it as the Mountie was opening the door.

"Good luck," Tom said to Richard Saks.

The man hardly seemed to recognize Tom, but he managed a small smile before sitting down wearily in the car. The Mountie got in, started the engine and drove quickly away, the wheels throwing dust up into the still, night air. Tom turned and walked slowly back to the train, unable to forget the sadness he had seen in the eyes of Richard Saks.

6

The next morning the sun was shining. Tom woke slowly, remembering the murder with a painful lurch of his heart. Poor Richard Saks.

He opened his eyes and glanced out the window. A huge mountain rose up into the sky, massive in the sunshine. He sat up wondering where the prairie had gone, then remembered the train was now in the Rocky Mountains.

The mountain was a giant slab of rock, its head reaching up among puffy clouds. Green trees clung to its side, and spread across the valley through which *The Canadian* was passing.

Tom pulled on his clothes while he enjoyed the view. The train struggled up a steep climb, then made its way carefully along a narrow passage cut into the face of a cliff. Looking down into the valley, Tom saw an emerald-green lake, absolutely still except for a V of water spreading out behind a red canoe.

Tom didn't want to give up the view for even a minute, but he was terribly hungry. Opening his curtains, he debated whether to awaken Dietmar, then decided to go alone to the dining-car.

Only a few passengers were up this early, but one of them was the old lady, Mrs. Ruggles, wearing a black dress with puffy sleeves, and her shawl. Smiling, she beckoned Tom to her table.

"Good morning," he said, sitting down.

"Isn't it lovely?" Mrs. Ruggles said, pointing at the thick green forest in the valley below.

"It certainly is," Tom said, then glanced at his watch. "The Mountie's investigation sure put the train far behind schedule."

"Yes," Mrs. Ruggles said, "but it does give us extra time to enjoy the scenery."

Tom wrote out an order for Rice Krispies with cream, toast and milk, then stared out the window. "I wish Richard Saks could be looking at these mountains, instead of rotting in a cell."

"Yes, the poor man." Mrs. Ruggles shivered. "Please, let's not talk about it. Where do you live?"

"Winnipeg. My Dad is on the police force there."

"I live in Winnipeg, too. You must come for a visit, and we'll have some tea."

"Didn't you board the train in Brandon?"

"I was there visiting friends. Now I'm going to see my grandchildren at the coast," Mrs. Ruggles said and smiled happily. "I can't wait to see them again."

Tom poured cream into his bowl of Rice Krispies and picked up his spoon, which flashed silver in the sunshine. "Do you have a picture of them?"

"Who?"

"Your grandchildren."

"No, I'm afraid I don't."

"That's strange," Tom said, smiling. "My grandparents have fifty million pictures of me and my sister." Chewing his cereal, he looked up high to the top of a mountain, where the frozen whiteness of a glacier stood out against the rock. "Last week I dropped my alarm clock in the river, and it's still running."

"That's amazing!" Mrs. Ruggles said.

"Well, it takes a lot to stop a river running."

The old lady laughed. "Have you heard the Little Moron jokes?"

"No," Tom lied. "Would you tell me some?"

"All right," Mrs. Ruggles said, beaming happily. "Why did the Little Moron take oats to bed?"

"I give up."

"He wanted to feed his nightmare."

Tom laughed. "That's great."

"Why did the Little Moron jump off the Empire State Building?" Silence, while Tom pretended to think. "He wanted to try his new spring coat."

Smiling, Tom spread marmalade on his toast, then said, "Adam and Eve and Pinch-me went down to the river to swim. Adam and Eve were drowned, so who was saved?"

"Pinch-me."

"Okay," Tom said, reaching over and lightly pinching the old lady's arm.

"Oh, you devil!" Mrs. Ruggles said, laughing. She finished her tea, then reached for her cane and stood up. "It's been lovely chatting with you, Tom. Perhaps you'd like to come to my compartment for a visit later, and we'll have some fudge and tell jokes."

"Great," Tom said. "I'll see you after."

The old lady hobbled away leaning heavily on her cane. When she was gone Tom looked down into the valley, where tiny cars crawled along a highway. Then, everything went black.

Lights came on in the dining-car, and Tom realized the train had entered a tunnel. Leaning close to the window, he saw the train's lights bouncing off the jagged rocks of the tunnel wall. A few minutes later sunshine burst on to Tom's face, making his eyes sting. Finishing his toast, he stood up and walked back through the train.

Reaching his car, Tom pushed open the door and saw a little boy in a baseball cap looking in the door of a roomette, where the old porter was making up the bed. Turning toward Tom, the little boy pulled out a water pistol.

"Reach!" he said.

Smiling, Tom held up his hands. The boy fired, soaking Tom's shirt, then turned and ran.

The porter laughed. "That brat has been bugging me for an hour. I'd like to amputate his head."

Tom smiled politely, unpleasantly reminded of the knife that had been used on Catherine Saks. "Any more news about the murder?" he asked.

"Nope, nothing more," the old man said, his words making the curious whistling sound in the gap between his front teeth. "I guess that fella will spend his life in prison."

Tom glanced along the corridor, and saw the little boy sneaking toward him with the water pistol. Caught, the boy fired quickly and retreated. Wiping water off his face, Tom wondered how someone could look so innocent yet be such a menace.

Finished with his duties in the roomette, the porter lit a cigarette. "I was plenty nervous giving evidence last night," he said.

"Why?"

"Man, at night I'm supposed to sit on a little chair in the corridor, in case people ring for something. If I'd been at my post last night, I would have heard the fight and prevented the murder."

"Where were you?"

"Sneaking a nap in Bedroom E." The old man puffed on his cigarette, then shook his head. "If that conductor finds out, I'll be fired."

"Well, I won't tell him," Tom said. He turned to walk away, then stopped, curious. "Was it pretty awful last night, in that woman's bedroom?"

"Man, there was blood everywhere. And vomit, all over the corpse."

"Vomit?" Tom said, surprised. "I thought she was stabbed to death."

"That's right. I guess that fella was so upset, he got sick."

Tom looked carefully at the porter. "Can you remember if there was a smell in the bedroom?"

"Sure, it was awful, all that vomit and blood."

"But, was there an almond smell?"

The porter stared at Tom in surprise. "Man, how did you know? Did you sneak into that bedroom last night?"

Suddenly excited, but not wanting it to show, Tom shrugged his shoulders. "Nope, I wasn't there. Listen, are you sure?"

"Sure as the day I was born. I spent half the night trying to get that smell out of there."

Unable to contain his excitement, Tom grinned at the porter. "Thanks a million!" he said.

Tom turned and hurried through the car. Dietmar was crawling out of the upper berth, a big yawn on his face.

"Dietmar!" Tom said. "Have I got news for you!"

"The sky is falling," Dietmar said sarcastically.

"Richard Saks is . . ." Tom said, then faltered. The cookie-woman was staring at him, her ears flapping. Boy, he'd almost botched it again!

"Come on," Tom said to Dietmar, dragging him toward the washroom.

"I want my breakfast," Dietmar protested.

"Later, later." Tom opened the washroom door, hauled Dietmar inside and locked the door. Then he stepped to the sink and turned on the hot and cold taps.

"I'm old enough to wash myself," Dietmar said.

"That's not what the water's for," Tom whispered. "If the washroom is bugged, the running water will cover our words."

Dietmar laughed. "You're the one that's bugged, Austen."

"Listen," Tom said, eyes wide with excitement. "I just found out that Richard Saks is not the murderer!"

"Who is, the cookie-woman?"

"She might be. Everyone is a suspect."

"Why?"

"Listen to this," Tom said, dropping his voice lower. "Catherine Saks was poisoned with cyanide!"

"Says who?"

"Says me. The porter told me there was vomit on her body, and an almond smell in the bedroom."

"So what?"

"That smell, and the fact she vomited before dying, means cyanide poisoning."

"How do you know?" Dietmar asked, sounding less sarcastic.

"I read it in a detective book."

"You and your books," Dietmar said, shaking his head. "I think you're crazy. Richard Saks murdered his wife, and now he's in prison. Anyway, I heard she was stabbed to death."

"Sure, she was stabbed," Tom said, "but only after she was dead. That was to disguise the fact that she had been poisoned."

"Then Richard Saks must have given her cyanide."

"But why would he use both poison and a knife? No, someone else poisoned Catherine Saks and then stabbed the dead body to make it look like Richard Saks had murdered his wife in a drunken rage."

"Who?"

"I don't know," Tom admitted, "but I suspect every-one. For example, the cookie-woman might have given Catherine Saks a chocolate-chip-with-cyanide cookie."

Dietmar laughed, and opened the washroom door. "I'm going for my breakfast," he said, then thought of something and closed the door. "I may have a lead for you," he whispered.

"What's that?" Tom asked, excited.

"Last night I was standing beside a berth, Lower Two in Car 165, and I heard someone muttering in his sleep about bloody knives and dead bodies."

"Hold it!" Tom said, reaching into his pocket for the notebook he always carried. "Let me write that down."

Dietmar repeated the information, then left for his breakfast. Tom hesitated, uncertain how to follow up the lead, then decided to reconnoitre the car and see who occupied the berth. Leaving the washroom, he suddenly remembered he was already in Car 165. Not only that, Lower Two was his own berth!

Swearing he'd get even with Dietmar, Tom went to his seat and began to make notes on the murder. First, he made a sketch of Car 165, with a chart indicating who occupied the various berths and bedrooms. Then he noted what he'd seen and heard last night, and the evidence given to the Mountie. Finally, he recorded his suspicion that Catherine Saks had been poisoned.

Tom leaned back in his seat, staring at the notebook. Somewhere, in that tangle of evidence, were the clues which pointed to the real killer. He must work it out before the train reached Vancouver!

"Hi, mister."

Tom looked up from his notebook and saw the little boy in the baseball cap.

"I'm sorry I shot you, mister." The little boy took a package of gum from his pocket. "If you forgive me, I'll give you a piece of gum."

"Sure, kid, I forgive you." Tom only chewed Dubble Bubble, but he thought he should make the boy feel better. "Okay, give me some."

Smiling happily, the little boy held out his hand. Tom reached for a stick of gum, and was pulling it out of the package when there was a buzzing sound, and a flash of pain shot up his arm.

"Ow!" Tom yelled, dropping the gum.

The little boy laughed with joy, grabbed the booby-trapped gum from the floor and ran quickly away. Across the aisle, the cookie-woman tried to smother a laugh.

His face red with embarrassment, Tom did his best to smile at the woman. "That kid," he said. "I'd like to amputate his head."

"Don't you dare!" the woman said, shocked.

"Okay, maybe just one foot. Then I can catch him when he tries to run away."

The woman gave Tom a dirty look, then sniffed and turned her head. If she was looking for the killer, Tom realized, he would be the number one suspect.

Enough wasting time. Tom turned back to his note-book, studying the evidence, searching for a lead. As he worked, Dietmar returned and slumped down in his seat, a toothpick in his mouth.

"The butler did it," he said, grinning.

"Drop on your head," Tom muttered, busy with his pen.

"Have you got a magnifying glass?"

"What for?"

"I can't wait to see you crawling around the floor, searching for clues like Sherlock Holmes."

"Funny, funny." Tom would never admit it to Dietmar, but he had already tried to picture how Sherlock Holmes would investigate this case. Probably he really would start by crawling around for clues. "Hey," Tom said, "I've got an idea!"

"Kill it before it grows."

Tom leaned toward Dietmar. "I'm going to get into Bedroom C, and search for clues," he whispered.

"How?"

"Maybe the door is unlocked." Tom stood up. "Coming?"

"I don't know," Dietmar said, trying to sound bored. "Okay, I guess so."

Tom led the way to Bedroom C. He glanced up and down the corridor, then tried the door, but it was locked. "Rats!" he said. "What a bad break."

"Why don't you ask the porter to open it?"

"Good thinking, Dietmar. Maybe I'll hire you as my assistant."

The porter was busy in Bedroom A, but Tom noticed there was no sign of its occupant, the man with the attaché case. He wondered briefly why he hadn't seen the man around lately, then looked at the porter.

"Hi," he said, "how's it going?"

"Okay, man. I hear you got zapped by the brat."

"What happened?" Dietmar asked.

"Nothing," Tom said, waving his hand. "Listen, sir, could you do me a favour?"

"What's that?"

"Let me see inside Bedroom C."

The porter laughed. "Man, you are some bloodthirsty kid."

Wanting to hide his real reason for seeing the bedroom, Tom bared his teeth like Dracula. "Blooooood, blooooood," he hissed, "give me blooooood."

Chuckling, the porter reached into his pocket for a key ring. "Okay, but let's make it fast."

"Great!" Tom said.

The porter led the way to Bedroom C. As he turned the key, Tom trembled, afraid of what he might see inside. But the porter had worked hard to clean up the bedroom, and the sun beamed happily through the window.

"There's nothing to see," Dietmar said, disappointed.

Tom opened the door to the toilet and looked inside. Nothing. He checked the cabinet over the sink, but the porter had done his work well. His heart sinking, Tom glanced around the carpet, then walked to the window, hoping for fingerprints.

"I gotta get back to work," the porter said.

"Okay," Tom said unhappily. Turning from the window, he noticed a small ashtray mounted in the wall. Inside was a cigarette butt.

"Here's something you missed," Tom said.

"What?" The porter walked to Tom's side, and laughed. "A butt! Man, I'm glad you're not president of this railway or I'd be fired. Here, I'll get that."

"No, let me," Tom said, reaching quickly for the butt. He slipped it in his pocket, and smiled at the porter. "Well, thanks a lot, man."

The porter laughed. "See you later."

The cookie-woman looked up suspiciously when they returned to their seats, so Tom dragged Dietmar on to the washroom. Locking the door, and turning on the taps, he took the cigarette butt out of his pocket.

"This could be a lead," he said hopefully.

"No," Dietmar said, "it's a butt."

Tom examined the butt closely, trying to make out the brand name. "I think it says Players," he said, "but this lipstick stain covers most of the name."

"What brand did Catherine Saks smoke at breakfast?"

"I don't know," Tom said, ashamed of his ability as a detective. Every book told him to concentrate on being observant, and now he'd failed. He strained his memory of the breakfast table, but all he could recall was how elegant the long cigarette holder had made Catherine Saks look. "Well," he sighed, "maybe it's nothing."

Returning with Dietmar to their seats, Tom pulled out his suitcase and found one of the envelopes his mother had given him for writing home. He put the cigarette butt inside, then wrote on the envelope the date, time of day, and his initials. Putting it in his pocket, he picked up the notebook.

"Back to square one," he said mournfully.

"I told you," Dietmar said, putting his feet on Tom's seat, "the butler did it."

Before long, Dietmar was asleep. Tom laboured over his notebook, too busy to look out at the beauty of the mountains. A waiter had just walked through the car announcing lunch, and Dietmar was snoring noisily, when Tom snapped his fingers and looked up, delighted.

"Hey," he said to himself, "I think I've got it!"

7

Tom grabbed Dietmar's arm. "Quick," he said, "wake up!"

Dietmar's eyes flew open. "What?" he shouted. "Murder? Murder?"

"No, no," Tom said, holding up his notebook. "I've figured it out!"

Across the aisle the cookie-woman snapped shut a book she'd been reading. "You boys stop making all that noise, or I'll ring for the porter."

"Yes, ma'am!" Tom said, grinning. Pulling Dietmar out of his seat, he headed for the washroom.

"That woman must think we're crazy," Dietmar said, "always going to the washroom together."

"Nuts to her," Tom said, so excited he forgot to turn on the taps. "I know who the killer is."

"Who?"

"The man with the attaché case!"

"Why?"

"It's all in here," Tom said, slapping his notebook. "When we were playing bingo, that man called Richard Saks a drunk, and said he was no good."

"So what?"

"I thought it was strange he knew Richard Saks by name, but he pretended he'd seen it in the newspaper." Tom looked closely at Dietmar. "If he'd only heard of Richard Saks from the newspaper, why would he say 'the man is no good'?"

"Yeah, that's weird. But why kill Catherine Saks?"

"I'm coming to that." Tom opened the notebook and checked his information. "When I asked him what was in his attaché case, he said it was paper worth a million dollars. There's the motive."

"I don't get it."

"Blackmail!" Tom waited for a reaction, but Dietmar only stared. "Haven't you read anything by Agatha Christie?"

"Nope."

"You illiterate," Tom said, shaking his head. "Well, in her detective books you always have to watch for a blackmail angle. When I remembered that, my case fell together."

"I still don't get it."

"I think Catherine Saks did something bad in Hollywood. That man found out, and has the details on the paper in his attaché case, which is why he won't let it out of his sight. He threatened to reveal the truth, so Richard Saks paid blackmail. But the man kept asking for more and more money, until finally Richard Saks threatened to go to the police."

"Okay so far."

"The night we played bingo, that man followed Catherine Saks to her bedroom and poisoned her. Then he stabbed her to make it look like Richard Saks was the murderer. That way, no one will believe Richard Saks if he ever claims he was being blackmailed."

"Well," Dietmar said, "it's pretty complicated, but it all adds up. Are you going to tell the conductor?"

"Yes, but first I want to get some additional proof. I'm going to find that man and ask a few innocent questions, then try to get a look inside his attaché case. If I could see those blackmail papers, it would really seal my case."

Dietmar swallowed nervously. "You'd better be careful," he said. "If he suspects anything, he'll murder you, too."

Tom smiled as bravely as possible. "Don't worry, I won't accept any poisoned food."

The washroom door creaked as Tom opened it. He hadn't noticed the creak before, but now his nerves were on edge. He looked up and down the train, then hurried back to his seat, heart thumping. It was one thing to read the Hardy Boys stories, but something else to be actually chasing a killer.

"What next?" Dietmar whispered.

"I'm going to find that man," Tom answered. "Wish me luck."

"Okay, but be careful."

Tom put the notebook in his pocket and walked toward the bedroom corridor. At the far end, the porter sat on a folding seat, a cigarette smouldering in his fingers. Seeing Tom, the man smiled.

"Hiya, Dracula," he said. "Going to the bar for a bottle of blood?"

Tom smiled. "Maybe later. Right now, I'm going to visit that man in Bedroom A."

"You can't do that."

"Why not?"

"He's gone to the dining-car for lunch."

"Oh," Tom said, hesitating. "Well, I'm kind of hungry myself. Think I'll go have a steak."

"Hey, a moneybags. I'll expect a giant tip when we reach Vancouver."

Heading for the dining-car, Tom stopped to check his finances. His parents had only given him money to buy a cheeseburger for lunch, but he had to follow the man. Well, he could spend his dinner money now and starve tonight.

In the dining-car, Tom saw Mrs. Ruggles sitting alone with a pot of tea. She smiled happily and beckoned to him, but at the same moment he spotted the man with the attaché case, alone at another table.

Slowly, Tom walked over to Mrs. Ruggles. "Hi," he said, his mind searching rapidly for excuses.

"Sit down, please," Mrs. Ruggles said. "How wonderful of you to come, just when I was feeling lonely."

"I'd like to sit with you, but I can't."

"Oh," Mrs. Ruggles said, unable to hide her disappointment. "Aren't you having lunch?"

"Yes, but . . ." Tom's face was beginning to burn. "I, uh, promised to have lunch with someone else."

"Oh." Obviously Mrs. Ruggles knew Tom was

lying, but she smiled. "Have fun, then, and perhaps I'll see you later."

"Sure," Tom said miserably. He walked away, feeling terrible about hurting the old lady's feelings, but a detective had to be ruthless.

The man with the attaché case was reading a letter. As Tom approached he quickly put it away and pretended to be staring out the window.

"Hi," Tom said, sitting down at the man's table, "mind if I join you?"

The man looked at Tom with a thin smile. "I don't seem to have much choice."

Tom held out his hand. "My name is Tom Austen."

"You can call me Mr. Faith." The man's handshake was quick, and limp. "Or Mr. Hope, or Mr. Charity."

Aliases? Tom's mind prickled with suspicion as he studied the man's grey hair, the dry skin of his narrow face, his tiny brown eyes. Certainly the face of a killer, but that was no proof. Get to work, Austen, he told himself.

"Going far?"

Again, the thin smile. "I thought so, when I was a young man. But life's plans often go astray."

"No, I mean on this train."

"Oh, I see." Mr. Faith looked out the window at the passing forest, and his attention seemed to drift. "This is the most important journey of my life," he said at last.

Tom waited for more, but obviously the man didn't intend to give a direct answer. Not wanting to arouse his suspicions, Tom pretended to lose interest and picked up the menu. The cheapest item was a Spanish omelette, which sounded horrible, but he had to order something.

"Ah yes," Mr. Faith sighed, "I have dreamed my dreams, and reached for the stars."

Was this guy nuts? Perhaps committing that gruesome murder had pushed him over the brink into insanity. Tom looked around the dining-car to see who could help in an emergency, but Mrs. Ruggles was gone and the only other passenger he recognized was the short, fat man, who seemed half asleep in the sunshine.

As he waited for the Spanish omelette to arrive, Tom considered and rejected various approaches, finally deciding to attack directly. Summoning courage, he looked at Mr. Faith.

"Do you know Richard Saks?"

Startled, the man turned from the window. "What?"

"Is Richard Saks a friend of yours?"

Mr. Faith laughed bitterly. "Certainly not," he said. "I hate him."

Tom almost gasped, he was so surprised that his theory was right. As he stared at Mr. Faith, a waiter arrived with a steaming yellow mass on a plate.

"Your omelette, sir," the waiter said, depositing the plate on the tablecloth.

"Thanks," Tom said weakly. He cut into the omelette, but was sickened to discover it full of green things.

Mr. Faith smiled unpleasantly at Tom. "*Bon appétit*," he said, lifting his water glass in a mock toast.

Bon appétit? The same curious words the dining-car steward had spoken to Tom at breakfast. Perhaps the two men were partners in crime, and the steward had provided the poisoned food used to kill Catherine Saks. His hands trembling, Tom looked down at the omelette, thankful he hadn't yet taken a bite.

"Not hungry?" Mr. Faith asked.

Tom shook his head.

"Then why waste money ordering that omelette?" Mr. Faith said, wrinkling his small mouth disapprovingly. "If you were my son, I'd make you eat it."

Tom shivered, pitying any kid who had Mr. Faith for a father. Glancing out the window, he saw the diesel slowing as it approached a tunnel. Afraid the man might try something while the train was in the tunnel, Tom pushed back his chair and got ready to run.

"Not another tunnel," Mr. Faith said as the train entered the darkness and the dining-car lights came on. "This is ridiculous."

The train continued to slow down until it was only creeping, increasing Tom's nervousness. For a horrible moment he thought even the engineer was part of the plot, then realized that was silly. Still, he greeted the return of sunshine with relief.

"Eat your omelette before it gets cold," Mr. Faith said. "You mustn't waste it."

Tom was caught. He couldn't eat the poisoned omelette, but he must not make the man suspicious. Slowly, he picked up his knife and fork, then put them down and reached for his water glass.

"Do you know any jokes?" Tom said, hoping to distract the man's attention from the uneaten omelette.

"This rail service is a joke," Mr. Faith said, looking

out the window as the train crept into another tunnel. When the lights came on, he raised his hand and snapped his fingers. "Come here, my good man," he called.

Tom turned, and saw a conductor about to sit down for a meal at the crew table. Hearing Mr. Faith call, the man walked down the car.

"Yes, sir?" he said.

"Why is this train moving so slowly?"

"Repair work in the tunnels, sir. There's a risk of falling rock."

"What a nuisance." Mr. Faith pulled back his cuff and tapped the face of his watch. "We're already late because of that wretched murder, and now more delays. I must get to Vancouver as soon as possible."

"Yes, sir," the conductor said, touching his cap. "I'll ask the engineer to pedal faster."

"None of your cheek," Mr. Faith said, his dull skin turning red. "I can get you fired."

"Yes, sir. In the meantime, may I eat my lunch?"

Mr. Faith watched the conductor walk away, then looked at Tom's plate. "Ah, I see you've eaten your omelette."

"Yes, it was delicious."

"That's better," Mr. Faith said, the tense lines on his face relaxing. "I've never had much money, so I hate to see anything wasted."

Tom's lap was becoming very warm. He glanced down at the omelette, which lay in the middle of a napkin on his lap, where he had shoved it during Mr. Faith's argument with the conductor. Keeping his eyes on the man, Tom carefully folded the linen napkin around the omelette, and dropped it on the floor.

That danger past, Tom returned to the attack. "Why do you hate Richard Saks?" he asked, watching for Mr. Faith's reaction.

"Oh, look," the man said, pointing out the window, "that's rather pretty."

Tom looked out at a stream which lay beside the tracks, its emerald waters shaded by trees along the bank. A fisherman wearing hip-waders stood in the stream, flicking his line toward a pool of deep, cold water.

"I needed some money," Mr. Faith said, "so I went to the bank where Richard Saks was manager. He turned me down."

"Why?"

"He said I was a poor risk," Mr. Faith said bitterly. "He said I should get a job if I needed money."

"Don't you have one?"

"Not a typical job, like driving a bus or pulling teeth." Mr. Faith paused, and swallowed some water. "I work on my own, and only get money from time to time. That's why I needed the loan."

The evidence was piling up. Everything Mr. Faith was saying showed that he was a blackmailer with a strong motive for revenge against Richard Saks. All that remained was somehow to get a look inside the attaché case.

"Richard Saks is a scoundrel," Mr. Faith said. "Because of him, an innocent person went to prison."

"What happened?"

"A few years ago, some money was embezzled from his bank, which means it was stolen by someone who worked there. The police suspected Richard Saks, but at his trial evidence turned up which led to the conviction of a cashier. She went to prison, and Richard Saks was set free, but a lot of people think he framed the cashier."

"Was there any proof?"

"No, but that's just the sort of double-cross that he'd do." The tension had returned to Mr. Faith's face, pinching the skin round his eyes and mouth. "You can never trust a man with a beautiful wife."

"Well," Tom said quietly, "he doesn't have her any more."

"That's true," the man said, cheering up. "And I can't say I'm sorry."

Someone was approaching. Tom looked up, and saw the conductor, cap in hand. "Excuse me, sir," he said to Mr. Faith, "but you'll want to know we'll be stopping for fifteen minutes at the town we're approaching. I regret the inconvenience, but the diesel has difficulty working unless given fuel."

"I know how diesels work," Mr. Faith snapped. "Anyway, I'll be happy to get off for a walk, away from smart-alec conductors."

"I'll come with you," Tom said, standing up.

"I'd rather go alone." Mr. Faith wiped his mouth delicately with his napkin, then took the attaché case from his lap and stood up. "Goodbye, young man."

Mr. Faith put some change on the table and walked away, the silver chain clinking at his wrist. Quickly, Tom counted out enough money to pay for the omelette, then rushed after Mr. Faith.

He found him standing in the vestibule between the

dining-car and the next sleeping-car, waiting for the train to stop. The rattle and bang of the wheels made speaking difficult, so Tom just smiled at Mr. Faith and looked out the window.

The train pulled to a stop beside a little station made of red bricks. The young porter, Dermot, opened the door and threw back the steel panel covering the steps, then descended to the platform.

"Fifteen-minute stop," he said, as Mr. Faith quickly left the train.

Tom caught up to Mr. Faith on the platform, and fell into step at his side. "Hi," he said brightly, "doesn't the mountain air smell good?"

No answer.

"Wow, look at those peaks," Tom said, pointing up at the frozen snow sparkling in the clean air. "Wouldn't you love to climb up there?"

Mr. Faith made a sudden left turn off the platform, cut between two cars in the station parking lot and hurried away. Tom was caught flat-footed, but he ran after the man and reached his side as he started along a street of ancient wooden houses.

"Why are you going to Vancouver?" Tom asked.

Mr. Faith stopped walking, and stared down at Tom. There was a long pause, the only sound the rusty creaking of a swing in a front yard, then Mr. Faith took a coin from his pocket.

"Why don't you go buy a Coke?" he said, holding out the money.

"Thanks, but there are no shops here."

Mr. Faith turned impatiently to look up and down the street. "There!" he said triumphantly, pointing toward an old building with a flickering neon sign reading CAFÉ.

"It looks awful," Tom said, staring at the café. "I'm nervous to go there alone."

"Come on," Mr. Faith said, taking Tom by the arm. "I'll buy you a Coke, and then you can leave me in peace."

No chance of that, but Tom didn't say so. By sticking close to Mr. Faith, he was deliberately applying mental pressure which would eventually make the man crack. Then he would make a mistake, and Tom would get his final proof.

"What kind of papers do you have in your case?" he asked.

No answer from Mr. Faith, who seemed lost in thought. They passed a general store, its window displaying faded merchandise and a sleeping cat, and crossed the street to the café.

Mr. Faith opened a screen door and they stepped into a dim interior smelling of greasy food. Tom blinked, adjusting his eyes to the darkness, and saw a waitress wearing a stained uniform.

"Off the train?" she said. "What'll you have?"

"A Coke for this young man," Mr. Faith said, "and I'll have a coffee if it's hot, and made today."

The woman looked angrily at Mr. Faith and turned to open a small hatch leading to the kitchen. "One Coke, one coffee!" she hollered, then banged the hatch shut.

Mr. Faith sat down at the counter, putting the attaché case on his lap. As Tom sat down on a stool, Mr. Faith took a paper napkin from a dispenser and carefully wiped the counter.

"How about playing some music?" Tom said, pointing at a juke-box sagging in one corner of the café.

"Rock and roll," Mr. Faith muttered, then looked at the waitress. "Is there a washroom?"

"Through there," the woman said, pointing at a door.

Mr. Faith stood up, and went through the door. As he did, Tom caught a glimpse of a kitchen with a man in a cook's hat leaning over a stove. The door swung shut, and Tom did a couple of spins on his stool, then wandered over to look at the juke-box titles.

"Here's your Coke," the waitress called. "Better drink up fast, the train's leaving soon."

"Thanks," Tom said, smiling at her. His Coke waited in a tall glass on the counter, beside it a cup of coffee. But there was no sign of Mr. Faith.

Tom sat down, glancing nervously toward the kitchen door. Mr. Faith wouldn't have time for his coffee if he didn't hurry. He reached for the straws which stuck out of his glass, and used them to swirl the ice cubes while he wondered what was keeping the man.

"Drink up," the waitress said, "there's a good boy."

Where was Mr. Faith? The fifteen minutes were almost gone, and they still had to walk back to the station. Tom leaned forward to sip his Coke, but he felt too nervous about the train to drink. Pushing the glass away, he stood up.

"I'll be right back," he said to the woman.

She pointed at his drink and started to say something, but Tom was already through the door into the kitchen. A frying-pan spluttered on the stove, music came from a radio, and the cook was washing a big pot in a sink full of dirty water.

"Where's the washroom?" Tom asked the cook.

The man lifted a dripping hand out of the water and gestured toward a door. The way to it was cluttered with mops and brooms and cartons of food, but Tom got past them as quickly as possible and knocked on the door.

"Mr. Faith?" he called. "We've got to hurry, the train's leaving."

There was no answer, so Tom knocked again, louder this time. The seconds ticked away while Tom waited, until finally he could stand the suspense no longer. Reaching for the wooden handle, he pulled open the door. The washroom was empty.

8

Tom stared into the tiny room, then slammed the door and turned toward the cook.

"Where did he go?" he asked desperately.

The man didn't seem to hear. He pulled the plug in the sink, and watched as the grey water seeped slowly away.

"Please!" Tom said. "Where's the man gone?"

The cook reached for a towel hanging over the sink and began to dry his hands carefully. As he did, he made a nodding gesture with his head.

"Please," Tom repeated, "help me."

Again the man nodded, and this time Tom realized he was gesturing toward a door half hidden in a corner. He ran forward, hearing the last of the dishwater gurgle down the drain, and pulled open the door.

Sunshine struck his face. Blinded, Tom stumbled ahead, tears streaming from his eyes. As he began to make out the dim shapes of walls, a car, some trees, he heard the whistle of the train.

Wiping at the tears on his face, Tom began to run. The whistle came again, a warning to hurry. Slowly Tom's eyes adjusted to the sunlight, but they still stung as he dashed down the long dusty road toward the station.

Outside a house, two women were laughing together, unaware that the boy who rushed past was in such trouble. Not only tricked into missing the train, but tricked into botching his murder investigation! Unable to believe what had happened, Tom raced across the station parking lot as the whistle blew a final time.

The porter stood in the doorway of the sleeping-car, waving his arm. "Come on, man!" he yelled. "Move those feet!"

His breath red-hot in his throat, Tom stumbled across the platform and reached the sleeping-car. He saw the conductor wave toward the diesel, then the porter pulled him on to the steps of the car and the train lurched forward.

"Man," the porter said, "I had to make them hold the train."

"Thanks," Tom gasped, holding tight to the railing as he sucked air into his lungs.

"What happened?" the porter asked. "Mr. Faith said you were hanging around in a café, or something foolish like that."

"Is he on the train?"

"Sure is. Man, if you'd missed the train, I'd have lost my giant tip."

Tom smiled at the old man, feeling happy to know there was one person on the train he could trust. Where was Mr. Faith now? He had to find him, and demand an explanation for his trickery.

"Thanks again," Tom said, climbing the steps on shaky legs, glad to be safe inside the train instead of abandoned in the mountain town.

Inside the sleeping-car, Tom stopped at Bedroom A and knocked loudly. Now he really was afraid of Mr. Faith, but he was also angry, and that gave him a sense of courage. When there was no answer he knocked again, then looked up and down the corridor wondering where the man was hiding.

The dome car was a possibility. As Tom started toward it, the short, fat man appeared ahead in the corridor. Tom kept walking, but the corridor was narrow and the man approached like a bull elephant apparently ready to flatten Tom if he didn't get out of the way. At the last second Tom saw an open bedroom door, jumped inside, and watched the man rumble past.

"Tom! You've come for your visit!"

Oh, no. What incredibly bad luck! Tom realized he had blundered into the bedroom occupied by Mrs. Ruggles. Remembering his promise to visit the old lady for jokes and fudge, and the way he had snubbed her in the dining-car, Tom closed his eyes miserably. He couldn't snub her again.

"Why did the Little Moron throw the clock out the window?"

Slowly Tom turned, trying to smile.

Mrs. Ruggles was sitting in a chair, a book on her lap. "Because he wanted to see time fly."

Tom managed to find a laugh, and pushed it through unhappy lips. This sort of thing never happened to the Hardy Boys, but he couldn't hurt the old lady's feelings again.

"Your turn for a joke," she said, pulling the shawl tighter around her shoulders. "Close the door, and come join me."

Fighting the urge to run from the bedroom and continue his search for Mr. Faith, Tom reluctantly closed the door and turned to Mrs. Ruggles, who smiled in anticipation of his joke.

"Uh, let's see," Tom said, "uh, this kid went into a barber shop and the man asked if he wanted a haircut. 'No,' the kid said, 'I want them all cut.'"

Mrs. Ruggles didn't get it. She waited for the punch line, then smiled vaguely. "Very funny," she said, frowning in confusion.

Feeling sorry for the old lady's fading mind, and her loneliness, Tom resigned himself to spending half an hour with her before looking for Mr. Faith. He sat down facing Mrs. Ruggles and tried to think of a joke that she could understand.

"Here's a riddle," he said. "You know that a horse goes on four legs, right?"

"Yes."

"And a human goes on two legs."

Mrs. Ruggles nodded.

"So what goes on one leg?"

The old lady scrunched her forehead in concentration, and Tom could practically hear the wheels grinding inside her head, but it was no use. Smiling hopelessly, she looked at Tom for the answer.

"A boot!"

This time she understood, and laughed brightly. Reaching for her handbag, she took out a piece of fudge for Tom, then a cigarette package. "Do you mind if I smoke?" she asked.

Tom shook his head. Chewing the rich chocolate fudge, he looked around the bedroom. "What's that?" he asked, pointing at something that looked like a statue of a bald head, resting on the floor in a corner.

"Oh, that." Mrs. Ruggles lit her cigarette, and shook the match until it puffed out. "It's a wig stand."

"What's it for?"

"You put your wig on there at night, so it doesn't lose its shape overnight."

"Do you wear a wig?"

Mrs. Ruggles didn't answer, but instead looked confused and upset. Tom blushed, realizing he'd said the wrong thing. The poor old lady was probably as bald as a billiard ball, but naturally she didn't want anyone to know.

"Got another joke?" he asked, trying to change the subject.

"Let me think," Mrs. Ruggles said vaguely, puffing on her cigarette. "I used to know so many."

As the old lady strained her memory, the train rolled into a tunnel and its speed dropped to a walking pace. This tunnel was very long, and Tom smiled when he thought how annoyed the train's slow progress must be making Mr. Faith. But where was the man hiding?

"I must go soon," Tom said.

"Why?" Mrs. Ruggles asked, disappointed.

Tom smiled, embarrassed. "I'm working on a case," he said shyly.

"A case? What do you mean?"

Suddenly it all poured out of Tom. It felt good to talk to someone kind and sympathetic, and now he told the whole story of the cyanide and Mr. Faith and almost being left in the mountain town.

"And that's why I couldn't sit with you at lunch," he finished, thankful he could at last explain the snub.

During the story, Mrs. Ruggles had listened quietly, nodding her head, occasionally asking questions. Now she lit another cigarette and looked carefully at Tom. "Very, very clever," she said. "You really are a detective."

Tom grinned happily, unable to hide his pleasure. "Maybe you could help me!" he said. "We can find Mr. Faith, and then you ask him some questions about his attaché case. That might catch him off guard."

"That sounds like fun," Mrs. Ruggles said. She gave Tom more fudge, then stood up and walked to the washroom. "Excuse me a minute. I'll need fresh lipstick if we're going out in public."

The washroom door clicked closed, and Tom settled back with the fudge. He had consulted his notebook while talking to Mrs. Ruggles, and now he flipped through the pages, checking details. Realizing he'd forgotten to make a note on the cigarette butt, he took the envelope from his pocket and copied out the details.

"What's that?" Mrs. Ruggles asked, returning from the washroom.

"Oh, I thought this was a clue," Tom answered, ripping open the envelope and removing the butt. "I found it in Bedroom C."

"A clue?"

"Well, the killer might have left it behind by mistake." Smiling, Tom pointed at the red smear on the butt. "However, I don't think Mr. Faith wears lipstick."

Mrs. Ruggles laughed. "I hope not."

"I tried to make out the brand name of the cigarette, but this lipstick stain covers most of it. Anyway, it's obvious Catherine Saks left it in the ashtray." Tom thought back to the beautiful woman at the breakfast table, looking so elegant with the long cigarette holder in her fingers. Then, with a shock, he thought of something.

"Hey!" he said, staring at the butt.

"What?" Mrs. Ruggles asked.

"Hey, just a minute. Catherine Saks used a cigarette holder, which means her cigarettes never touched her lips. So this lipstick stain can't be hers."

"That doesn't make sense, Tom," Mrs. Ruggles said, sitting down in her chair and picking up her handbag from the floor.

"Sure it does!" Tom said, excited. "Some other woman was in her bedroom that night, smoking."

Mrs. Ruggles laughed. "Really, Tom, that is farfetched. If you want me to help with your case, you'll need to have better theories."

"You don't understand," Tom said, impatient that the old lady's mind worked so slowly. He was trying to think of another way to explain about the lipstick, when his eyes fell on one of her butts still smouldering in the ashtray. "You'd better put that out," he said.

"Oh, yes."

Mrs. Ruggles reached for the butt, and ground it firmly out. As she did, Tom realized that it had a red lipstick stain. A cold, sick feeling spread through his body as he lifted his eyes to stare at Mrs. Ruggles.

Smiling, the old lady reached one hand to her head and lifted off her wig, revealing thick black hair which shone in the light from the window. At the same moment, she took a small revolver from her handbag and pointed it at Tom.

"Congratulations," she said. "You just found the killer."

9

"I don't understand," Tom said, feeling sad and stupid.

Mrs. Ruggles returned the wig to her head, adjusting it carefully. "A few more hours and I'd have been safely off the train," she said, her voice no longer that of an old woman. "I didn't figure on a kid wrecking my plans."

A million thoughts tumbled inside Tom's head, surprise, foolishness, despair. Fear of the black revolver which pointed straight at his heart. He had found the killer, and he was trapped.

"Why you?" Tom said unhappily. "I like you."

Mrs. Ruggles smiled. "And I like you. You did okay, solving this case."

"Are you going to kill me?"

"Only if necessary."

Tom stared at the revolver, wondering if he should throw himself at the old lady and wrestle with her for it. But she wasn't an old lady, and she had already killed one person.

"Who are you?" he asked.

"Be quiet, while I think," Mrs. Ruggles said. There was a long silence, then she nodded her head. "Yes, that's a good plan."

"Who are you?" Tom repeated.

"I'm the cashier from the bank."

"What?" Tom said, surprised.

"Mr. Faith was right, when he suspected Richard Saks had framed me for the robbery." Mrs. Ruggles leaned toward Tom. "But it wasn't Richard's fault, it was that rotten Catherine. She made him do it."

"Were you with her in Hollywood?"

"Yes, we went there together to become stars, but Catherine couldn't act. She got sick of trying to succeed, and insisted that we return to Winnipeg. She always got her own way, so we came home and found jobs at Richard's bank. Before long, we were both in love with Richard." Mrs. Ruggles smiled, but her mouth was bitter. "Guess who got him?"

Tom remembered the way Catherine Saks had treated her husband at the breakfast table. "She didn't seem to be in love."

"It didn't last long." Mrs. Ruggles looked down sadly, and for a second the gun wavered in her hand. "All she wanted from Richard was money, so she forced him to steal from the bank. I knew about it, but I didn't say anything, because I loved Richard."

"Do you still love him?"

"Yes, but I wanted revenge, especially against Catherine. When I read in the newspaper they were taking this trip, I planned the perfect murder."

Mrs. Ruggles seemed to have forgotten the gun, and it drooped lower and lower as she spoke. "Two weeks ago I terrified Catherine by phoning her to warn I wanted revenge. Then, to avoid suspicion, I went to Brandon and boarded the train acting my role of little old lady."

Mrs. Ruggles paused, looking pleased.

"Catherine never recognized me. Last night, after she fought with Richard in the bar, I followed her to their bedroom and offered a sympathetic ear. Catherine told me all her woes, and then I gave her a piece of fudge."

"Filled with cyanide," Tom said, shivering.

Mrs. Ruggles nodded. "She popped it in her mouth, and started chewing. As she did, I took off my wig and smiled at her. Catherine used to say I was a poor actor, but she didn't think that as she died."

Tom stared at the woman, realizing what a vicious person was masked by the make-up and wig.

"When she was dead, I stabbed her body and went to my bedroom. When I heard Richard return, I raised the alarm, pretending I'd heard a fight."

By now the revolver was almost pointing at the floor. Gathering courage, Tom thought of another question to keep Mrs. Ruggles talking. "If you loved Richard Saks, how could you set him up for a murder rap?"

"I just wanted him to have a taste of what I went through. When they get Catherine's body to a city, they'll find the cyanide and fudge in her stomach and know Richard wasn't the killer. By then old Mrs. Ruggles will be off the train and gone forever."

No you won't, Tom thought. He bunched his muscles to spring at the woman, but there was a knock at the door and the gun snapped up.

"Who's there?" Mrs. Ruggles called in her old lady's voice.

"Porter, ma'am. Shall I bring you some tea?"

"Not this afternoon, thank you."

"Everything fine?"

"Hunky-dory," Mrs. Ruggles said, smiling at Tom. "A young man has come by for some fudge."

"Have fun, then," the porter called.

Fudge. Tom felt sick, realizing how easily he might have been poisoned. His detective work had landed him in a real mess, and there was no way out.

"And now," Mrs. Ruggles said, "it's time to eliminate young Tom Austen."

"You wouldn't shoot me," Tom said, trying to sound tough.

"Want a bet?"

Keeping the gun aimed at Tom, Mrs. Ruggles leaned close to the window and looked toward the front of the train. "Good," she said, "here's a chance now."

"You won't get away with this," Tom said. "Give yourself up to the police."

Mrs. Ruggles laughed. "You sound like a TV show. Now listen carefully, sonny. We're going to leave the bedroom and walk to the end of the sleeping-car. I'll have the gun under my shawl, and if anything goes wrong I'll kill you."

"If you do, you'll go to prison."

"You forget I've already killed. One more corpse won't make any difference."

Tom trembled, remembering the grey blanket which had covered Catherine Saks when her body was taken away. He'd better obey, or he too would leave the train feet first.

"Open the door."

Tom did as ordered, hoping foolishly that a dozen Mounties would be waiting outside to ambush Mrs. Ruggles, but the corridor was empty and silent except for the lonely clack-clack of the wheels.

"Quickly," Mrs. Ruggles said, poking Tom in the back with her cane.

They hurried down the corridor and past the roomettes without seeing anyone. As they stepped into the vestibule between the cars, Tom looked out the window and saw darkness. For a confused second he thought it was night, then realized the train was inside a tunnel.

"Open the outside door," Mrs. Ruggles said.

Tom was beginning to understand what she planned. He looked at the woman, hoping for sympathy, but the cold look in her eyes showed he must obey. He un-latched the door and swung it open, hearing the sounds of the train magnified by the tunnel.

"Now the floor panel," Mrs. Ruggles said above the noise.

Tom lifted it away, and the steel steps lay waiting.

"Hurry up," Mrs. Ruggles said, pushing Tom with her cane. "Go to the bottom, and jump."

Tom started down slowly, the diesel fumes filling

his nose. He reached the bottom step and looked out fearfully, knowing the train was moving slowly but afraid to step into darkness.

"Jump," Mrs. Ruggles called.

Tom turned, and looked up at the woman. "I can't," he whispered. "I'm afraid."

"Do as I say!" Mrs. Ruggles said angrily, leaning forward to poke Tom with her cane.

Fear was tight in Tom's throat. "I can't jump," he said, dodging the cane.

"You must!" Mrs. Ruggles came down two steps, trying to shove Tom out the door, but he kept jumping away from her cane.

The woman came down one more step, leaned forward, and pushed Tom with her hand. As she did, Tom threw up his arm in self-defence and his fingers tangled in her shawl; he toppled backwards clutching the shawl, and the two figures fell together out of the train.

Metal burned into Tom's back, his head hit something, and a roar filled his ears. He gasped for air, sure that he was dying, then opened his eyes and saw the dim shape of the train's wheels rolling past.

Tom turned his head, feeling it throb, and saw Mrs. Ruggles lying on her back. He sat up painfully and crawled to her side, hoping to find the gun, but her eyes opened and she grabbed his arm. As she did, the last car of the train went past and its lights faded away down the tunnel.

Now there was only silence and darkness.

Tom tried to pull away from the woman's hand, but her grip was firm. He could hear the sound of her breathing, but saw nothing.

"I've got my gun," Mrs. Ruggles whispered. "Give me one excuse, and I'll gladly kill you."

Tom was silent, not wanting his voice to reveal his fear. The woman's strong grip hurt, and the rocks of the tunnel floor were cutting into his knees, but he could only think of escaping the cold, damp air which choked around his head.

"Help me get up," Mrs. Ruggles said.

The silk of her old dress rustled as she stood up, leaning heavily on Tom's shoulder, then pulled him to his feet.

"This is all your fault," the woman's voice said angrily. "When we're out of this tunnel, I'm going to get rid of you for good."

Tom listened to the terrifying words echo inside the tunnel, knowing he must act now to save his life. Without warning, he kicked out and felt his shoe connect with the woman's leg. She cried out with pain, and her grip loosened; with a quick motion Tom tore free, turned, and ran.

"Come back!" Mrs. Ruggles shouted.

There was a red flash, followed by a loud bang, and a bullet crashed against the tunnel wall. Tom stopped running, realizing she had shot toward the sound of his feet, and stood waiting in fear. The black air was silent while long seconds passed.

Then, he heard footsteps.

Mrs. Ruggles was coming slowly in his direction. Tom heard her feet stepping cautiously as she worked her way forward in the darkness. His heart thumping, he bent down for a rock, and threw it in her direction.

For a moment he heard nothing, then the rock smacked against the tunnel wall. Mrs. Ruggles shouted in surprise and fired toward the sound, the flash and roar of the gun huge inside the tunnel.

Again, silence spread through the darkness. Tom listened, waiting for movement, and at last heard the woman's cautious footsteps. Closer they came, the rocks crunching under her feet, until she was so close that Tom could hear her harsh breathing.

Every muscle in his body was rigid with fear as the feet went past. They walked on into the darkness, and suddenly stopped.

The railway tracks were humming.

Tom turned his head, listening to the strange sound which quivered in the rails, then heard a distant rattle. It hung in the black air, died, and came again. The hum grew louder, and a dim glow began to melt the black air. Somewhere far down the tunnel, still out of sight but coming this way, was a light, its beam gradually pushing aside the darkness which surrounded Tom and Mrs. Ruggles. Very soon she would see where he was standing, and shoot.

Tom leaned over and picked up a rock in each hand. He looked toward the darkness where he had last heard footsteps, drew back his arm, and threw.

The rock clattered against the tunnel wall, and the gun roared.

With all his energy, Tom threw the second rock toward the place where he had seen the gun's flash. This time there was a cry of pain; Tom turned, and was running toward the distant glow when he heard a bang and the sound of a bullet.

Tom put down his head and ran faster. The light was close now, glowing in the darkness ahead, and he could hear the sound of a motor. Seconds later, a headlight burst around a distant bend.

Gasping for breath, Tom threw himself forward. As the headlight grew stronger, he raised his arms to wave, and heard the rasp of steel against steel as brakes were applied.

"Who are you?" a man's voice shouted.

Tom shielded his eyes against the headlight and ran toward the voice. When he was past the glare, he saw two men sitting in a railway scooter piled high with repair tools. Thrilled to see them, Tom raised a shaking hand and pointed down the tunnel.

"Please help me!" he said. "There's a woman with a gun."

The men looked at each other. "I told you those were shots," one said.

The second man reached down to Tom. "Climb aboard," he said, helping Tom into the scooter.

"She'll shoot," Tom warned. "Be careful."

The scooter started forward, its headlight gleaming along the rails. At first there was no sign of Mrs. Ruggles, but then Tom saw a distant figure, running.

"There she is!" he shouted.

The scooter picked up speed, the throb of its motor echoing around their ears. As they closed in on Mrs. Ruggles, she fired a shot over her shoulder, but the bullet went wide of the scooter. Stopping to aim, she squeezed the trigger again, but nothing happened. Once more the woman tried, then threw the empty gun in their direction.

It smacked against the front of the scooter and clattered to the tunnel floor. Mrs. Ruggles turned to run, but one man was already out of the scooter and managed to catch her arm. She struggled desperately, but the man twisted her arm painfully behind her back and led her to the scooter.

Mrs. Ruggles looked at Tom and held up a bleeding hand. "You hit me with a rock," she said, almost crying. "How could you do that, when you said you liked me?"

There was no way Tom could answer her question.

10

Mrs. Ruggles was bundled into the scooter, and it rolled quickly out of the tunnel and along the tracks to the next station. From there, the police were called and a message radioed ahead for *The Canadian* to be stopped.

Once Tom had given a statement to the Mounties and watched Mrs. Ruggles being driven away under guard, the scooter crew gave him a ride to the waiting train, which had stopped on a siding overlooking a green lake surrounded by mountains.

Some of the passengers had left the train to stretch their legs and take pictures of the scenery. Rumours had already begun to spread about Tom and Mrs. Ruggles, and the scooter was surrounded by curious faces the moment it stopped.

"What happened?" Dietmar asked, shoving through the crowd to stare at Tom.

"Nothing much," Tom answered. "I fell out of the train, and these guys gave me a lift back."

But such modesty did not apply to the scooter crew, one of whom stood up and looked around at the crowd. "This kid and us are heroes!" he said proudly. "We just caught a murderer."

"Who?" someone asked, and other voices joined in: "Where? Why? When?"

"Just a minute!" It was the conductor, pushing through the passengers. "Everybody climb on board, so the train can get moving. Then you can all gather in the dining-car, and let this young fellow tell what happened."

Inside the train the smiling steward provided refreshments and Tom told his story to the people who crowded into the dining-car. Then, questions were asked to fill in the blanks.

"Did you have any idea that Mrs. Ruggles had murdered Catherine Saks?" one man asked.

"No," Tom admitted, "but there were several clues which should have told me she was the killer."

"What were they?"

"First, there was the cigarette butt with the red lipstick stain. Because of Catherine Saks's cigarette holder, I should have realized another woman had been in Bedroom C."

Tom paused for a drink of pop.

"During bingo Mrs. Ruggles mentioned that Catherine Saks had five lines in one movie. Why would she know the exact details of a stranger's movie career?

That was a tip-off I missed, plus it was odd that Mrs. Ruggles didn't have any pictures of the grandchildren she claimed to be going to visit. Most grandparents carry at least a dozen pictures of beaming babies."

Mr. Faith raised his hand to ask a question. "Were there any clues to indicate the killer was a woman?"

"Yes," Tom said. "At the breakfast table I learned that Catherine Saks worked at the bank with a friend. Later, you told me that Richard Saks was thought to have framed a cashier at his bank. I already suspected that someone wanted Richard Saks to look guilty of murder, so I should have realized it was the cashier who'd done it for revenge."

As Tom spoke, the train's speed dropped and it entered a tunnel. Even though he knew he was safe, Tom shivered as he looked out at the darkness.

"You know," he said, "it's too bad she didn't stay in Hollywood, because she was a really good actor."

"She fooled us all," Mr. Faith said. "With that rouge and powder covering her skin, I never realized she might be a young woman."

Someone was tugging at Tom's sleeve. He looked down, and saw the cookie-woman sitting at a table with her tin of goodies open. "Have one of these," she said, smiling. "I think you're a fine young man."

"Thanks," Tom said, selecting a large chocolate-chip cookie. "By the way, did I mention that you were a suspect?"

"Me?" the woman said, annoyed.

"Yes," Tom said, quickly gulping the cookie before the woman could ask for it back. "I thought you might have given Catherine Saks a cookie laced with cyanide.

Of course you hadn't, but I should have remembered that Mrs. Ruggles was passing around fudge, which could also contain poison."

The woman turned to her husband. "Imagine," she said, "thinking my cookies would kill someone."

This produced a laugh from the other passengers, and even the cookie-woman's brittle face broke into a smile when she realized how foolish she sounded. Some people got up to leave, and others came forward to shake Tom's hand.

Among them was the little boy in the baseball cap. "Congratulations, mister," he said, holding out his hand.

Too late, Tom saw the water pistol. The boy fired a deadly stream into Tom's face and turned to run, but this time Tom reached out quickly and caught his collar.

"Come here," he said, leading the squirming boy into the empty corridor.

When Tom reappeared he was smiling, but the little boy didn't look as if he'd been damaged. More passengers swirled around, patting Tom's back and calling him a fine specimen of humanity, and then he spotted Mr. Faith about to leave the car.

"Mr. Faith!" he called, pushing through the passengers. "Just a minute!"

"Yes?" the man said, pausing by the door.

"Please open your attaché case and show me what's inside."

"I can't do that," the man said, but other people were crowding around, and a woman suggested he open it as a reward for Tom. Reluctantly agreeing,

Mr. Faith shielded the case's combination lock and spun the dial.

"I can't wait to see this," Tom said, leaning close. "I bet it's full of diamonds and rubies."

But Tom was wrong, for all he could see inside was a stack of paper. He looked up at Mr. Faith, disappointed.

"I knew you didn't believe me," the man said. "No one believes in me."

"I don't get it."

"I'm a writer. This is my latest manuscript, which I'm taking to a publisher in Vancouver."

"But how can it be worth a million dollars?"

"Arthur Hailey made a million dollars for his book, *Airport*. With luck, I'll do the same with this book."

"What's it called?" someone asked.

"Oh no you don't." Mr. Faith closed the lid of the attaché case. "No one is going to get my title."

"Why do you have the case locked to your wrist?" Tom asked, pointing at the handcuffs.

"All Hemingway's early manuscripts were stolen in a railway station," Mr. Faith said. "That will never happen to me."

"Boy," Tom said, "I've never met a writer before. I'll be watching for your book to come out."

Mr. Faith looked pleased. "I've already had some paperbacks published, under the pen names William Hope and Robert Charity. Why don't you buy those, too?"

"Hey!" Tom said, snapping his fingers. "I'll bet you've got another pen name."

"What?"

"Franklin W. Dixon!"

"Never heard of him."

"Oh," Tom said, surprised. "It's strange that you haven't, because he's the greatest. He writes the Hardy Boys stories."

"What are they about?"

Tom stared at Mr. Faith, shocked at his ignorance. "About two brothers who are detectives. You see their books everywhere."

"Do you?" Mr. Faith looked interested, and studied Tom carefully. "You're quite a detective yourself. Maybe I'll write a book about you, and earn a million dollars."

Tom grinned. "That would be great!"

"On second thought," Mr. Faith said, "I don't think it would make any money. Let's forget it."

Tom was disappointed, but didn't let it show. He was about to turn away when a man with red hair and a beard spoke up from a corner of the crowd.

"I'll write about you," he said to Tom. "You'll be the most famous character since Puck of Pook's Hill."

Everyone laughed, including Tom. "One final thing," he said to Mr. Faith. "Why did you desert me in that town? I almost missed the train."

"I got tired of your questions. Anyway, trains are like girlfriends. If you miss one, there'll be another along soon."

Picking up his attaché case, Mr. Faith left the dining-car. As the other passengers began to drift away, Tom saw Dietmar standing by a table, picking at cake crumbs on a plate.

"Still hungry?" Tom said, walking over. "Would

you like a stick of gum?"

Dietmar nodded. "Okay."

"You know," Tom said, as he held out the package to Dietmar, "I never forgot that bomb trick you played on me."

"Poor Tom," Dietmar said, laughing. And then, he pulled the gum out of the package . . .

The Lost Treasure
of Casa Loma

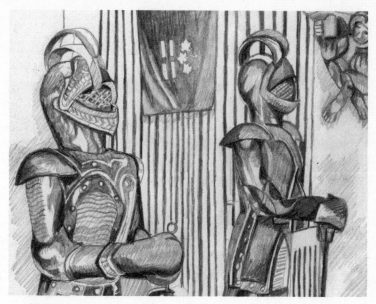

1

"We fear it was murder."

The butler's gloomy face was lit by a flash of lightning. "But please come in. Mr. Winter will tell you all the details about Sir Nigel's disappearance."

Tom shivered with excitement as he stepped into Casa Loma, a castle in the heart of Toronto. He put down his backpack and followed his sister Liz and their Uncle Henry to the castle's Great Hall.

A log fire roared, throwing an orange light on suits of armour and crossed lances on the walls.

"Welcome to Toronto, Mr. Austen." A handsome dark-haired man came forward to shake Uncle Henry's hand. "I'm Vince Winter, a close friend of Sir Nigel's."

After the introductions were over, Uncle Henry went to the enormous fireplace to warm his hands.

"This is a sad occasion. I was very fond of Sir Nigel."

Vince looked thoughtfully into the flames. "We don't know that he's actually dead."

"What happened?"

"I'll tell you in just a minute. First, if I may, let me introduce Sir Nigel's private secretary."

A young woman in a wheelchair came across the Great Hall toward them. "I'm Tia Nightingale, Mr. Austen."

"Please, Tia, first names only."

She smiled. "That's a nice idea. But you may get objections from the new butler, Smythe. He's only been at Casa Loma a few days, and seems a bit stuffy."

Tom glanced toward a distant corner of the Great Hall, where the butler stood under a carving of an evil-eyed jester. Had he heard Tia?

Vince motioned to Smythe. "Sherry, please, and Cokes for Tom and Liz."

"Very good, sir."

Vince led Uncle Henry through a doorway. "This is the library. Let's have our sherry in here, while I tell you as much as I know about Sir Nigel's disappearance."

Smythe appeared with a silver tray, and passed around the drinks. Tia sipped hers cautiously, then nodded. "I'm pleased this is actually sherry. Yesterday Smythe served us brandy by mistake."

Tom thanked the butler for his Coke, and accepted a tiny sandwich served by a pretty maid named Irene. Then he waited impatiently for details of Sir Nigel's mysterious disappearance, which had brought Uncle Henry to Casa Loma. Tom and Liz had been staying with their uncle when the news had arrived, and they had been excited by the prospect of accompanying him to Toronto.

But, before anyone could speak, a thin man of about sixty came into the library and approached Uncle Henry. "May we have a word in private, Mr. Austen?"

"We don't have secrets out West, where I come from. Please speak your piece."

The thin man swallowed nervously, and glanced toward Smythe. "My name is Hatfield, and I am Sir Nigel's personal servant—his valet. I have been in his service for many years now. Is it correct you are taking over Casa Loma?"

Uncle Henry nodded, and his glasses caught the light. "Sir Nigel is my cousin. If he can't be found, I will inherit the castle."

"Then, sir, I must warn you something is terribly wrong! Some of the new servants, including Smythe, don't even know their jobs. But it's the stables I must tell you about. I . . ."

At that moment the lights went out. Startled cries sounded in the room, then Smythe's reassuring voice was heard.

"The storm must have blown down the power lines," he said. "I'll fetch some candles."

Suffocating darkness filled the library, and Tom's nerves prickled with tension as the minutes passed. Why was Smythe taking so long?

At last a match flared into life and the yellow light of several candles cut the darkness, revealing the shadowed faces of the assembled company.

"Well, Hatfield?" Uncle Henry said, looking around for the valet. "What were you saying?"

"He's not here, Unc," Liz said.

"But where has he gone?" said Irene, the pretty maid. On her face was total astonishment.

"Let's not worry about Hatfield now," Vince said. "I was about to tell you what happened to Sir Nigel. Come along, and I'll show you the room where he disappeared." Picking up a candlestick, Vince led the way to a long dark hallway. "This is called Peacock Alley. Over here is the door to Sir Nigel's study. Nothing in it has been moved since he disappeared."

Opening the door, Vince stepped into the study. Then he gasped. "Oh no! It can't be!"

The horror in his voice made Tom's hair stand on end. Stepping closer, he looked into the study. Sprawled in the room, the twisted features of his face yellow in the candlelight, was Hatfield.

2

"Everyone get back!"

Vince slammed the study door and gestured to the maid. "Irene, go phone the police!"

"Yes, Mr. Winter."

"I insist we all wait together until the cops arrive."

Tom nodded his head in agreement as he glanced around at the other faces in the yellow candlelight. Had one of them attacked Hatfield and then dragged the valet to the study while the lights were out? Obviously Uncle Henry and Liz were not involved, but that still left several other suspects.

"Mr. Winter," Irene called, hurrying back toward them along Peacock Alley. "The phone is dead, so I can't call the police."

"Surely the storm hasn't affected the phone as well?"

"Perhaps someone cut the line. Could that be possible?"

"That's *very* possible, Irene." For several long moments Vince gazed thoughtfully at the young maid, until finally she dropped her eyes. "Well, I'd better drive to a police station and make a report. But, first, we'll have to find out what happened to Hatfield."

Tom edged closer, his heart beating rapidly as he watched Vince open the study door and look inside.

The room was empty.

"That's impossible!" Tom stared into the study. "There's only the one door, and no windows!"

Suddenly the lights came back on and everyone crowded into the room, staring at the place where they had seen Hatfield's body only moments before.

"We can't *all* be crazy!" Vince tried to smile. "I'm sure the police will find an explanation. But, first, let's go back into the library so I can tell you about Sir Nigel."

Tia shivered as she turned her wheelchair to leave the study. "A second mysterious disappearance within a few days. I think I'll look for another job."

"Please don't," Uncle Henry said, walking beside her into the library. "I'd be lost, trying to run this place alone."

Vince sat down and stretched his long legs, then glanced at his fancy watch. "I'm sorry, it's getting late, but I do want you to hear about Sir Nigel."

"Yes," said Uncle Henry. "We'd better hear quickly, before someone else disappears." No one returned his faint smile. They were all too nervous.

Tia leaned forward in her wheelchair. "As you know, Sir Nigel Brampton purchased Casa Loma a year ago, after retiring here from Britain. The castle cost a mint, but Sir Nigel had earned millions from oil and gold."

Vince smiled. "Millions? I'd have said jillions, or maybe zillions."

"Sir Nigel was fascinated by Casa Loma and tried to find out as much history as he could. One unusual thing he learned was that the original owner was so horse-crazy that he had false teeth made for a favourite charger, but that's not—"

"Excuse me," Liz said. "I'm a horse freak, too. Did the false teeth work?"

"I don't know," Tia answered, smiling. "Anyway, one day Sir Nigel discovered an old coded document. When he broke the code, it led him to a cache of hidden diamonds."

"Diamonds! How fabulous!"

"Fabulous is right. I saw them once, shortly before Sir Nigel hid them again, and they were gorgeous. Tiny, radiant perfection."

Uncle Henry frowned. "You say he *hid* them again?"

"Yes. Sir Nigel wouldn't trust a safety-deposit box, so he found a new hiding-place in Casa Loma."

Vince gulped down the last of his sherry. "Shortly afterwards, I was introduced to Sir Nigel by Tia, and we became close friends. I urged him to put the diamonds in a bank, but he refused."

Tia shook her head. "That was a mistake. The police are convinced that criminals are behind Sir Nigel's disappearance. They're after the diamonds."

"Exactly what happened?" Liz asked.

"A week ago, Sir Nigel was working in the study. A maid had just taken him a cup of tea when she heard a terrible cry. Rushing back to the study, she found Sir Nigel lying face-down across his desk, apparently dead or at least unconscious."

Vince shuddered with the memory. "I was a weekend guest of Sir Nigel's at the time. When the maid raised the alarm, I rushed to the study and . . ."

"Yes?"

"And the study was empty."

"Just as it was with Hatfield!"

"Exactly. Sir Nigel disappeared into thin air. Not one word has been heard from him since."

For a moment no one spoke. Tom glanced at Liz, wondering what his sister thought about the strange events at Casa Loma. Suddenly there was a loud crash somewhere in the castle. Tom and Liz both stared toward the sound.

Vince smiled. "Don't worry, Casa Loma doesn't have ghosts. Sometimes the wind slams a door."

"What about that horrible creaking?" Liz asked.

"That's only the teak floors."

"Are you sure? It sounds more like a pack of zombies roaming around."

Vince smiled, then turned to Uncle Henry. "And so, as Sir Nigel's closest relative, you have been summoned from Winnipeg to look after Casa Loma. Should Sir Nigel not be found, the castle will be yours."

A mournful grandfather clock tolled midnight. Uncle Henry ran his hand nervously through his hair.

"Sir Nigel had better be found. This castle gives me the creeps."

* * *

The next morning Tom felt groggy. He hadn't slept well, despite the luxury of a massive bed in the Round Room, which had once been occupied by the Duke of Windsor.

Tom went down to the Great Hall in search of breakfast, and found Liz already there combing her dark hair in front of a gold-framed mirror.

"Guess what?" she said happily. "The shower in my suite has perfumed water."

"My bathroom's so big, I could use a bike to get around. But there's only a bathtub."

"One of the servants told me Sir Nigel's private suite has a fabulous shower with six taps. Apparently Sir Nigel never bothered using it, but I'm sure no one would object if you tried."

Smythe appeared. "Breakfast is served, young sir and madam."

The butler's glum face was an upsetting reminder of Hatfield's disappearance the night before. The castle was spooky even in daylight; Tom and Liz followed Smythe into the breakfast room, where Uncle Henry was eating a huge serving of bacon and eggs while talking to the young maid, Irene.

"Good morning, kids! How'd you sleep?"

"So-so," Tom said, sitting down in a gigantic chair carved with sea serpents and dragons. "Have the police arrived yet?"

Uncle Henry shook his head. "Not yet. Vince drove

down to make a report last night after you'd gone to bed. They'll probably be here later this morning."

"Great! I can't wait."

Uncle Henry smiled, looking a bit sheepish. "I hate to be a killjoy, but I've already planned your morning. You'll be with Irene. You've only got a week's spring holiday from school, so I figured you'd want to explore Toronto before you fly home."

Irene grinned at Tom and Liz. "How about us seeing a human scalp this morning?"

"Hey," Tom said. "That sounds all right!"

Just then, Tia entered the room in her wheelchair. "Planning to visit Fort York? I'd enjoy showing you round. Before my accident, I was a guide there."

"Then take the morning off," Uncle Henry said. "With Smythe and twenty-five servants, the castle should survive! Right, Smythe?"

The butler nodded solemnly. Dark circles under his eyes, and several shaving cuts on his chin, made him an unattractive sight this morning. Tom was glad Smythe wasn't going to Fort York with them.

* * *

The first sight of the fort was a Union Jack, being tossed by the cold, rainy wind. As they drove into the parking lot, they heard a cannon boom.

"Want some help?" Tom asked, as Tia wrestled her wheelchair out of Irene's car.

"No thanks, I'm used to this. I drive myself to work, using hand controls."

Tia wheeled the chair toward the fort, leaving two

long tracks behind her on the muddy path. "During the War of 1812," she explained to Tom and Liz, "American forces invaded this area. Fort York was the headquarters of the British defenders."

Irene smiled. "These days, the American invaders are all tourists."

Tia smiled. "And some of us like Canada so much, we stay."

"Are you from the USA, Tia?"

She nodded. "Look, there's the Fort York guard, drilling with Brown Bess muskets. Aren't their red uniforms splendid?"

"Where's that scalp?"

"Follow me," Irene said, laughing.

The scalp—long black hair and a bit of skin attached to a wooden stretcher—was displayed inside a barracks. Then Tom and Liz followed the others to the fort's magazine to see a shot-oven. This, Tia told them, had been used for heating cannonballs to set enemy ships on fire.

Next, they went into the officers' kitchen, where an aproned girl was making cinnamon doughnuts over an open fire. Copper pots reflected the flickering flames, and the circles of sizzling dough made Tom's mouth water.

The girl gave each of them a doughnut, and Tom wandered outside eating his.

Hatfield was standing in the yard.

Tom nearly choked on his doughnut. He hurried toward the man.

"Hatfield! You're alive!"

The man's face went white when he saw Tom. He

turned to the two small children at his side. "Go and find Granny. I'll be there in a minute."

When the children were gone, he looked at Tom. "O.K., so I'm Hatfield. What of it?"

"What happened last night? And what were you going to say about the stables?"

Hatfield glanced nervously at some passing people. "Just that the blacksmith was pounding cold iron. Now, please, leave me alone."

Hatfield started away, but Tom followed. "What happened to you after the lights went out?"

Hatfield's face was marked by tension. "Listen to me. They've threatened my family if I talk to anyone about Casa Loma. So please get away from me."

"*Who* threatened you?"

Hatfield stared at Tom with fear written on his face, then he hurried toward the parking lot. Puzzled, Tom watched him get into a car with a woman and the two young children.

After making a note of the car's licence plate number, Tom walked back toward the officers' quarters. He was greatly relieved to discover that Hatfield had not been murdered the night before, but he was completely mystified by the strange events that had happened at Casa Loma.

Speaking of the castle, what was all this about a blacksmith? Tom stopped to jot *blacksmith pounding cold iron* in his notebook, then continued on with a big smile on his face.

Excellent lead!

3

"Guess what?" Tom exclaimed, as the others came out of the officers' quarters. "Hatfield is alive!"

Tia was shocked. "You must be joking!"

"He was right here at Fort York, large as life and happy as a clam. Happy, that is, until I gave him the third degree and he spilled a clue that points me straight at a major suspect."

"A suspect? Who is it?"

"I shouldn't say, in case my man's innocent and I ruin his reputation."

Tia studied Tom's face thoughtfully. "I admire that." She wheeled her chair toward the parking lot. The others followed, and they were soon heading back to the castle.

The towers of Casa Loma were magnificent as they approached. "What a sight!" Liz said. "Unless the crooks have found them, the diamonds must be hidden in one of the castle's ninety-eight rooms. I wonder which one?"

Tia brushed back her thick curls. "Sir Nigel once teased me with a clue, but I couldn't figure it out."

"A clue! Please tell us."

"These were his exact words: 'It's the same place as pictures are sent, when they've made a mess of things.'"

"Weird."

* * *

Back at the castle, Tom and Liz found Uncle Henry in the billiard room. They told him about Hatfield, and he was equally puzzled by the man's strange behaviour. Although the police still had not arrived to investigate yesterday's events, the morning had been busy, and unpleasant, for Uncle Henry.

"The servants are complaining about Smythe, and threatening to quit if the former butler doesn't return."

"But where is the original butler?" Liz asked.

"No one knows. He left shortly after Sir Nigel disappeared, then Smythe came as his replacement. According to the other servants, Smythe is making a mess of things. They say he's incompetent."

"Why don't you boot him out?"

Uncle Henry made an unhappy face. "I tried to, Liz, but I just couldn't do it. I talked to Smythe, said he had to leave, and the poor man was so upset that I changed my mind. But I warned him he'll have to shape up or ship out."

Liz smiled. "Get on the ball, Smythe, or get on the boat."

"You bet!" Uncle Henry tried to look stern.

"Say, Unc, may we explore the castle's towers?"

Uncle Henry nodded, smiling. "Let's ask Smythe to take us. It might cheer him up."

* * *

Not long afterwards, they were climbing stairs which spiralled up inside a gloomy tower. Tom half expected to be attacked by bats, and was pleased to step out into the open air.

"Be careful," Smythe warned as they approached the stone rampart around the roof. "The rain has made it slippery up here."

"Far-out view," Liz said, looking at the city's famous CN Tower and the skyscrapers gleaming along the shore of Lake Ontario. "This was a great place to build a castle."

"Casa Loma is Spanish for 'house on the hill.'"

"Some house!"

Tom and Liz crossed over to the other side of the tower roof. Leaning over the rampart, they looked down at the red tiles and stone unicorns below.

"Those must be the stables," Tom whispered, pointing at a distant building. "Got time to investigate them?"

"Because of what Hatfield told you?"

"Yes. He said that—"

Suddenly there was a terrible cry. Whirling around, Tom saw Uncle Henry and Smythe struggling at the edge of the rampart. For an awful moment Tom thought Smythe was trying to push Uncle Henry over. Then he realized that in fact the butler had kept his uncle from falling. Tom ran to help, but before he reached him, Uncle Henry had managed to scramble back to safety.

"I almost fell! I leaned against the rampart and something slipped. Thank heavens, Smythe, that you were right beside me!"

A closer look revealed a loose stone in the rampart. Uncle Henry seemed satisfied that this had caused the nearly fatal accident, but Tom still kept a long way from Smythe as they descended the tower's narrow stairs.

"Let's try those stables," Tom whispered to Liz, when they were alone.

It was now pouring with rain and the water bounced off the road as Tom and Liz ran to the stables. "I'm soaked!" Liz wiped her foggy glasses. "We should have asked the chauffeur to drive us over."

Tom laughed. "This rich life suits you, Liz. Soon you'll be taking baths in milk."

Liz glanced into a feed room, but it was empty. Cobwebs were thick in the corners. "The stables must be . . . Yikes!"

A huge man appeared from around a dark corner. For a moment he stared at them with unsmiling eyes. "Get out of here," he said, gesturing menacingly with an enormous hand.

"Hey," Tom protested. "We want to see the stables." When there was no reply, he swallowed nervously and added, "Please."

"There's nothing to see. The horses are at winter quarters in the southern USA."

"We still want to look around," Tom said.

"Not a chance."

"Oh, well," Liz shrugged. "We'd better come back with Uncle Henry. You'll let your new boss look around, won't you?"

The man looked hostile. After a moment, he pointed down a dark passage. "Follow that and you'll find the horse stalls."

"Thanks."

Tom and Liz stumbled along the dark passage but it led to a blank wall. Returning, they heard the sound of metal ringing against metal and followed it to a large room containing two rows of enclosed horse stalls. Near a forge, a blacksmith—the same unfriendly man they'd seen earlier—was pounding a horseshoe on the anvil. Tom shivered, wishing there was a fire in the forge to warm the chilly air.

"Let's go," he shouted to Liz above the noise of the blacksmith's ringing blows.

As they reached the outside door, footsteps sounded from the dark passage and a man came out, carrying a tray of steaming food. It was the chauffeur who'd met them at the airport yesterday.

"Oh," he said. "You startled me! I, uh, brought my lunch over from Casa Loma. I like eating in private."

"How about a ride home after you've eaten?" Liz asked.

The chauffeur smiled, but a nerve twitched in his eyelid. "Afraid not, Miss. The limousine's parked at the castle."

"Oh, your clothes are dry, so I thought you must have driven over here."

The chauffeur mumbled something as he headed for the horse stalls. Outside, Liz turned her face to the rain.

"Did you notice the horses' names in gold on the doors of the horse stalls? I bet there's enough room inside those huge stalls for a horse to entertain several friends to tea."

"All I noticed was that blacksmith's arms. If the diamonds are hidden under the castle, he could just lift it up for us. I wonder why he lied about the location of the horse stalls?"

Tom had planned to question the blacksmith about what Hatfield had said concerning the stables, but one look at those muscles and the plan had evaporated. Embarrassed by this failure, and feeling miserable after the rain, he decided to drown his blues in a hot shower.

Remembering the fabulous shower in Sir Nigel's private suite, he headed there after receiving permission from Uncle Henry.

His footsteps were silenced by a thick carpet as he entered the suite. Then he stopped in surprise. Standing beside a table and holding a photograph in a silver picture frame was the maid, Irene.

She didn't notice Tom, and he didn't speak. After studying the photograph for a few moments, Irene put it down and turned toward the door.

"Tom! What a scare you gave me! I, um, I was checking that everything's O.K. in here."

Tom glanced toward the wooden bedstead, carved

with forked-tongued serpents. "But this suite hasn't been used for a week."

Irene smiled, pushing her black hair away from her face. "You're right. Actually, I was walking past the room and saw the secret panel was open. I came in to close it, then noticed that photograph of Sir Nigel and your uncle."

"A secret panel! May I see it?"

Irene went to the fireplace. "There's a button hidden under the mantel. You just push it, and presto."

A thin panel beside the fireplace swung open, revealing narrow shelves holding books and papers. "Disappointed?" Irene smiled. "I bet you expected to see the diamonds."

"This secret panel hardly seems secret."

"You're right. All the servants know about it. But I wonder who opened it, and why."

When Irene had left, Tom went into Sir Nigel's bathroom. The marble walls were streaked with colours, and the many fixtures included a telephone linked to the castle's private phone system.

Dropping his clothes on the floor, Tom stepped into the shower. Six separate taps controlled the spray from silver rails which enclosed him. The hot, stinging water coming from all directions was so invigorating that Tom began to sing.

Perhaps in protest, the main pipe clunked loudly and the water died to a trickle. Tom was disappointed! Unable to get the water flowing again, he grabbed a fluffy towel and rubbed his hair until it stood up in red spikes.

Then Tom noticed that a tube of Sir Nigel's toothpaste had been cut neatly in half. The toothpaste had been squeezed out and hadn't yet hardened. It looked as if someone had suspected this was the hiding-place for the diamonds—someone who had very recently been in the bathroom.

A shiver passed through Tom. Close by in the castle there was someone, perhaps well known to Tom, who was behind the disappearance of Sir Nigel and the determined search for the diamonds.

But who?

4

Vince and Tom walked along a sidewalk, jostled by the shoppers crowding Toronto's Kensington Market. Vince had purchased a couple of Jamaican hot beef patties, and Tom was eating his while he tried to puzzle out a meat market sign reading *Grande Especial Carne de Porco*.

"Big special on pork chops, I guess. What language is that?"

"Portuguese. Toronto is home to people from all over the world, including yours truly. I'm from San Francisco."

Tom looked in the door of a music store, where music blasted and a straw-hatted clerk danced behind the counter. The boy gave Tom a friendly wave, inviting him to join in, but Tom shyly shook his head and hurried on.

A sweaty teenager came their way, trundling a cart loaded with red snappers on ice; as the fish passed, their huge, dead eyes seemed to stare at Tom. "They're as unpleasant a sight as the face on that Casa Loma blacksmith. There's something strange happening in the stables, Vince. I'm going to poke around there this evening."

"So you said earlier. And I repeat my warning: don't chance it."

Tom bent to rub the head of a mongrel sprawled in a doorway. "Why'd you move here from the USA, Vince?"

"I was offered a sportscasting job by a local TV station. I'm pleased to say the station's ratings are now huge. We're number one."

"Which sports?"

"You name it, I report it. Most of the pro athletes in town are close buddies of mine."

"Like who?"

"Dexter Valentine, for one."

"Dexter Valentine is your friend? I don't believe it!"

"Then why don't I prove it?" Vince crossed the narrow street. "Let's ring this doorbell, and see if Dexter's home."

Tom waited, doubtful that the famous shortstop for the Toronto Blue Jays baseball team would really open the door.

When he did, Tom's jaw fell open. He was still struggling for speech after he'd been introduced and they'd gone up a flight of stairs to an apartment overlooking the market.

"Liveliest view in town," Dexter said, leading them

onto the balcony. "Plus fresh fruit and vegetables, right on our doorstep."

Tom tried to think of an intelligent comment, but could only stare in awe at the man. He'd seen him so many times on television! His wife came onto the balcony carrying a baby, and Tom was introduced. The Valentines then produced some refreshments, and Tom gradually began to relax.

"This is delicious," he said, taking another bite of a crunchy, corn-meal fritter as he looked down at the market from the balcony.

Vince looked at his watch. "I should be heading for the TV station soon. Hey, Tom, how about you and Liz seeing tomorrow night's baseball game as my guests?"

"Fantastic!"

"Then, with the Valentines' permission, I'll use their phone to make the arrangements."

When Vince had left the balcony, Tom worked up the courage to ask Dexter Valentine how he liked being a star baseball player. The man laughed good-naturedly, and told some fascinating stories about life in professional baseball.

"The player under the most pressure is the pitcher, who's the focus of constant attention. When he has a bad game, and makes such a mess of things that another pitcher must take over, it's a long and unhappy walk to the showers."

"Wait a minute," Tom suddenly exclaimed. "That's it!"

"Huh?"

"Tia got it wrong! Sir Nigel didn't say 'pictures,' he said 'pitchers'!"

As the Valentines stared in amazement, Tom did a joyful jig around the balcony. Vince returned, and Tom blurted out, "Guess what? I know where the diamonds are hidden!"

Vince laughed briefly, but then looked thoughtful. "I believe you mean it." Tom grinned happily. "So? Where are they?"

"I'd rather not say, in case I'm wrong. But let's head for Casa Loma, and I'll test my theory."

"Hold your horses. We can't just leave in the middle of visiting the Valentines."

Tom choked back his disappointment as Vince sat down and accepted another cup of coffee from the Valentines, then explained to the puzzled couple why Tom was so excited. All three then did their best to get the secret out of Tom, but he just grinned and shook his head.

"What if I'm wrong? I'd look like a prize turkey."

Smiling, Vince stood up. "It's clear Tom can't be moved, and I must get going. One more phone call, and then we'll say good-bye."

Vince was gone some time, and Tom tried to calm his excitement while he bounced the gurgling baby in his arms. But at last Vince was ready to leave, and they were soon hurrying through the market. Tom barely noticed the delicious smells from bakeries and spice sellers in his eagerness to get back to the castle.

"Listen, Tom," Vince said, "I'm already late for an on-air interview with Jacques Savard, the ice hockey player. You'll have to take a streetcar to Casa Loma."

"Sure, Vince, and thanks. It was great touring the market and meeting the Valentines. Liz made a big mistake, deciding to visit the Science Centre today."

Several streetcars passed, and Vince grew anxious and impatient as he stared along the street.

"At last! O.K., Tom, this next streetcar is yours. Get out at Prince Edward Drive, and ask someone the way to Casa Loma." He made sure Tom was safely on board, then waved good-bye. "I hope you find the diamonds. Save a couple for me!"

Tom walked to a seat at the back of the streetcar as it swayed along the tracks. Only a few passengers were on board; Tom glanced at them, then looked out the window at some kids playing baseball on a school's concrete playground.

Two men in bulky raincoats and floppy hats were waiting at the next stop. The first dropped into a seat at the front as the second struggled into the streetcar on crutches.

The driver offered to help, but the man shook his head and slowly made his way down the aisle. Tom smiled at his choice of both a raincoat and wrap-around sunglasses; the man was obviously prepared for any weather.

Tom shifted closer to the window as the man sat down heavily beside him. Tom wondered briefly why the man hadn't selected an empty seat, then he looked out the window at a push-cart displaying shiny red candy apples and hot cashews. A candy apple would be a perfect reward for finding the diamonds; he wished the streetcar would double its speed.

"Pickpocket! Pickpocket!"

The cry came from the man beside Tom. As the streetcar ground to a halt, the other passengers turned to stare. The man struggled up onto his crutches and pointed an accusing finger at Tom.

"This boy stole my wallet!"

"What?" Tom couldn't believe his ears. "Are you crazy?"

"It's in your pocket!"

Tom looked down, and was stunned to see a worn leather wallet, clearly visible in his pocket. "Hey, what . . . ?"

"You sneaky little thief! Stealing from the handicapped! You should be behind bars."

The other man who'd boarded at the last stop came along the car toward them; close up, the raincoat and hat no longer hid his identity from Tom.

"Hey! You're—"

"Just you be quiet," the man demanded, his strong voice overpowering Tom's. "I'm a police officer, son, and you're under arrest."

"What are you—"

But again Tom was drowned out as the man called for the driver to open the rear doors. He dragged Tom out of the streetcar and toward a van with dark windows. It was parked in an alley. Tom looked round desperately for help, but the alley was deserted. Suddenly he found himself being thrown roughly onto the floor of the van. With a burst of power, it shot off into the traffic of the main street.

Fear pounded through Tom as he looked up from the floor and saw the blacksmith from the stables at Casa Loma leaning menacingly over him.

"Don't move, don't speak," the man said to Tom and then turned toward the driver. "Better slow down. We don't want to be stopped for speeding, especially after I posed as a cop!"

The van slowed down. Tom tried to fight his fear by concentrating on the driver, who he couldn't see from the floor. Who was it? Where were they taking him, and why had he been kidnapped?

As the questions whirled inside Tom's head, he began to panic. He closed his eyes, and tried to think about Liz and the others at Casa Loma; when he didn't return, they'd be sure to call the police.

Time passed, and the van rolled on. Tom's eyes grew heavy, and unwillingly he fell into a troubled sleep.

* * *

He awoke to find the blacksmith shaking his shoulder. "Come with me."

Cold air was blowing in the open door of the van. Tom stumbled out into the black night, and was dragged toward the door of a building. He was bundled down a hallway and shoved into a dark room.

The door closed behind him, and a key turned in the lock.

Light seeped around the locked door, outlining chairs and a sofa; in one corner of the dark room Tom could make out a fireplace.

Low voices came from the hallway on the other side of the door. Tom moved closer, and his stomach tightened in fear as he heard the blacksmith say, "I'll break that kid. He'll tell the truth. It'll take two seconds, or less."

There was a reply from a second voice, probably that of the driver of the van. Tom strained to hear what was said, but the voice was so low it was barely a murmur.

"Not yet," the blacksmith said. "First, I'm gonna watch the game on TV."

The other voice murmured something.

"I like him," the blacksmith said. "He's got style, with that twenty-four-hour watch and everything. I'm getting one of those when he pays me for this job."

A murmur.

"O.K., so I'm working for *both* of you! Sure, it was you who discovered the study has a latch instead of a button, but you're still not the boss type."

There was the sound of a TV being turned on and suddenly Tom's heart leapt when he heard a voice he knew: Vince Winter.

* * *

Good evening, Vince said. *It's a perfect night for baseball.* As his deep voice went on, describing the baseball game, Tom was filled with an aching loneliness. Would he ever see Liz again, and Uncle Henry?

If only he could escape!

Fantastic! Vince exclaimed. *What a catch by Dexter Valentine!*

The memory of the happy scene on the Valentines' balcony only a few hours before made Tom even more determined to escape. He knew he had to seize the chance provided by the baseball broadcast.

Carefully, he examined the room. There was only the one locked door, and the window had been nailed shut. He was trapped.

Or was he? Tom looked at a small wooden chair in the corner, and considered his chances. Then he went quickly to the chair, picked it up and approached the window.

Using all his strength, Tom swung the chair. With a terrible *crash* the glass broke, showering splinters everywhere. Startled cries came from the hallway as Tom knocked away loose bits of glass and then jumped to the ground.

A light went on inside the room and Tom was caught in its glare. He plunged into the darkness, almost collided with a tree, then stumbled on into the bushes.

"Come back!" the blacksmith shouted.

Tom fought a path through the bushes until he reached the rocky side of a hill. He scrambled on, pausing occasionally to listen for sounds of pursuit. Apart from the cold stars above, he was surrounded by darkness. There was no sound except the shrill calling of frogs, and Tom knew he'd escaped safely.

For a moment this thrilled him, but then a gust of wind chilled his face and he looked around. Where could he possibly go in the endless, empty darkness?

5

For a while Tom blundered on.

He climbed another hill, hoping for signs of civilization, but found only darkness. He thought he heard traffic, but he was mistaken.

Finally, shivering with cold and fear, Tom sat under a tree and hugged his body for warmth. It was hopeless to go further until dawn.

Throughout the long night he dreamed of fireplaces with roaring flames, and of a luxurious hot bath in which he was soaking, while diamonds sparkled nearby. He woke often, his body stiff, then returned to his dreams.

* * *

Birdsong came before morning. The dawn's faint light revealed a white fungus clinging to a dead stump, then the bare branches of a tree overhead.

At last the sun arrived, and he saw a forest of barren trees, wrapped in mist. Standing, Tom stretched his cramped muscles. If he went toward the sun, which was glowing feebly behind the thick grey mist, he would avoid walking in circles and must eventually find help.

Twigs snapped underfoot as Tom started down the hill. Suddenly he stopped. Was that a car he'd heard? No, it was just the wind gusting through bare branches.

At the foot of the hill, Tom came to a dirt road. A hawk rose from the ditch with something in its talons; briefly it was silhouetted against the cold grey sky before disappearing.

"Wow," Tom whispered. "What a sight."

Hoping that the hawk was a lucky sign, he walked in the direction it had gone. The road was surrounded by the browns and greys of the forest; although it was April, the air was far too cold for the trees to be budding yet.

Despite his stiff muscles, and the hunger which ached inside his stomach, Tom felt cheerful as he followed the road up a hill. People must live around here somewhere, and soon he'd be safe.

At the top of the hill Tom stopped dead in his tracks. Parked on the road ahead was the van used by his kidnappers the previous evening!

Dropping to the ground, Tom studied the van. It was parked near a phone booth, in which Tom could see the blacksmith gesturing with his hand while talking to someone on the phone. The blacksmith hung up and went to speak to a man leaning against the van; with a jolt of surprise, Tom recognized the chauffeur from Casa Loma.

Both men wore red-checked wool coats, and their breath came out in puffs as they nodded agreement at each other. Then they split up, the chauffeur going into the nearby woods while the blacksmith entered the trees on the other side of the road.

When they were lost from sight, Tom hurried toward the phone booth to call the police. He was so cold and tired that he needed help soon, and he was sure the men would take their time searching the woods.

Tom glanced at the back of the van, then reached for the phone. His hand was shaking so much he could hardly hold it.

"Please answer," he whispered, listening as a phone rang in some distant office. "Please!"

As he waited, Tom looked again at the van. Someone was inside, on the driver's side—Tom saw eyes reflected in the rear-view mirror. A ski mask hid the person's face—only the eyes were visible. They darted back and forth across the road, watching the scene.

The ringing stopped, and a voice answered. "Police."

"Uh." Tom stared at the person in the ski mask. He knew those eyes, but where from? "Hello, police?" he whispered.

"Would you speak up? The line's so bad, I can hardly hear you."

"I need help," Tom whispered, slightly louder.

"Please make your call again. I can't hear anything."

"Listen—"

As the line went dead, the eyes spotted Tom. For a moment the person stared in shock, then the van's horn blared. The morning air was shattered by the terrible sound as Tom stumbled out of the booth and started running.

Soon Tom reached the woods—for a second he paused. The horn was still blaring, so the driver must have chosen to signal for the others instead of giving chase. This was a real break, and Tom used it to plunge deeper into the trees.

At last the horn stopped. Tom reached a stony outcrop and looked down into a deep river, swollen with the spring flood. Crawling behind a rock, he tried desperately to think. How could he save himself?

A minute later, Tom had a plan. Putting his shoulder against the largest boulder on the outcropping, he worked it loose. Then he waited until he could hear the sound of feet crashing through the trees.

Tom pushed with all his strength against the boulder. It hesitated, then rolled over the edge of the outcropping, and plunged down toward the swirling black water below. As it fell, Tom cupped his mouth and screamed, "No!"

The boulder hit the water with a tremendous splash. Tom scrambled along the outcropping to the shelter of a big tree and dropped behind it, shaking with fear.

"That was the kid," the blacksmith shouted from somewhere in the trees. "He must have fallen in the river!"

"Perfect," cried the chauffeur. "Let's go fish him out."

The chattering of an angry squirrel announced the approach of the men. Tom held his breath.

"Look at that water," the blacksmith exclaimed. "He didn't have a chance. I can't even see his body."

"We'd better get outta here."

They hurried away, but Tom remained in hiding long after he'd heard the van drive off. It was possible the men suspected a trick, and one had remained behind to watch the woods.

Finally hunger and cold forced Tom to move. He worked his way cautiously back toward the road until he could see the phone booth. There was no sign of the men. He hurried to the phone booth, desperate now to contact the police. But the phone was dead.

"They've cut the line! I don't believe it."

Tom stared at the useless instrument, feeling his spirits ebb away. What should he do now? Slumped against the booth, Tom stared at the grey mist and barren trees.

The men might return at any moment. Tom knew he must move on, yet he couldn't find the energy; it didn't seem worth the effort. Then, to his surprise, a porcupine came out of the woods and lumbered slowly across the road. Tom looked at its sharp quills, smiling at the porcupine's rolling gait. It looked like a near-sighted gentleman, bound for the Millionaires' Club.

One more try. Tom started along the road on feet that felt like blocks of ice, blowing on his pinched fingers for warmth. A tiny bird swept out of a pine tree and swooped round Tom's head, defending its nest. Tom trudged wearily on.

Then Tom saw a lake. In the distance, along the shoreline, there was a large cabin with a twist of smoke rising from its stone chimney.

"People! At last, real people! I'm saved!"

At this moment, as if in a final effort to break his spirit, rain began to fall. Big drops splattered on Tom's face as he left the road to follow the shoreline to the distant cabin.

"Don't be a mirage," he begged. "Please stay where you are."

A flock of small birds explored the wild grass along the shoreline. A blue heron took off from the shore, rising gracefully over the still lake where raindrops were forming hundreds of perfect circles.

Reaching the cabin, Tom noticed a ribbon of road winding out of the woods to a garage with a moss-covered roof. Both doors of the garage were closed. The road was littered with dead branches from winter storms, giving it a deserted appearance, but recent tire tracks and fresh footsteps leading from the garage to the cabin suggested that the cabin was in active use. Beside the footsteps in the wet ground were two long, thin tracks.

Tom thumped on the cabin's side door with his hand, and called for help. When there was no reply, he hit the door again, feeling his numb hand throb with pain.

"Who's there?" a voice shouted from inside.

The thrill of hearing the voice, and knowing he was truly safe, fed energy into Tom's system. "Help me," he cried.

"Be right with you."

134

Tom stepped back from the door, blowing on his cold hands. Moving about to keep his blood circulating, he went around to the front of the cabin.

One of the windows was smashed.

Tom stared at the scattered glass, refusing to believe his eyes. Then he heard the cabin door open, and his heart jumped as he turned to see the blacksmith.

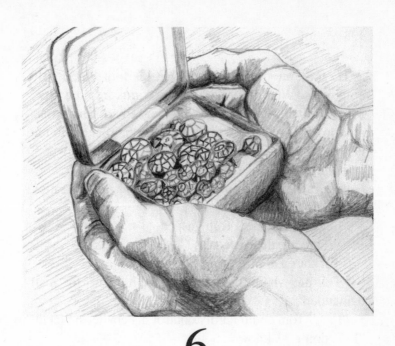

6

The man glared at Tom.

"So you tricked us, boy."

"No," Tom whispered. "Please, leave me alone."

The blacksmith walked forward, his huge hands clenched. Tom stared past him at the woods, realizing he couldn't reach their safety, then he ran toward the lake.

A pier stood over the water. Tom's feet slipped on the pier's wet surface as he ran to the end. There were no boats. He looked at the rain falling on the black water. Knowing it was foolish to even consider swimming across the cold lake, he turned to face the blacksmith. The pier was narrow, and there was no hope of darting past the man to safety.

"Get away from me," Tom begged, backing away.

He took another step back, but his foot found only emptiness. With a cry he fell backwards into the lake! Freezing water closed over his head, then Tom struggled to the surface and swam toward the pier. With the last of his energy he climbed a ladder from the water, and collapsed at the blacksmith's feet.

The man lifted Tom in his powerful arms. "Enjoy your swim?"

"Leave me alone," Tom gasped. "I'm . . . I'm . . ."

"Where are the diamonds?"

Tom stared at him.

"Tell me where the diamonds are hidden," the man demanded.

"I . . ." Tom could hardly control his chattering teeth. "I . . . don't . . . know."

The blacksmith stepped toward the water. "In you go."

"No! I'll tell."

"You've got two seconds, then you're back in the lake."

"They're . . ." Tom gasped for breath. "They're in . . . Sir Nigel's . . . shower."

The blacksmith's piggy eyes studied Tom's face, and for a terrible moment the man seemed ready to throw him into the lake again. Then he nodded.

"I think you're telling the truth."

"I . . . am!"

"For your sake, I hope so."

Carrying Tom in his powerful arms, the blacksmith returned to the cabin. Soon Tom was lying in a hot bath, feeling it draw the chill from his bones.

Later he sat at a rough-cut wooden table, watching the blacksmith throw chunks of log into a potbellied stove. Despite what had happened, Tom was too hungry to feel anything but thankful as the man dropped bacon, and then eggs, into a sizzling frying pan.

Tom's clothes were drying beside the stove. The blacksmith had provided an old dressing-gown; Tom pulled it tighter around himself.

"Where's the chauffeur?"

No reply.

"And the driver of the van. You know who I mean. I don't see them around."

The blacksmith scooped the bacon and eggs onto a tin plate, and dropped it in front of Tom on the table. He looked at Tom without speaking, then returned to the stove.

The first taste of food was marvellous. "This is great! May I have some toast, please?" Tom swallowed quickly, loving the crispy bacon and the superb eggs. "You three will be arrested for kidnapping. Doesn't that worry you?"

The blacksmith poured coffee from a blackened pot, then downed the hot beverage in one long swallow. He hadn't spoken a word since leaving the pier.

"You're a terrific cook," Tom said, trying to get the silent man talking. "You should be a chef, not a criminal. You don't seem the outlaw type to me."

The blacksmith glanced at Tom, and something flickered in his eyes. "It's time for you to get some sleep," he said gruffly. "I'm tired of your questions."

Tom fell silent, afraid he had pushed the man too far. He was led to a room with a bare mattress and a sleeping bag. Crawling into it, he burrowed a warm place and closed his eyes. With vivid clarity, Tom re-enacted in his mind the scene as he had approached the cabin. He recalled the rising smoke and the dead branches on the road, but he was sure the memory held something else that was really important. He'd almost figured it out when he fell asleep.

Some time later, the blacksmith shook him awake. Barely able to focus his eyes, Tom dragged on his clothes and was taken outside, where the van was waiting. Someone wearing a ski mask sat at the wheel.

Tom dropped into the rear seat and wearily closed his eyes. Then suddenly, without warning, he was blind-folded and shoved onto the floor by the blacksmith.

"Oh no! Hey, it's horrible down here. Please let me up."

His pleas were in vain. The van was soon under way, and Tom remained on the floor. Again he slept, but fitfully.

* * *

Tom was awakened by the squeal of brakes. Rough hands seized him, and he was pushed out of the van. Tearing off his blindfold, Tom tried to get the licence plate number but he was unsuccessful. He watched the vehicle disappear from the small park in which Tom had been abandoned.

Delighted to be free, Tom looked around the park. There was no sign of people, so he hurried toward the sound of traffic to find help.

By the time he reached the street, he'd had time to think. It would be better if he found the diamonds before contacting the police. He stopped a woman and asked her where he could catch a streetcar to Casa Loma.

She pointed at a TTC sign. "Take the subway to the Dupont stop."

"Thanks."

It was a long ride and Tom tried to curb his impatience by sitting in the front car, where he watched signal lights flash past as the train raced through twisting tunnels beneath Toronto. At Dupont he climbed to the street and hurried toward Casa Loma; in just a few more minutes he could tell Uncle Henry about the shower and help him to take it apart. He just hoped that the crooks hadn't got there first.

Tom rushed from room to room until he spotted Liz and his uncle in the conservatory.

Swinging open a door, he hurried in. "I'm back!"

Liz glanced his way. "Hi, Tom."

Uncle Henry smiled. "Enjoy your swim? I hope the water wasn't too cold."

Staggered, Tom stared at the two. Surely they weren't involved in his kidnapping? His shock then turned to amazement as they returned to their conversation.

"Hey," he cried aloud. "I'm safe!"

Liz looked his way, puzzled. "Have you been nibbling mouldy crackers again? Of course you're safe."

"Well, don't you care?"

"You're spoiling our fun, Tom. We're trying to act nonchalant, so you won't know we've got a secret."

"But don't you realize I was *kidnapped* yesterday?"

"Sure you were," Liz said. "And the cow jumped over the moon."

"Listen to me! I was grabbed by the Casa Loma

blacksmith and chauffeur, taken to some cabin, chased through the woods, I don't know what all happened. Then I come home to *this*! Where do you think I've been all this time?"

Uncle Henry polished his glasses thoughtfully. "The chauffeur's wife phoned last night, Tom. She said you'd be staying overnight. You were delighted because their apartment building has a swimming pool."

"Lies!"

"So I gather." Uncle Henry looked concerned. "What actually happened?"

Tom told the full story, including his theory about the diamonds' hiding-place. Liz and Uncle Henry glanced at each other when he mentioned the jewels, but remained silent.

Uncle Henry polished his glasses again. "This is serious, Tom. We must contact the police."

"What's the use? Both men will be in hiding by now. Besides, I've got no proof against them, and I haven't clue one where that cabin is located."

"What about the third person?"

"I could only see the driver's eyes. I couldn't make an ID. Hey, I'm starving. Do you think Irene would fetch me a snack?"

"Irene's left us."

"Irene? I don't believe it!"

Uncle Henry shook his head unhappily. "I'm afraid it's true. According to the other servants, Irene suddenly announced she was quitting. She walked out and didn't say good-bye."

"What a rotten thing to do."

Uncle Henry sighed. "I don't understand. After she's been so friendly."

"Do you think she quit because of Smythe?"

"Who knows? Anyway, we've seen the last of Smythe. He's quit too."

"*What!*"

Uncle Henry tried to smile. "It seems I'm not a very successful employer. The staff of Casa Loma is in tatters, and I've only been here three days."

"Surely no one else has gone?"

"A couple of others resigned, and Tia had to go home yesterday. She's got the flu. I can't get replacements until she's back, and can interview the candidates."

His face was so bleak that Tom almost smiled. Running a castle wasn't proving to be much fun; any more staff losses and Uncle Henry's entire day would be spent cleaning the fifteen bathrooms and replacing Casa Loma's five thousand light bulbs.

"Cheer up, Unc. Let's check Sir Nigel's shower for the diamonds."

"I almost forgot!" Uncle Henry smiled at Liz. "We haven't told Tom our secret."

They led Tom down Peacock Alley to the door of Sir Nigel's study. Uncle Henry unlocked it, waved the others inside, then secured the door against intruders.

Puzzled, Tom looked at the oil paintings of ancient gentlemen in wigs, then at the chandelier and the mahogany walls. He wondered what the big secret could be. Liz went to stand by the marble fireplace, while Uncle Henry sat at the desk and ran his fingers over one of its carved eagles.

"Look at this, Tom." Uncle Henry opened a drawer.

He slid aside a secret panel, then took a small velvet box from hiding.

Tom shivered with excitement as the box was put in his hands. He lifted the top, and his eyes were dazzled by the white fire inside.

"The diamonds! I don't believe it!"

7

For a few minutes, Tom could only stare.

"But . . . ? How . . . ?"

"It was simple." Uncle Henry put his feet on the desk, and fiddled happily with an old quill pen. "Want to know how we found them?"

"Of course!"

"Well, we just opened the secret drawer." He smiled. "Of course, we had a little help before that."

"What help?"

"Someone phoned this morning, Tom. He wouldn't give his name, but he explained exactly where to find the diamonds. Vince Winter was here having coffee, so the two of us plus Liz and Smythe dashed to the study . . . and you know the rest."

"Brother! After all my running around in the woods,

and a ducking in the lake, I finally get set to dig out the diamonds and you've beaten me to it!"

"Sorry, Tom. Maybe we should have waited for you."

Tom tried to smile. "I'm glad you found the diamonds. Too bad Sir Nigel wasn't in the desk too."

"I agree. He could have his crazy castle back." Uncle Henry looked at his watch. "I'd better go and arrange for afternoon tea. The cook may forget, now there isn't a butler to keep things happening on time."

When he'd left, Liz smiled. "We were in the kitchen this morning. The stove is actually big enough to roast a whole ox."

"Is that right, eh?"

"You sound blue, Tom."

"Yeah." He put his finger in the velvet box, and pushed around the glittering jewels. "Shouldn't these be somewhere safe?"

"Uncle Henry is leaving them hidden in the desk overnight. Tomorrow they're going into a safety-deposit box at the bank."

"Will they be O.K. here?"

"Sure. The rest of the servants will probably soon resign, so there'll be no one to steal them."

Tom watched Liz put away the velvet box, then close the secret panel.

"There's still a lot of unanswered questions, Liz. For example, the clue Sir Nigel gave Tia doesn't fit with a desk drawer, although I suppose he could have been just teasing." Tom walked over to the marble fireplace. "There's also that weird thing I overheard the blacksmith say. When I was being held prisoner at the cabin."

"What was that?"

"Something about the study having a latch instead of a button. I thought maybe he was talking about this study, since this is where Sir Nigel disappeared."

"Well, it beats me." Liz commented.

Still chilly from his night in the open, Tom decided to take a shower. Leaving Liz sitting in the study, staring at a scrap of paper on which she'd written *study-latch-button*, he went off to Sir Nigel's private suite to use the fancy shower.

To his delight, it decided to co-operate this time, and thin needles of hot water hissed from the rails until Tom had nearly drained the castle's boiler. Lazily he dried himself. He was sorry he hadn't been correct about the shower concealing the diamonds, but he was glad they were safe.

Returning to the study, he found Liz with her feet on the desk and a wrap-around grin on her face.

"I deserve a large medal," she said.

"What happened?"

"Tell me again about Irene opening the secret panel in Sir Nigel's bedroom?"

"Well, she just pushed a button under the mantel, and the panel swung open."

"Don't you get it? In the bedroom a button, in the study . . ."

"A latch!"

"Watch this." Liz crossed the luxurious rug and reached under the wooden mantel above the fireplace.

Silently, a mahogany panel swung open in the wall.

"Good grief!" Tom went forward to gaze at the narrow stairs leading down into darkness. "Well done, Liz."

"Thanks," she said, smiling.

"Where do they go?"

"Don't ask me. I'm too chicken to go down there alone."

Gingerly, Tom put his foot on the top stair. It creaked, and he stepped quickly back.

"Come on," Liz said. "Let's try them together."

Tom followed her into the darkness. The narrow wooden stairs spiralled down, and soon the light of the study was left behind. The air was musty and freezing cold.

"Concrete," Liz whispered. "I think we've reached a tunnel."

"There must be a light." Tom stretched out his hand, and his fingers touched cold cement. He felt his way along it, but found no light switches.

"Want to turn back?" Liz whispered.

"No way. Let's see where this leads."

Liz's face was a dim white smudge in the darkness. She started along the tunnel, then disappeared.

"Slow down," Tom said. "I can't see anything."

"Keep your hand on the wall as a guide."

"What if there's an open pit ahead? Filled with alligators."

"Nice thing to say, when I'm going first."

They both fell silent. The only sound came from their hesitant footsteps and nervous breathing as, slowly and carefully, Tom and Liz worked their way forward through the cold black air.

"This is crazy," Tom whispered after a while. "We could walk forever."

"The tunnel must lead somewhere."

"Two more minutes, then we turn back."

"O.K."

Tom's nerves were on edge as he pictured water-filled pits and spiders with fangs waiting in the darkness. He was beginning to wish the secret panel had remained a secret when an urgent *hssst!* came from Liz.

"Stairs," she whispered. "Leading up."

The wooden stairs creaked underfoot. At the top Liz searched the wall for an opening. Suddenly there was a *click*, and pale light seeped through a narrow crack.

"We're in the stables!"

"Are you sure?"

The crack grew wider as Liz pushed open a panel in the wall. Tom could see the narrow passage that led to the horse stalls.

"So! This is how they got Sir Nigel and Hatfield out of the study."

Liz nodded. "The blacksmith probably did the dirty work. He must have knocked Sir Nigel over the head, then hauled him through the tunnel to the stables. Ditto with Hatfield."

"But then what happened?"

"Listen!" The urgency in his sister's voice made Tom's hair stand up.

From somewhere in the stables came a muffled thudding. Tom grew tense as he followed Liz along the passage toward the sound; what if the blacksmith was waiting with one of his mallets?

Turning a corner, they found themselves at the horse stalls. The thudding was much louder.

"It's coming from that end stall," Liz said.

They hurried across the tiled floor to the stall's padlocked door. Tom found a pair of the blacksmith's tongs, and used them to force the padlock off.

Liz gave the door a quick shove, and with a squeal of metal, it swung open to reveal a small cot.

Lying on the cot was Sir Nigel Brampton.

His face was flushed from the effort of kicking the wall, and his eyes goggled as he tried to speak through the gag over his mouth. "*Mmmmmph!*" he said, gesturing with his bound hands.

"It's O.K.," Tom replied. "We'll get you untied."

As Tom bent over the knots, Sir Nigel continued to make anxious sounds. The moment Liz removed his gag, Sir Nigel burst out, "The diamonds! Are they safe?"

"They sure are." Liz smiled. "And now you're safe, too."

"The jewels . . . are you positive?"

"We've just been looking at them. Now try to relax, Sir Nigel. Tom's almost got those knots undone."

"Thank goodness my diamonds are safe. Those crooks tried everything to make me reveal the hiding-place, but I refused!"

"That's great."

As Tom released the final knot, Sir Nigel sat up on the cot. He smoothed the white hair which fringed his bald head, then smiled. "Thank you for rescuing me. I've kicked and kicked that wall, but no one ever heard." He tried to stand, then sank back with a groan.

"You're not well," Liz said anxiously. "We'd better get help."

"Nonsense. I'm fine." Sir Nigel staggered up, but again he collapsed. "Perhaps you're right. I do need assistance."

Tom went to the door. "Wait here. I'll ask Uncle Henry to phone for an ambulance." Hurrying through the stables, he noticed the forge and suddenly realized why the blacksmith was always pounding cold horseshoes. Obviously it was to drown out Sir Nigel's efforts to attract attention when anyone came to the stables.

A second puzzle was answered when Tom remembered the chauffeur with the tray of food. He must have brought it through the tunnel for Sir Nigel, which explained his dry clothes.

The jigsaw was slowly falling together, and yet Tom didn't feel elated. Somehow, he sensed the mystery and danger were far from over.

8

The big man swung hard.

There was a loud *crack* as bat and ball connected. Dexter Valentine dove for the ball, then threw it with lightning speed to first base.

"You're out!" the umpire shouted, as the batter reached the base a split-second after the ball.

Thousands of cheering voices filled the night, and another Blue Jays baseball game was under way.

"Did you see that play?" Tom exclaimed. "That was my buddy, Dexter!"

Liz laughed. "Your buddy? You didn't know the guy two days ago."

"I make friends fast." Tom turned to look at Vince Winter inside a nearby glass-walled broadcast booth. Vince could be seen describing Dexter's sensational play; although the booth was sound-proofed, it was clear that Vince's words were filled with awe at the player's skill.

A cold wind came off nearby Lake Ontario, slicing through Tom's clothes. He shivered, and looked longingly at a man who was carrying a steaming container through the crowd. "Hot dogs," the man cried. "Get your giant red-hots here!"

"You hungry, Liz?"

She nodded. "I'm going for a Salty Pretzel. Can I get you a hot cat?"

"You bet!"

Tom leaned against the railing which separated the broadcast area from the crowd, and returned to watching the action on the stadium's ultra-green artificial turf.

Dexter was first up for the Blue Jays. He let two strikes past, then sent the ball flashing into left field for a clean single. As the crowd erupted in cheers, Liz returned with the food. "Why the thanksgiving? Is the game over?"

"Funny, funny. Dexter just happens to be a hero, yet again."

"I'm frozen solid." Leaning over the railing, Liz pointed at a man whose head was hidden inside a tuque that read *Go Jays Go*. "I'd love one of those tuques. It would be a great souvenir of Toronto."

The next pitch was fouled off into the crowd. There was generous applause for the girl who proudly held up the ball after a mad scramble among the fans.

"That's the souvenir I'd like," Tom said. "Or even a broken bat."

Seconds later, as the pitcher unleashed a knuckle-ball, Dexter broke for second base. The crowd rose, screaming, as the throw to second seemed to have Dexter trapped, but with a burst of speed he slid to safety under the tag. The cheering continued as he brushed dirt off his uniform, then grinned.

"Fantastic," Liz said. "Your buddy puts on a great show."

"I predict he'll score the first run."

On the next pitch, the batter rattled a double off the wall, and Dexter crossed home plate to put Toronto in the lead.

The Milwaukee pitcher was in deep trouble, and Tom felt sorry for the man as the team's manager walked slowly to the mound, frowning. They spoke briefly, then the unhappy pitcher handed over the ball and started toward the dugout.

"He's heading for the showers. Maybe he'll get lucky and find some diamonds there!"

On the stadium's huge screen, the pitcher was seen trudging woefully across the field. As this image froze and was replaced by a junk-food commercial, Tom remembered Sir Nigel's clue to Tia about where he'd hidden the diamonds. The clue couldn't possibly have referred to the desk drawer, and again Tom felt uneasy.

"Why am I nervous about the diamonds?"

"Because it was all so simple. One anonymous phone call, and suddenly the mystery is solved." Liz looked thoughtfully at the cold darkness beyond the stadium, where a winking neon sign advertised a TV station. "Something about the discovery of the diamonds smells like a very old egg."

The new Milwaukee pitcher quickly got his team out of trouble, and Toronto clung to its one-run lead as the fast-paced action continued. During the seventh-inning stretch, Vince joined Tom and Liz. "I've brought some binoculars, if you'd care to try them."

Tom smiled at the sportscaster. "Can't you arrange for Dexter to foul one up here, so we'll have a souvenir?"

"Although I've worked many miracles, Tom, that one could be difficult. However, I do believe you'll be leaving with a souvenir."

"Wow! What is it?"

"Patience, patience."

Using the binoculars, Liz studied the people huddled under blankets and shaggy coats. "You know something?" she said at last. "I'm sure that's Smythe the butler down there."

Vince grabbed the binoculars. "Let me look!"

Vince carefully studied the man Liz pointed out. Then he smiled. "You're wrong, Liz. His nose is a different shape."

"What about that hacked-up chin?"

"Some other guy with a dull razor blade. Not everyone is wise enough to buy the electric shavers I advertise on TV."

Liz tried again with the binoculars. "That *is* Smythe. I noticed him a while ago, because he kept looking up here. I wonder what's going on?"

Vince laughed. "The only action is in your imagination, Liz."

Vince returned to the booth and Tom tried the binoculars, but saw only the man's back as he hurried toward an exit. "Why would Smythe be here? I remember him saying only kooks like pro sports."

With a roar, the crowd rose to its feet. A Blue Jays slugger had connected solidly, and the ball was high in the air, gleaming against the black sky. Tracing an arc through the night, it landed beyond the wall for a home run.

"I don't believe it!" Tom released a war whoop, and pounded his hands together. "What a hit!"

The Blue Jays left the dugout to congratulate their latest hero, and the crowd applauded for several minutes. Then they settled back anxiously, wondering if Milwaukee would stage a comeback.

By the time the game was over, Tom's fingernails were a mess and the Blue Jays had a 2–0 win. After studying the remains of the money he'd saved for his holiday, Tom decided he could afford hot dogs for Liz and himself.

As they ate, Vince joined them. "You two interested in meeting the Blue Jays? I'm just about to do some interviews."

"For sure!"

Deep inside the stadium, happy talk and laughter came from the Blue Jays' dressing-room. In a separate room, a TV camera was set up for Vince's interviews with some players.

The last to be interviewed was Dexter Valentine, and afterwards Tom proudly introduced him to Liz. Vince then handed Dexter a large carton. He whispered something to the baseball player, who then smiled at Tom and Liz.

"Liz and Tom," Dexter said, sounding rather self-conscious and strained, "I understand you rescued Sir Nigel today?"

"Sort of, I guess," Liz replied. "We just looked in the right place."

"I've been asked to present you both with a souvenir, to mark his rescue."

"Thanks!"

Tom and Liz grinned at Dexter and then thanked Vince, who waved his hand. "You deserve it, kids."

Dexter opened the carton to reveal two satin team-jackets with thick crests reading *Toronto Blue Jays*, and baseball caps with crests. Tom and Liz were delighted, and immediately put them on.

"You look good," Vince said. "Let me get a picture of you with Dexter."

The camera flashed, then Dexter said good-bye. Vince smiled at Tom and Liz. "Feel like a day at Niagara Falls? I'm going there to interview a retired tennis pro. Would your uncle let you go as my guests?"

"He'd better!"

"Then let's drive up to the castle. You can collect your toothbrushes, and we'll leave tonight. That way we'll get an early start on the sights of Niagara Falls."

Uncle Henry gave permission for the journey, but seemed depressed about something. They left him slumped in front of the fireplace waiting for Sir Nigel, who had insisted on being discharged from hospital and was expected at any minute.

"I wonder what's wrong?" Tom said, as they walked towards Vince's sports car. "Do you think

Uncle Henry is feeling blue because he won't be taking over the castle?"

Liz shook her head. "No, something else is bothering Unc."

"Maybe it's the diamonds. I still say there's something weird about how you found them so easily."

9

Rocking and bucking, the little boat headed toward the Horseshoe Falls.

From high above, emerald-green water plunged down with great force, forming a steaming white spray.

"This is fantastic!" Tom had to shout above the thundering roar of the falls.

Liz laughed as her face was lashed by needles of spray. "I'm drowning!"

Wrapped in rain-slickers, they stood with Vince in the bow of the *Maid of the Mist* as it fought the seething green water. Tom could now see nothing except the white spray which stung his face until he was blinded. He was worried that the captain had taken them too far in and the boat would be crushed to pieces by the terrible fury of the falls. For many years, tourists have ventured deep into the heart of the falls in these brave little boats.

The captain put the boat into reverse and the *Maid of the Mist* slipped slowly out of the spray. Licking water off his lips, Tom grinned.

Vince pulled back the hood of his slicker, and shook water out of his wavy brown hair. Then he pointed up to the top of the falls, where a crowd of people were watching the *Maid of the Mist* from a high cliff. "That's called Table Rock House. From there, elevators take tourists deep inside the rock to tunnels which lead to openings behind the falls. Let's go take a look."

"Is it safe?" Tom asked.

"Let's hope so!"

The boat swung around, and started toward its dock. Tom watched gulls dipping and soaring in the air currents caused by the cascading falls. A fine mist drifted over the gorge's green waters, and the air smelled wonderfully fresh.

"What a day! The best of my life."

Vince smiled. "The excitement isn't over yet."

After they'd docked, and returned the rain-slickers, Vince and Liz paused at mirrors provided by the company to comb their damp hair. Tom ran a quick hand through his hair, then put on the Blue Jays cap and adjusted his team-jacket, anxious to start the next part of the adventure.

They took an elevator to the top of the gorge where Vince had left his sports car. "There's Rainbow Bridge," he said, pointing. "It crosses to the American side of the falls."

"You mean that's the USA, just across the gorge?"

Vince nodded. "We'll cross the bridge and look at the falls from the American viewpoint after we've seen those tunnels."

"*If* we survive the tunnels," Tom said, attempting a laugh.

* * *

A short while later, they were walking toward Table Rock House when Liz suddenly pointed at a newspaper box. "Hey, look at that headline!"

Under a photograph of Sir Nigel, a huge black head-line read: BORDER ALERT FOR GEMS. Inserting a coin in the box, Liz seized a paper and quickly scanned the article.

"That explains everything!"

"What's it say, Liz?"

She looked up from the newspaper, her eyes shining with excitement. "Those so-called diamonds we found at Casa Loma were fakes! They were cheap imitations made from quartz. The police figure the real diamonds have been taken from the castle."

"Why the border alert?" Vince asked.

"Apparently the police think a couple of Americans are the masterminds behind the theft, and may be heading for the USA with the diamonds. Travellers are being questioned at border checkpoints, and some people are being searched."

"What a great story!" Vince looked envious as he read the article. "Sometimes I'd love to be in TV news, not sports. Then for sure I'd dig up lots of hot news items like this. I could become an anchor on net-work TV."

Tom began reading the story. "Thank goodness Sir Nigel came home last night, and discovered the truth about the diamonds."

Liz shook her head. "Keep reading, Tom. The police knew the diamonds were fakes long before Sir Nigel got home."

"But how did they know that?"

No one could suggest an answer. Tom turned to the sports page, hoping to find the photograph Vince had taken of them with Dexter Valentine, but the only picture showed Dexter making a sensational diving catch. Under the photograph, a caption read: *Dexter Valentine—America's greatest player of all time!*

Vince looked at his watch. "Come on, people."

Outside the entrance to Table Rock House, they paused to gaze down into the gorge. Far below, the *Maid of the Mist* was just disappearing into the white spray; Tom shivered with excitement as he looked at the massive weight of green water plunging down.

"Imagine going over those falls. You'd be knocked to pieces."

Vince nodded. "A lot of people have died here. But a few survived."

"Went over the falls and lived? Impossible!"

Vince pointed at the wide river which rushed through a series of rapids before dropping over the falls. "Back in 1901, a widowed teacher was set adrift on the river inside an oak barrel. She was looking for instant fame and fortune by being the first to survive the plunge."

"Did she live?" Liz asked.

"Yes, but the only money she made was from selling autographed pictures of herself beside the barrel.

She died a pauper. Then some guy went over safely in a barrel, only to die later after slipping on a piece of orange peel."

Tom stared at the roaring water, finding it hard to believe that such strange events had happened right here. "I think Mr. Stones told our class about some kid surviving the falls."

Vince nodded. "A seven-year-old boy was in a boating accident on the river. His life-jacket kept him afloat all through the rapids, and he was so light that he was then thrown straight out over the falls. He landed beyond the rocks, and was picked up by the *Maid of the Mist*. No damage done, except a couple of cuts."

Liz looked at a log trapped between two boulders near the lip of the falls, then stared at the foaming white rapids. "Imagine boating on such a dangerous river. If I ever do that, please have my head tested."

Vince laughed. "You're right, Liz. Although I'm an avid sportsman, a boat ride through the Niagara rapids is one thrill I'm not after."

"Speaking of thrills, how about those tunnels?"

"Follow me!"

Inside Table Rock House, they were directed to a changing-room which looked like a scene from a science fiction movie. Attendants dressed in yellow prepared the tourists for the tunnels by replacing their shoes with huge gumboots and wrapping each person inside a black rubber rain-slicker and hood. At Vince's suggestion, Tom and Liz kept their Blue Jays caps and team-jackets on under their slickers. "Those outfits are valuable," Vince said, smiling.

Tom waddled toward the elevator, his feet sliding around inside the gumboots. His head was buried beneath the greasy rubber hood. Smiling, he watched a large group of tourists chattering happily in a foreign language as they posed for pictures in their black gear.

Then everyone jammed inside the elevator for the trip down. The noisy conversation continued until the elevator doors opened without warning and the tourists were silenced by the roar of the falls.

The booming thunder of the water filled the narrow tunnel. A little child belonging to one of the tourists started to cry. He was picked up as the group shuffled out of the elevator.

"This way," Vince yelled, pointing along the tunnel.

Tom nodded and smiled, but his heart was beating fast. The deafening noise of the water made him wonder if they should keep away from the plunging falls. But then he realized that it must be safe, or tourists would not be allowed down here.

"Fabulous, eh?" he shouted to Liz.

She smiled nervously. "I hope Vince knows what he's doing! I'd hate to fall in."

"We'll be fine!"

The long tunnel was lined with orange, white and red lights. Tom was again reminded of a scene from a science fiction movie as he looked at the eerie figures of the other tourists, hidden inside their identical black slickers. A person could commit a murder here, and never be identified.

Rounding a corner, he suddenly saw the water.

It fell in a solid sheet of white, roaring down to the

rocks and steaming up in clouds of spray through the narrow tunnel opening. Tom stared at it in fascination.

Finally he backed away, and followed a second tunnel toward another opening. There were yet more tourists here, and he had to wait his turn to approach the flimsy wooden railing which warned *Danger: do not climb over*.

At that moment, a man at the railing turned his head.

It was Smythe.

10

The Casa Loma butler returned to studying the plunging water, and was again camouflaged by his hooded slicker. Tom's heart thumped fearfully, and he moved carefully away, hoping he wouldn't be spotted.

Tom hurried to the other tunnel. "Vince," he shouted, going from figure to figure until he found him. "I just saw Smythe!"

Vince looked stunned. "Are you certain?"

"Yes! It was him, shaving cuts and all. He's in the other tunnel!"

Vince was silent for a moment. Then he led Tom and Liz away from the other tourists. "Listen carefully," he said. "It's time for the truth. I'm a Mountie, working undercover on the Casa Loma case. Things are getting hot. I'll need your help or the crooks might get away!"

"Wow," Tom exclaimed. "Sure thing!"

"The real reason I'm at Niagara Falls is to watch for Smythe, in case he tries to cross the border with the diamonds. Thanks to your quick eyes, Tom, he's been spotted."

Tom glowed. Liz patted his back.

"I can't tackle him alone, in case he's armed and someone gets shot." Vince quickly outlined a plan, then Tom rushed back to the tunnel where he'd spotted Smythe.

It was jammed with tourists, and Tom's spirits sank as he hurried from figure to figure without finding Smythe. Had the suspect made a getaway? Then suddenly Tom spotted the man.

"Smythe! Please help me!"

Looking shocked, the man stared at Tom.

"Quick," Tom cried. "My sister's in terrible danger!"

Tom started to run. He glanced over his shoulder at Smythe close behind, then pushed through the tourists toward the thundering water where Liz stood waiting.

She turned, her face wet with spray, and screamed when she saw Smythe. Her legs buckled, and she collapsed to the rocky ground beside the thundering falls.

"Help her!" Tom cried.

Smythe pushed Tom aside, and bent over Liz. Just then Vince came along the tunnel with two muscular-looking men in slickers. "That's him," he yelled, pointing at Smythe. "You see, he's tried to push that girl over the side. Grab him!"

Smythe glanced up, puzzled, then gave a startled cry as the men seized his arms and shoved him against the rock wall. Liz scrambled to her feet, and quickly followed Tom along the tunnel. Behind them, Smythe shouted something but his words were lost in the roar of the water.

Vince joined them at the elevator, his eyes bright. "Good work! Those men will hold Smythe until we return with police help."

The elevator doors closed on the fury of the water. The silence was a sudden contrast to the noise which had been pounding inside Tom's head. Releasing a deep sigh, he looked at Vince.

"Who's your second suspect?"

"What?"

"The newspaper said two Americans are behind the theft."

"Oh." Vince paused to shake water out of his hair. "I'm sorry, but I can't give you that information."

"Is it someone I know?"

Vince smiled. "O.K., I admit you know the person."

"Then . . ."

Vince raised a hand. "No more questions."

Tom tapped his foot impatiently as the elevator rose slowly inside the cliff. "Is it a man or a woman?" he asked Vince.

At that moment the elevator reached the top. Soon they were running across the crowded parking lot to Vince's car. He pulled out of the parking lot at top speed and headed through the crowded streets of the tourist town.

"Where's the police station?" Tom shouted, hanging on tight as they flew around a corner.

"Not far."

Liz looked at Vince. "Isn't that the Rainbow Bridge straight ahead?"

Vince nodded. "We're crossing to the American side to alert the FBI to increase their border guard. Smythe's partner is almost certainly here too."

Reaching the middle of the bridge, they passed the flags of Canada, the United Nations and the USA. Tom looked beyond the flags to the distant Horseshoe Falls, then straight down at the swirling waters of the gorge far below.

"Hopping horntoads! That's a long drop."

Vince laughed. "How'd you like to cross this gorge on a tightrope?"

"No thanks! Not for every diamond in the world."

"The Great Blondin did a lot of tightrope stunts over this gorge." Slowing down on the bridge, they joined a line of vehicles waiting to pass through the border checkpoint. "The Great Blondin did back-somersaults, rode a bike across, even cooked an omelette out there."

"Cheese or mushroom?" Liz asked.

Vince laughed, then gestured impatiently. "What a time to be delayed! Come on, traffic, move!"

"Put on your siren, and pass the others," Tom suggested.

"This sports car didn't come with a siren." Vince chewed a fingernail, then relaxed as they moved closer to the checkpoint. "It's O.K., kids! We're going to make it safely."

"Did the Great Blob ever fall?" Liz asked.

"Nope. But he came close, when he carried a man across on his back and the tightrope swayed wildly. But they managed to reach safety."

Liz shook her head. "Men are crazy."

"A woman did stunts, too. She walked the tightrope backwards, then crossed with her head covered by a bag. Another time she had her feet inside peach baskets."

"What a way to make a buck!"

"You're right, Liz." Vince smiled happily. "I'm making lots of bucks, but not by risking my neck."

They drove toward a row of booths where multi-coloured flags flapped in the wind and uniformed officials questioned occupants of the vehicles coming off the bridge.

"I'll do the talking," Vince said, stopping the car at a booth. Getting out, he had a short conversation with the official, but only his charming laugh could be heard from inside the car.

"This is no laughing matter," Liz said. "Smythe could have escaped by now."

"Not with those two big bruisers holding him. But I still wish Vince would hurry!"

Finally Vince got back into the car, and drove to a nearby parking lot. "They need me inside the customs office. I won't be long. You kids, stay here."

"Have the officials seen anything of Smythe's partner?"

"Apparently not."

Vince disappeared inside the customs office. Long moments passed and still he didn't reappear. What could be keeping him? At last they saw him leave the customs building, smiling broadly, and come their way with an official.

"Hop out, kids! You've got some questions to answer."

Tom gave Liz a puzzled glance as they got out. The official consulted his clipboard, then studied their faces. "Where were you born?"

"Winnipeg."

"Bringing any goods into the USA?"

"No, sir."

"Staying more than twenty-four hours?"

"No."

After a few more questions, the official gave Vince's car a thorough examination. Then he nodded, and walked away.

"We did it," Vince exclaimed. "Let's get going."

Gunning the engine, Vince took the car out of the parking lot on smoking wheels.

"Is this really the USA?" Tom said, feeling disappointed as he looked at hotels and stores lining the wide streets. "It's just like Canada."

Vince smiled. "Could be, but it looks like home to me."

"Oh yeah, I forgot. You're from the USA."

Liz's grip tightened as the sports car swerved around a corner, then she frowned. "Are you an American, Vince? I didn't know that."

"Yeah, I'm from good old San Fran. I think that's the first place I'll visit, now I'm home again."

"But aren't you going back to Canada?"

"Sure, sure. I'm just talking about the extended holiday I'm planning."

Leaving the buildings behind, they drove into a park. This early in the year, the park was empty. The occasional person could be seen walking a dog, but otherwise the park was deserted as they followed a road toward a wide body of water.

"Is that the Niagara River?" Tom asked.

Vince nodded. "It flows through the rapids, then

drops over the falls. You see all those trees on the far side of the river? That's Canada."

Liz glanced at the river, then returned her puzzled gaze to Vince's face. "A park seems a strange place for an FBI office. Anyway, you could have phoned."

"You're right, Liz." Vince swung the wheel, and the car pulled to a stop behind a fast-food stand. No other vehicles were in the lot. "Wait here while I phone. Can I bring you something to eat?"

"A hot dog for me, please," Tom said.

Liz shook her head. "Nothing, thanks."

When Vince was gone, she rubbed her cheek thoughtfully. "Remember what I said about the discovery of the diamonds smelling like a very old egg? Well, my nose is twitching again."

"You think there's something strange about this trip?"

Liz nodded.

"Me too. I tell myself that Vince has been good to us, but another voice inside keeps asking a lot of questions. Like, if Vince really is a Mountie, why were we held up for so long by the customs officers at the bridge?"

"And here's another question: why are we the only customers at this stand? Can the food be that bad?"

"Either that, or it's closed."

"Then why hasn't Vince come back?"

"Maybe he's decided to swim to the FBI office."

"Anything seems possible with Vince." Liz opened the door. "Let's investigate."

A cold wind whipped up whitecaps on the river, and the bare branches of trees rattled as Tom and Liz cautiously approached the front of the stand and found it closed. A notice said, *See you in the summer!* There was no sign of Vince.

"So where is he?" Liz commented.

"In those woods, I think," Tom said nervously. "Look."

Someone was pushing toward them through thick bushes. As Vince stepped out, they glimpsed the roof of a parked vehicle. Then the bushes closed behind Vince, and he smiled.

"Got tired of waiting?"

Liz nodded. "What's happening, Vince? You're not really a Mountie, are you?"

"Don't you believe me?"

"We want to, Vince. But you're acting so strangely."

"O.K., my friends, it's time for the truth." Vince came forward, grinning, and put his hands on their shoulders. "You've been more help than you realize."

Liz smiled happily. "Well, that's good."

"Let's go for a walk while I explain."

Vince led them along a narrow path through the trees. "All truth-seekers, follow me," he exclaimed happily, trying to click his heels.

Tom gave his sister a worried look. "He's gone nutty, Liz," he whispered. "Let's turn back."

"I think he's harmless. A bit vain, but hardly dangerous."

The path ended abruptly. To one side a dirt road curved toward the place in the woods where Tom had noticed the parked vehicle; to the other side was open land sloping down to the river bank. A woman in a wheelchair sat on a small dock, watching the waves lap around the pilings.

As she turned and waved cheerfully, Tom gasped in surprise. "It's Tia!"

"Hi, there," she called. "Why'd you take so long?"

Vince smiled as they approached the dock. "They wanted to look behind the falls, so we went to Table Rock House. I figured one final treat wouldn't hurt, after all the help they've given us."

"I approve, Vince. Even young law-breakers deserve some fun."

Tom stared at Tia, trying to understand what she was saying. Then she reached under the cushion of her wheelchair, and his heart lurched as she produced a small pistol.

"Nobody move," Tia ordered. Her face was grim. "I'm not afraid to use this gun."

11

For a moment there was only silence.

Then a gull screamed over the river, and Tia chuckled. "Surprised, kids?"

"But . . . ?"

"What a moment of triumph. I'll remember it forever."

Suddenly Tom understood. On the path between the dock and the woods there were two long tracks, identical to those near the cabin where he'd been held prisoner. They were the tracks of Tia's wheelchair.

"So, *you* were the driver of the van!"

Tia nodded, still chuckling. She looked at Vince. "Tell him what happened, partner."

Vince smiled. "Remember refusing to say where you thought the diamonds were hidden? I phoned Tia and she arranged for the men to grab you on the street-car. We wanted to learn your theory."

"So the diamonds *were* hidden in Sir Nigel's shower?"

"Yes. As soon as you'd coughed that up, Tia phoned from the cabin and I raced to Casa Loma. People were used to me at the castle, so I wandered up to Sir Nigel's bathroom and locked the door. In a few minutes the main pipe was off, and I was holding a small metal tube full of diamonds."

"No wonder the shower stopped working for me. The water must have shifted the tube, and it blocked the main pipe."

Vince started to speak, but Tia cut him off.

"I decided to hide fake diamonds in Sir Nigel's desk. The old fool had shown me the false drawer."

"He's not an old fool," Liz protested. "He gave you a job, and trusted you. It's terrible how you've treated him."

Tia's cheeks turned red. "Be quiet, you."

"I won't be quiet. You're a thief and you should return the diamonds immediately."

"But I don't have the diamonds, and neither does Vince."

"What?"

Tia laughed. "That's shut you up. Now, as I was saying, once the real diamonds were safely out of Casa Loma, the chauffeur phoned your uncle with the tip to look in Sir Nigel's desk. That discovery gave Vince time to make preparations for the jewels to cross the border."

"But you don't have the diamonds."

"*We* don't have them, but you do."

"*What?*"

Tia broke into delighted laughter. "If you could see your faces!"

Vince laughed too, but only briefly. "Come on, Tia. Time's a-wasting."

Suddenly she turned the gun his way. "I said *nobody* move. That includes you, partner."

"Are you crazy?"

"No, just greedy." Tia smiled. "I've been thinking, Vince. It's stupid to settle for a half-share, when all the diamonds could be mine."

"Why, you crook! You double-crosser!"

Vince's face turned dark with fury. He started toward Tia but her finger tightened on the trigger, and he stopped dead.

"That's right, partner. Take it easy, or you'll suffer severe lead-poisoning." Tia's eyes flicked toward the river, where a small motor boat with *Niagara Rentals* lettered on its sides was bobbing beside the dock. "Get in that thing."

"Why should I?"

"Because I had it specially delivered, just for your getaway. Soon you'll be across the river in Canada, and you can find a nice tree to hide in from the Mounties."

"What about the kids?"

"They're staying with me as hostages."

"Keep the diamonds, Tia, but let Tom and Liz come with me."

"Not a chance. Get in that boat."

Tia turned to Liz. "Take off your jacket."

"So that's it," Liz exclaimed. "I should have known."

Tia chuckled. "You're a clever young lady, but not clever enough. Give me the jacket!"

Reluctantly, Liz took off the splendid satin jacket and watched Tia tear at the Blue Jays crest. Finally it came apart, and a shower of diamonds sparkled into Tia's lap.

"Beautiful," Tia whispered softly, letting the diamonds run through her fingers. "What a treasure, and it's all mine."

"May I have my jacket back?"

"Sure." Tia pocketed the diamonds, then tossed the jacket back to Liz. "Now yours, Tom."

When the diamonds from Tom's crest were safely in her pocket, Tia aimed her gun at the motor boat. "It won't go far with a leaky hull, partner, so get travelling. Otherwise I'll try some target practice."

"You rat! You couldn't have pulled off this operation without me."

"Hogwash. I was the brains, and you were just hired help. Now take a ride. My finger is getting itchy."

Muttering angrily, Vince reached for the starter and the engine rumbled into life. On Tia's instructions, Tom went to release the boat's mooring lines.

"Sorry, kid," said Vince quietly. "I didn't like tricking you, but how else could I safely smuggle the jewels?"

"I wish we weren't staying with Tia. I'm scared she'll use that gun."

"She'd plug me in two seconds, but not a couple of kids." Vince glanced toward Tia, then dropped his voice even lower. "Say, good buddy, may I have your cap? I'm afraid I'll get sunstroke out on the water."

"But you'll be across the river in fifteen minutes."

"That's true. But it would be a good disguise."

From behind, Tia's wheelchair squeaked as she rolled closer. "You two quit whispering. Tom, step back so I can get a clear shot at that dude."

Looking frightened, Vince put the boat into gear. He started to speak to Tom, then heard the click of the gun's hammer and quickly accelerated. Foam and spray flew from the boat as it swept away from the dock.

Tia laughed. "Good riddance to bad rubbish," she called, then motioned at Tom and Liz. "Walk ahead of me into the woods. We're going for a nice ride."

As Tom started walking, he heard the motor boat drop speed. He glanced back quickly and saw that Vince had stopped outside gunshot-range, and was looking their way. Vince was waiting for them, if only they could escape from Tia.

Hoping to distract Tia, Tom started talking. "Was it the chauffeur who pretended I'd stolen his wallet?"

"Yes. Then he drove to the cabin after you'd escaped, to help search for you."

"Why'd you wear the ski mask in the van?"

"So I wouldn't be recognized."

Tom looked at Tia; the pistol rested in her lap while she turned the wheels of her chair. "Why'd you park in these woods?"

"So you wouldn't see my van when you arrived with Vince. Boy, you're certainly one for questions."

Straight ahead, a long branch dangled low across the narrow road. Tom grabbed the branch as he passed; when it was bent tight as a spring, he let go. The branch snapped straight back at Tia.

"Run, Liz," he shouted.

Tom plunged through the bushes, hoping desperately

that Tia would not start shooting. He raced out of the trees with Liz and headed for the dock, waving to Vince.

With a roar of power, the motor boat leapt through the water toward them. "Hurry," Tom shouted. His heart was hammering, and he expected gunfire.

Approaching the dock, Vince slowed the engine and yelled. There was no time for the motor boat to stop; they would have to jump, and Tom tensed every muscle as he waited for the right second.

"Now," Liz cried.

Together, they jumped through the air and landed safely in the boat. For a moment Tom was winded, then he staggered up as the boat shot away from the dock.

"I did it," Vince yelled into the wind. "Victory!"

Tom tried to thank him for the rescue, but was ignored as Vince looked back at the shore, then started laughing. "Here come the cops! Right on time!"

Amazed, Tom heard the howl of sirens in the park. The van, with Tia at the wheel, burst from the trees. Then, with a screech of metal, it veered to the right and stopped in a cloud of dust. As police cars surrounded the vehicle, Tia raised her hands in surrender.

"Yahoo!" Vince was beside himself with glee. "What a sight! That'll teach the dirty double-crosser!"

"But what happened?"

Vince grinned. "From the start, I planned to trick Tia. I knew her van would be hidden in the woods. Before letting the air out of her wheels so she couldn't drive anywhere, I phoned the Mounties in Canada to say the diamond thief they wanted was in the USA, in Riverside Park."

Vince paused, chuckling.

"I knew it would take time for the message to get from the Canadian Mounties to the American FBI, and then to the local cops. Before they could reach the park I planned to grab the diamonds from you two, then leave Tia to be arrested while I made my getaway."

Tom looked at the spectacle of lights whirling on the police cars in the park. "Well, Tia is certainly under arrest. But you're still out of luck, Vince."

"How's that?"

"The police will recover the diamonds from Tia. You went to all that trouble for nothing."

Vince grinned happily. "You think I'm stupid? Don't forget, I never trusted Tia."

"I don't understand."

"Think about it, kids. If fake diamonds have been used once, why not twice? And where else have you got crests, besides on your jackets?"

Vince broke into delighted laughter. Then he seized the caps from their heads, and waved them happily. "You guessed it! Knowing Tia might try to double-cross me, I told her the diamonds would be in the jacket crests. Those I filled with fakes, and put the real diamonds in the crests on your caps. Wasn't that a fantastic plan?"

Liz shook her head. "You've also been lucky, Vince."

"Sure I'm lucky, but so what? We're halfway across this river already. I'll get away once we land. The Mounties will never find me, and I'll be rich beyond my wildest dreams!"

Feeling betrayed, Tom looked unhappily at the man he'd liked and trusted. "When we were going with Tia to her van, I thought you were waiting to rescue us. But you only wanted the diamonds from our caps."

Vince flashed one of his charming smiles. "Don't take it hard, Tom. You're still my good buddy, and so is Liz."

She snorted. "Everything you say is a lie, Vince. You robbed your friend Sir Nigel, and left him to die in the stables."

"That old geezer deserved to die! He's got more money than the King of Siam, and he still hoarded the diamonds. Why didn't he give them to the needy?"

"The needy like you?"

"Sure like me! I'm just an ordinary guy struggling to make a living, and meanwhile Sir Nigel eats caviar in a castle. It made me sick, pretending to become his friend so I could worm out where he'd hidden the diamonds."

"Other people are greedy, but you're not?"

"That's enough backtalk, young lady. You like twisting things around so you can look smart."

"If you're not an undercover Mountie," Liz said, "then I bet Smythe is."

"Yes! I'll never forget his face when he was grabbed in the tunnel, and I made my getaway. Don't you see, the Mounties couldn't arrest and search me in Canada because they had no proof, so Smythe's job was to follow me until I tried to cross the border, then have the customs officers conduct a legal search for the diamonds."

"But they wouldn't have found them," Tom pointed out.

"Right again. I'm such an ace guy, I came up with the great idea of having you two carry the diamonds across the border. And you saw what happened. The customs officers searched me closely, but never thought to check you kids."

The motor coughed. Vince glanced at it, then whistled cheerfully as he turned his face to the sun. "I think I'll visit Florida to work on my tan."

The motor sputtered again and then cut out completely. Vince looked at the fuel tank. "It's empty! That double-crossing woman must have drained most of the fuel."

Liz smiled. "I guess she didn't trust you, Vince."

"Wipe that smirk off your face, and grab an oar! We're starting to drift."

Tom was surprised by the urgency in Vince's voice. Then he heard a sound that seized him with fear.

Whirling round, Tom looked downriver. "We're heading for the rapids!"

Liz grabbed an oar, and began paddling frantically. "Look what's beyond them!" she screamed.

In the distance, where the river appeared to end abruptly, a cloud of spray was rainbowed in the sunshine. It marked the deadly place where the river plunged over the falls to the rocks far below.

Seizing an oar, Tom tried to help Liz drive the boat to safety. But the current was strong, and carried the boat steadily toward the terrible booming of the rapids.

"It's hopeless," Vince shouted. "Drop those oars and hang on!"

A huge rock loomed straight ahead. Tom shut his eyes, then felt the surging water toss the boat away from the rock. Cold spray stung his face, and he cried out in fear.

The cry was lost in the thunder of the rapids and Tom could only stare helplessly at the white water leaping around jagged rocks. The boat veered past a huge boulder, then spun into a sickening whirlpool and as quickly whirled back into the roaring torrent.

Suddenly the rapids ended. Tom's grip on the boat loosened, but his relief was short-lived. He shook the spray from his face and saw that within seconds the ruthless water would carry them to the brink of the falls.

"That log," Vince screamed. "Grab that log when we hit it!"

Ahead was a log jammed between two boulders. Tom somehow managed to seize a branch as the boat hit the log. He pulled himself out of the boat—just before it was swept over the falls.

Stunned, Tom stared at the place where the boat had disappeared. Then he crawled higher up the log and his heart leapt with relief when he saw Liz and Vince.

"We're safe," Tom shouted above the deafening noise of the falls. "I can't believe it!"

"*Safe?*" Vince cried. "You call this *safe?*"

Water was churning angrily around the log. Tom shifted his position and the log trembled; with the weight of three people on it, the log was likely to break free at any second.

Filled with fear, Tom looked toward the shore. At Table Rock House, people stared and pointed. Only a short while ago, Tom had been safely standing there, joking about people who'd gone over the falls.

A tremor passed through the log, and the river foamed higher as if determined to tear it loose from the rock. Tom looked desperately at the crowd on shore, wishing they could somehow help.

Liz cried out and Tom's head snapped round toward the sound, afraid she had fallen in. But his sister was pointing at the sky.

"Look!"

Tom stared at a giant rescue helicopter. As the huge machine descended slowly out of the sky, he shouted with joy and relief.

"You see?" he called to Vince. "We really are safe!"

The man's face was pale with fear. His grip tightened as the whirling blades created a windstorm that shook the log. A hatch opened in the belly of the helicopter and a rescue basket dropped down. Vince glanced at the basket dangling beside him, then clung even tighter to the log.

"Hurry, Vince," Liz shouted. "Before it's too late!"

Tom saw terror in Vince's eyes. At any moment the log would break loose; Tom knew he must hurry. Moving carefully along the slippery log, he reached the basket and within seconds had been whirled to the safety of the helicopter, where he was wrapped inside a blanket.

But the danger was not over, and Tom's body shook as he watched the basket drop again to the log. "Hurry, Liz," he whispered, watching his sister crawl toward the basket.

Reaching it, she stopped to shout something to Vince. When he shook his head, Liz climbed into the basket; the helicopter's winch tightened and very quickly Liz was being bundled inside a blanket by a crew member.

Wiping water from her eyes, Liz looked at the woman aiding her. "Vince is afraid to let go," she called above the noise of the helicopter.

"I'll help him." The woman quickly assembled some equipment. "Vince Winter comes across so big and strong, but now we see the truth!"

"How come you know it's Vince Winter?"

"Oh, I've seen him lots of times on TV."

As she was lowered in the basket, Tom looked at the man operating the winch. "How'd you get here so fast?"

"This rescue chopper is based at Niagara Falls. People often get into trouble."

Tom looked through the hatch. The woman was standing fearlessly on the log, strapping a harness around Vince. Then she signalled to the winch operator, and the machine whined.

As the harness ropes tightened, the woman forced Vince to release the branches and he rose away from the log. Spinning slowly like a giant beetle, Vince Winter was lifted to the helicopter and deposited on the deck.

The woman followed Vince through the hatch, and quickly undid the harness. When he was free, Vince stumbled to a seat and dropped into it with a sigh of relief.

"I did it, kids," he said, raising a triumphant hand to show he was still clutching the baseball caps. "Despite all that, I saved the diamonds!"

"So what?" Tom replied. "You're heading for prison, and the jewels will go to Sir Nigel."

"Sure," Vince said eagerly. "But, don't you see, Sir

Nigel will have to give me a big reward for saving his diamonds!"

As the helicopter lifted away from the falls, Liz wrapped the blanket tighter round herself and grinned. "Boy, Vince, you're better entertainment than a dozen dancing bears. Life won't be the same without you."

12

As the little plane tilted, Tom felt his stomach lurch.

For a few seconds the plane flew on its side, one wing pointing at the swift blue river below. Then, with a sickening tumble, it was upside down.

"I can't watch," Liz moaned through her hands.

The plane righted itself, then swept into a narrow canyon over a stretch of seething white water.

"The rapids," Sir Nigel said. "Just like I promised you."

Uncle Henry laughed. "Haven't you kids had enough rapids?"

"Yes," Tom exclaimed.

The plane skimmed low over the water, then the scene was suddenly replaced by the image of a man's gigantic face. As he talked about the need to live in harmony with Nature, Tom wiped his forehead and leaned back in his seat; he'd had enough thrills lately.

The *World of Nature* film ended, and the lights went up. Sir Nigel smiled. "Was it as good as I promised?"

"For sure! Is this really one of the world's largest movie screens?" Tom asked.

"So they say. I see all the shows here at Ontario Place, but I confess to sometimes missing the cinemas in London, England."

"What's Britain like, Sir Nigel?"

"It's marvellous. I'll take you for a visit someday. I'm sure we can find you a spare mystery to solve."

A few minutes later, the group left the theatre to wander around Ontario Place. Sir Nigel had invited everyone responsible for the recovery of the diamonds to return to Toronto during the summer as his guests. Dexter Valentine and his wife had also joined the party.

"Who's hungry?" Sir Nigel asked, leading the way to a Chinese take-out stand.

Later, laden with chop suey and egg rolls, they found benches with a good view of a lagoon and its procession of floating bands, pedal boats and other vessels.

"Impossible," Liz said, reading the message in her fortune cookie. "I thought you could believe these things."

"What's it say?"

"I'm about to lose my head over a handsome stranger."

Uncle Henry smiled. "Liz is always cool, calm and collected. I'd love to see her lose her head."

Smythe lifted a sweet-and-sour sparerib with his chopsticks, but they slipped and red sauce spotted his shirt. "I'd better learn to operate these things before my next undercover assignment."

"What is it?" Tom asked quickly.

Smythe smiled. "That's a secret, but I can tell you it's a big change from being a butler."

"Can you tell us what happened to the original butler at Casa Loma?"

"Sure. He took a holiday at the request of the police, and I replaced him in order to investigate Sir Nigel's disappearance. I understand he'll be back at Casa Loma soon, along with the other servants like poor Hatfield. I must say he's welcome to the job!"

Uncle Henry looked at Smythe. "I still don't understand why you quit that day, and left me in the lurch."

Smythe tried again with the chopsticks, and more sauce splattered. "Do you recall showing me the diamonds you found in Sir Nigel's desk? When your back was turned, I tested their hardness and quickly discovered they were fakes, which meant the real diamonds had been removed from the castle."

"But why did you quit?"

"To shadow my chief suspect, Vince Winter. You see, I couldn't tell you the truth about the fake diamonds, in case word got to Vince and he went into hiding. The police wanted Vince to think his plan had succeeded, so we could nail him at the border-crossing with the diamonds."

"But the story was in the newspapers."

Smythe nodded. "But there was no publicity about us trailing Vince Winter, only a mention of two American suspects."

Tom blushed. "Then I spotted you in the tunnel at Niagara Falls."

Smythe laughed. "By the time I got out of the tunnel and rushed to join the American police, your motor boat was heading for the falls. You can imagine how terrible I felt."

"Well, it all worked out fine in the end."

A flock of ducks skidded to a landing on the water, and Tom tossed some chow mein in their direction. Then the group walked toward the waterslide, where kids shrieked joyfully as they twisted down long plastic chutes to plunge into a pool.

"Speaking of Casa Loma," Smythe said, "it was Vince who found a couple of petty crooks to pose as a chauffeur and a blacksmith."

"You know," Tom said, "I should have realized that Vince and Tia were secretly their bosses."

"Why's that?"

"I'd seen the tracks of Tia's wheelchair at Fort York, then the same marks were on the driveway at the cabin where I was a prisoner. Another tip-off came at the phone booth on the country road, when the driver of the van didn't chase me. That meant the driver was Tia, who couldn't run because of her disability."

"But what about Vince?"

"At first I couldn't understand why I had been grabbed on the streetcar," Tom explained. "Then the blacksmith asked where the diamonds were hidden. Who could have told him I had guessed? Only three people knew I had a theory."

Mrs. Valentine smiled. "My husband and I were two of them."

Tom nodded. "And Vince was the third."

"But we're Americans, like Vince and Tia. How could you tell we weren't the villains?"

"Two main reasons, Mrs. Valentine. First, because it was Vince who arranged for me to take the streetcar. He was setting me up for the grab."

"And the second reason?"

"When Hatfield disappeared from the study, Vince said he'd contact the police. But they never showed up—obviously because Vince didn't want them poking around."

Smythe shook his head. "Vince and Tia figured they had covered every angle, but there's always an unexpected event that makes a crime go wrong."

"Poor Vince," Liz said. "He won't like giving up his fancy clothes for prison stripes."

The group was drawn by loud cries from children coming from the distance. They stopped to watch the wild battles in the water-wars area and the foam swamp. Then they became aware of even louder screams coming from the distance.

"What's that?" Liz said.

Sir Nigel frowned. "It's coming from the stage, where they have the open-air shows, but I can't imagine what's happening. Nobody was screaming when I saw the Toronto Symphony there."

"Let's investigate!"

Hurrying toward the noise, they saw that all around the stage, police officers were struggling to hold back thousands of hysterical girls who were trying to reach a young singer.

"Big deal," Liz said. "It's a rock concert. Look at all those crazy girls, going gaga over some no-talent pretty face."

"It's somebody new," Tom said. "I've never heard of him before."

"How do you know his name?"

"It's on that sign. He's called Nick Nalini."

"*Nick Nalini!* Are you kidding me?"

"Nope. Read the sign for yourself."

Liz trembled. "It really is Nick Nalini! Why didn't someone tell me?"

Uncle Henry laughed. "But he's just some no-talent pretty face, Liz."

"Don't ever say that about Nick Nalini! He's the most perfect creature ever born, and he's *right here*!" Liz broke into a run and disappeared into the seething mass of fans.

Sir Nigel laughed. "The fortune cookie was right. Liz has lost her head over a handsome stranger, but I'm sure she'll survive the experience. I just hope her eardrums survive that music!"

"You know," Smythe said, "the blacksmith should have made you listen to Nick Nalini music in the stables. I'm sure you would have revealed the diamonds' hiding-place in no time."

Sir Nigel smiled. "You could be right. One's bravery has its limits."

Irene studied him thoughtfully. "I admire you, Sir Nigel. You really stood up to those crooks."

"I must say the admiration is mutual, my dear. Now, don't you think it's time for the others to learn your secret role in this affair?"

Irene nodded, then turned to Uncle Henry with embarrassed eyes. "I must apologize for letting you believe I was a maid at Casa Loma. You see, I was under strict orders not to reveal my true identity to anyone, including you."

"You mean you were never one of the servants?"

She shook her head. "I'm also a Mountie, and, like Smythe, I was at the castle as an undercover investigator."

For a moment there was silence, then Uncle Henry laughed with surprise and delight. "You had me completely fooled! I must say I was very surprised when you left Casa Loma without saying good-bye."

"I felt bad about that, but it was impossible to tell you why I was leaving. I couldn't risk having the truth leak to the people I was after."

"Who were they?"

"The blacksmith and the chauffeur. I'm happy to report we arrested them early this morning."

Uncle Henry smiled at Irene. "Hey, you're really something! How about having dinner with me tonight?"

"I'd love to."

Looking pleased, Uncle Henry turned to Tom with a wink. "When we get home to Winnipeg, nobody will believe everything that's happened to us. Especially if word gets out that it all ended with me dating a good-looking Mountie!"

Tom laughed. "Your secret is safe with me, Unc."

The Case of the
Golden Boy

For kids everywhere

A note from Eric Wilson

This story is dedicated to kids because you have made my books a success. When I was a teacher and a struggling would-be author, my students urged me to "try again, Sir" when I couldn't find a publisher for my stories.

Once I broke into print with *Murder on The Canadian*, kids told each other about the book, starting the "word of mouth" publicity that has built a following for my mysteries over the years.

I listen closely to my readers' comments, and I ask volunteer student editors for their thoughts on each new story as I work on it. So I turned to a grade six class at Toronto's Rolph Road School for advice when I thought about publishing, as an artifact, the first Tom Austen adventure I ever wrote. The class enthusiastically said, "Go for it!" so this story is now in print.

200

Like those students, I hope you will be interested to
see the beginning of my evolution as a writer. Here I
introduce some familiar characters, as well as people
you may recognize from other stories. You'll also detect
how I was intrigued enough with some ideas in this
story to explore them again later, as I developed as a
mystery author.

So, this book is for you, my readers and friends and
true supporters. With it, I give you my thanks—from
the heart.

Yours mysteriously,

1

It was night when Tom Austen and his friends approached the mystery house. "All right," Tom said in a low voice, "are your instructions clear?"

Matthew and Art nodded.

"Any last minute questions?"

None.

"Final check of watches." Tom pulled back his parka sleeve. "Total silence."

He ran his eyes over the deserted house. No signs of life, but he gazed a long time at the attic window. That's where he'd seen movement yesterday. No one had believed it, so Tom proposed a mission into the house. Only Art and Matthew had the courage to come along.

Spring would arrive soon, but the cold of winter still gripped Winnipeg. Branches rattled together in the icy wind, and the black sky was scattered with brilliant stars.

The house had been empty a year. People crossed the street if they had to walk past, and there were rumours of ghosts. Then, yesterday, a dog was barking at the house when Tom went past. Looking up at the attic window, he thought he saw a movement.

Tom motioned for Matthew and Art to stop. "Footprints," he whispered, pointing at a patch of snow. "Coming from the front yard."

"They go to that basement window," Matthew said. "It's been broken."

The window opened easily. The boys dropped down into the cellar. It was dark and smelled of old newspapers. Tom's nose wrinkled. He signaled to Art, who was posted as sentry outside the window. He'd go for help if they weren't back in 15 minutes.

The house moaned. Fear ran across Tom's skin. Another moan, then a long creak that shivered through the darkness. Outside the broken window, Art waited. His breath steamed in the cold air. He looked safe. For a second, Tom wished he was sentry, but he was leader and had to do the hard part.

Switching on their flashlights, they tiptoed to the stairs. As they started up, the house seemed to whisper *Stay away*.

Tom's scalp prickled. He looked at Matthew, wanting desperately to say something, but the rule was no talking. He looked up the stairs, knowing they had to keep going. Tomorrow at school, everyone would be asking questions.

What if someone was waiting upstairs with a gun, planning to spring a trap? Keep Tom and Matthew prisoner in the attic until they starved to death?

Tom stared at Matthew, wishing they could talk.

Maybe they should come back another time. What if someone really was lurking with a gun? Maybe it wasn't just his imagination that the house had whispered *Stay away*.

The steps creaked as they climbed from the cellar to the kitchen. Through the dirty windows, Tom saw the sky growing darker. He looked at the old enamel sink, the wooden cupboards, the thick dust on the floor. He heard a scrabbling sound, whirled, and saw a mouse rushing away.

Matthew was trembling. Tom squeezed his friend's arm and tried to smile as they entered the hallway. The plan was for Matthew to wait here as sentry while Tom climbed the dark stairs alone to the attic. That didn't seem like such a good idea anymore.

The house had stopped creaking, as if it was watching and waiting. Tom looked up the stairs.

BANG BANG BANG

The sound crashed down from the darkness. Tom jumped, then Matthew grabbed his arm. "*What was that*?" he whispered.

BANG BANG BANG

The crashing filled the air. Matthew said something and ran; Tom stared up into the darkness, then rushed into the kitchen. He heard Matthew crashing down the cellar stairs. "Art," he was screaming, "help, Art, help!"

Tom flew down the cellar stairs, certain that someone with a gun was close behind. Matthew was wiggling out the window. "Wait for me," Tom yelled, scrambling after him. "Hurry," he shouted, as they ran across the yard. "Hurry!"

When they reached safety, Tom turned to study the

deserted house. The attic window stared back, its secret still guarded. Tom promised himself he would return.

"That banging," Matthew gasped. "What was it?"

"I don't know," Tom said.

"What happened in there?" Art demanded. "One minute I'm waiting for you guys and the next minute we're racing across the yard!"

"It was a ghost!" Matthew's eyes were wide. "It made a slamming noise, warning us away."

Tom shook his head. "I don't think it was a ghost, Matthew. But I can tell you one thing—tomorrow we face some tough questioning at school."

"That's right," Matthew exclaimed. He looked at Tom. "What'll we do?"

"It's simple," he replied. "Tell everyone we've got some good leads, and our plans are top secret. Beyond that, *no comment*."

"It makes sense," Art said.

Matthew nodded. "If Dietmar Oban finds out, we're finished. Everyone will be laughing."

Tom looked at his watch. "Fortunately, my parents are away on a trip, but you guys are in trouble. It's getting late."

"Gosh," Matthew exclaimed, looking at his watch. "I'll be grounded for sure."

"Me, too," Art groaned. "Forget the detective business, Tom. It's just plain scary."

Tom shook his head. "No way. I'm on to a good case, I can just tell." When the others looked doubtful, Tom smiled. "Wait and see."

2

The next morning, Tom was reading *The Twisted Claw*—his favourite Hardy Boys mystery—when his sister Liz knocked the milk over. The cold white liquid splashed and gurgled as it rushed across the kitchen table at Tom. He leapt to safety, but the book got soaked.

"Oh, no," he cried. "Now the pages will stick together."

"I'm sorry, Tom."

"Frank and Joe were just entering the hideout of the Pirate King. I need to know what happens next!"

"But you were reading the same book at Christmas," Liz said. "You already know what happens."

"But. . ." Tom shrugged. "You've got to be in the detective business to understand."

After cleaning up the mess, they talked in the living room with their Uncle Henry, who was staying with them while their parents took a holiday in Mexico. Uncle Henry loved to tell stories about people like his cousin, who lived in a 98-room castle in Toronto.

"He keeps diamonds hidden there," Uncle Henry chuckled. "Can you believe it? Doesn't trust safety deposit boxes—what a character!"

"I'd like to visit that place," Liz said. She polished her eyeglasses. "Always smudged! Some day I'm getting contacts."

Tom opened another Hardy Boys mystery and Liz returned to her book about Green Gables. As they read, a police car pulled up outside. The car door slammed, and a man in uniform came to the door.

"It's Officer Larson," Tom said. "He looks upset."

"I'll get straight to the point," said the grumpy officer. "Some kids broke into the deserted house on Borebank Street. A neighbor saw, and complained to us." He stared at Tom. "My first guess was Tom Austen, playing detective again. Correct?"

Tom nodded solemnly. Liz was silent.

Officer Larson leaned over Tom. "Remember the green creatures from Mars? Remember starting the rumour they had landed?"

Tom's eyes were on the floor.

"When people found green blobs outside their houses, they almost died of shock, thinking the Martians were closing in." Officer Larson shook his head. "But it was only lime ice cream, courtesy of Tom Austen."

* * *

As Tom had predicted to Art and Matthew, a mob of kids surrounded them in the school playground. The sun was stronger today, and parkas were open.

Dietmar Oban was face-to-face with Tom. "I bet you were scared, Austen."

"Not a chance, Oban."

"What happened in the abandoned house?"

"No comment," Tom replied.

Dietmar turned to the other boys. "Did Austen panic in the house? I bet he ran screaming into the night."

"No comment," Matthew said.

"Yeah," Art added. "No comment."

Heads high, the three young detectives went into the school. People asked some more questions, then gave up. *No comment* was all they heard. Tom was satisfied by this damage-control, but still felt curious about the old house. He wanted to return, if only to solve the riddle of the terrible banging sound from the attic.

In the hallway, Tom talked to Elizabeth Whitman, a shy girl with friendly eyes and dark hair. Together they were editors of the school newspaper, which this month featured photographs of everyone who worked at Queenston School.

Tom smiled at Elizabeth. "Your pictures are great. I love the one of Mr. Nicholson, frowning."

"Just before I took the picture, I asked him to announce extra school holidays."

As Tom laughed, he saw a man approach. For many years, Pete Tyler had been the school custodian; in all those years, no one had ever seen him smile. He was very tall.

"Hi Pete," Elizabeth said. "Did you like your picture in our newspaper?"

"It was okay," he replied. "But I don't like pictures. Too many bad memories."

"What do you mean?" Tom asked.

"Nothing," the custodian replied, walking away.

Tom and Elizabeth shrugged at each other, then went into their classroom. A few minutes later, Dianne Dorchester arrived, and Tom's heart skipped a beat. She had blond hair and blue eyes, and he often gazed at her across the classroom. The one time she'd caught him staring, Tom had blushed crimson. Today she wore a soft sweater and a plaid skirt.

One of the girls smiled at Dianne. "Where'd you get the tartan skirt? In Scotland?"

She nodded. "My family was there last summer on holiday. It's a neat place."

"Listen, I've often wondered something," the girl said. "Why do you attend Queenston? Your family's so wealthy, you could be in a private school."

"This school's where I want to be," Dianne replied. "My friends are all here."

Their teacher, Mr. Stones, called for order, and announced his plans for a "Kids' Day" to celebrate his students. "I'll bring some food," he promised.

"Can we have pizza?" Dianne asked. "It's my favourite."

"Pizza gives me heartburn," Mr. Stones said, "but I'll get some for you, Dianne."

"Thanks, Sir!"

They all liked Mr. Stones, who had been a champion basketball player before becoming a teacher. He believed they could do anything in life, and wanted to help them succeed.

The day passed quickly. At 2:45, Mr. Stones looked up from his desk and nodded to Tom and Chuck. "You may go," he said.

Minutes later, Tom had buckled a school-patrol belt over his parka and was standing at the corner of Kingsway and Waterloo, where his job was to stop traffic whenever students wanted to cross. Unfortunately, it wasn't a busy corner and there was little to do, but Tom was very proud of the belt and his authority to stop cars.

A light snow powdered the streets, making the surface slippery. Tom checked the road for Skid Factor by taking several long slides, then waited impatiently.

The first students appeared in the distance. Tom stamped his cold feet and adjusted his belt, ready for business. As usual, he watched in dismay as almost every kid turned off at Queenston and Niagara, giving the patrol on those corners lots of business and Tom nothing.

But then Dianne came his way, the yellow of her parka bright in Tom's eyes. He adjusted his belt again, rubbing the silver buckle to make it glow, then glanced along Waterloo. To his delight, he saw that a pickup truck would reach his corner at the same time as Dianne. At last, he could hold up traffic for her. As she reached his side, Tom stepped into the road. He put up his hand, calmly signalling the driver to stop.

But Tom's timing was bad for such a slippery road. He saw surprise on the driver's face, then shock as he jammed on the brakes and the truck skidded out of control.

It was coming straight at them.

3

Dianne screamed.

Tom threw himself at her. They fell together in the snow as the truck hit the curb and bounced off, spinning in a circle until it stopped in the middle of the street.

Silence. Tom opened his eyes and saw sparkling white crystals of snow. He wondered if he was in heaven, then lifted his head and saw Dianne's blue eyes.

"Are we safe?" she whispered.

"I hope so." Tom was afraid to tell her they might be in heaven. He felt terrible—he shouldn't have tried to stop the truck.

"You crazy kid!"

Tom knew they were alive when he heard the angry driver. He got slowly to his feet.

"You crazy kid!" The driver's face was as red as the curly hair on his head. Despite the cold, he wore jeans and a light jacket displaying the name Red. "You almost got me and Dianne killed! Are you crazy?"

"I'm sorry," Tom said to the man. "Are you going to phone the police?"

"The cops? Not a chance."

Someone opened the door of a nearby house and a big dog ran into the yard. Turning pale with fear, the man immediately got into his pickup truck. The windshield was cracked, and rust stained the fading brown paint. He looked at Tom. "I've seen you before, kid. I live next to the abandoned house on Borebank Street— you were sneaking in with your buddies. That's a scary place to be, especially at night—you've got courage." He paused. "But you're also too snoopy."

Red's eyes stared at Tom. "Stay away from that place, kid. Got that?"

Without waiting for a reply, he gunned the engine and was gone.

Tom pulled out his notebook. "Have you seen that guy before, Dianne?"

"Nope."

"Very interesting," Tom said, jotting this down. "He knew your name. I wonder why?"

* * *

That night, Tom stood alone in the cellar of the deserted house and listened to it moan and creak. He felt the same shivering fear, but this time he was determined to get to the attic.

Trying not to listen to the sounds, Tom quickly climbed the cellar stairs. Standing in the front hall, he muffled the glow of his flashlight as he studied the abandoned furniture. There wasn't much, and it was drab.

Tom started upstairs. The landing was thick with dust and it tickled in Tom's nose. More stairs led higher, up to the attic.

BANG BANG BANG

The same terrible noise! It roared down the stairs from above. Tom stared up into the darkness, and then began climbing to the attic. His heart thumped in his chest, and his breathing was harsh. The noise continued—BANG BANG BANG—but Tom went higher.

The attic was small and empty. Tom saw a small closet with two wire hangers. The wind blew through the open window, causing venetian blinds to bang against the frame.

"So *that's* the noise," Tom said. "It wasn't a ghost!"

Then he glanced down the stairs. A flashlight shone somewhere below, and he heard the voices of two men.

They were coming his way.

* * *

Quickly, Tom looked for a hiding place. The closet was his only hope. He scurried inside, but the door wouldn't close properly. Through the opening, Tom saw the approaching flashlight beam, and then two men entered the room.

One was Red, the driver of the pickup truck. He was smoking a cigarette, and wore the same light jacket and jeans. The second man wore a parka fringed with a spiky white fur, and a dark ski mask that covered his head completely.

Tom leaned forward, straining to hear the low voice. It seemed familiar.

"You'll do as I tell you," Red said angrily, "or your family dies. I've been planning this a long time—you can't back out now. Understood?"

The other man nodded his shrouded head.

Red handed him an envelope. "Your instructions are inside. Memorize them, then burn everything. Our next meeting will be four o'clock Saturday at the Golden Boy."

* * *

After school the next day, Dianne stopped to chat with Tom at his school patrol corner. "Any sign of the red-headed man today?"

Tom stared shyly at the ground. "Actually, something did happen." He described the two men meeting at the mystery house. "I'll tell my parents when they get home tonight from their holiday."

"Do you think those men are criminals?"

"Possibly."

Dianne touched his hand. "Don't take any chances, Tom."

"I'll be okay," he replied bravely. "Don't worry about me."

For a moment her blue eyes studied his face. Then she smiled, "Bye, Tom."

"See you." He was too shy to say her name. "Bye." He watched Dianne until a twist of wind hid her yellow parka behind a flurry of snow.

Then, Tom had a strange feeling of foreboding.

He looked toward the school, decided that no more kids would be coming past his corner, and started quickly after Dianne. He knew it was against the rules to leave his post, but something made him want to stay near her. The wind carried the blowing snow into his face, as he hurried along Waterloo.

After crossing Academy Road, a busy street with small stores and some traffic lights, she turned into a quiet residential area. Tom continued to follow at a distance, still nagged by fear.

A small brown van pulled out from a side street and approached Dianne, moving quietly through the snow. The windows on the rear doors had been painted over and displayed the words *Blind Driver*; the person at the wheel was hidden from Tom's view.

The van stopped beside Dianne. She looked in the passenger window, which was open.

"Oh, hello! It's nice to see you."

The driver said something that Tom couldn't hear. If he moved closer, Dianne would see that he had followed her like a silly puppy.

"Thank you," Dianne said cheerfully. "A ride would be nice. It's cold today!"

She got inside, and the van pulled away. As Tom walked back to his patrol corner, he was nagged by a strange uneasiness. Although he tried to chase it away, the feeling remained when he reached home and took off his patrol belt. Once again he pictured Dianne getting into the van, and once again he felt sad and lost.

4

"Have you heard!?"

Art was yelling and waving his arms as he ran down the street toward Tom.

"Have you heard?"

Art stopped in front of Tom, panting, trying to catch his breath.

"Dianne Dorchester is missing!"

Tom stared at Art's face, looking for the grin that would tell him it was a joke, but all he could find was excitement and fear.

"It's true," Art said. "It was on the radio this morning. Dianne is missing! There's police searching for her and everything."

Tom was too shocked to speak. Why Dianne? Why would anyone want to take Dianne?

"They've got dogs out," Art said, "and they're searching the woods, and they've got roadblocks to stop cars, but they can't find her anywhere!"

But Tom didn't hear Art's words. He was remembering yesterday afternoon, the strange feeling that had made him follow Dianne. The brown van.

"Come on," he called to Art. They ran all the way to school. At the edge of the playground, they stared in awe and horror as three police officers came out of the school and drove off in a car with the emergency lights flashing. Students stood in groups, talking in low voices. Tom told Art and some friends about the brown van, then Tom entered the school alone.

The halls were empty all the way to his classroom. Tom tried not to worry about Dianne, but sadness tugged at his eyes when he saw her empty desk. She sat there just yesterday, he thought, and now she's gone.

"Yes, Tom?" Mr. Stones sat behind his big wooden desk. "What is it?" The morning light through the windows made shadows on his unhappy face.

Tom carefully closed the classroom door. "May I speak to you, sir?"

"Yes, Tom, you may." Usually Mr. Stones spoke with a deep, strong voice, but today it sounded weak and broken. Everyone knew that Dianne was his favourite student, even though he tried to hide it, and Tom felt sorry for him as he approached the desk.

"I have some information," Tom said quietly. "About Dianne."

"*What*?" The teacher's eyes widened. "Do you mean that, Tom?"

"Yes, sir." Even though Tom was upset about Dianne, it was exciting to be part of the drama.

"This isn't one of your jokes?"

"No, sir. I'm serious."

Mr. Stones stood up. "Then let's go to the principal's office. He'll want to phone the police."

"Yes, sir," Tom said.

The linoleum in the hallway was shiny. They walked in silence, and then Tom looked at his teacher. "Poor Dianne."

Mr. Stones nodded. "Yes, poor Dianne. Think, too, of her family and all the others. A child is kidnapped, and waves spread out. Many people will suffer because of Dianne's disappearance. Even the kidnapper must be in agony, jumping in fear whenever a police car passes by, terrified of capture and the prison cell that awaits. Yes, many will suffer."

"We've got to get her back, sir!"

Mr. Stones' eyes stared at Tom from their dark sockets. "I know you're constantly reading those Hardy Boys mysteries, but don't get involved. Your father's an officer in an excellent police department. They'll find Dianne."

Tom nodded, but in his mind he thought, *Maybe they'll need some help*.

* * *

Inside the office of Mr. Nicholson, the principal, Tom sat on a wooden chair. The principal's arms and legs were very long, so he was secretly called "Bones." He stood at the window, watching a few snowflakes drift down from the white sky. The trees looked cold, dancing in the wind.

"Poor Dianne," Mr. Stones said quietly, cracking the knuckles of his big hands.

The school bell jangled, and feet thundered past the office. By now everyone was probably talking about the brown van. Tom gulped, wondering if he'd made a mistake.

The door opened, and in walked Officer Larson with Tom's father. Inspector Austen wore his police uniform, and carried his uniform cap. Just home from Mexico, his skin was brown from the sun. "I understand you've got some evidence for us," he said to Tom. "Well done."

Mr. Nicholson gestured at two chairs. "Sit down, please, gentlemen. Mr. Stones and I haven't yet heard Tom's evidence, but he assures us it's important."

"What happened, son?" Inspector Austen asked.

"Well, Dianne passed my patrol post after school yesterday."

"What time was that?" Officer Larson asked.

"Exactly 15:22. That's when she passes me every day."

Inspector Austen smiled. "You kept careful track of her movements, Tom?"

Tom blushed. "I don't know. I guess so."

"Carry on, son."

"Well, after Dianne went by, I, well . . ." Tom faltered to a stop. He would have to confess his mistake. "Well, I left my post and followed Dianne. I know I shouldn't have, but I didn't think any more kids would be coming along."

Mr. Nicholson made a disapproving sound. He wrote something on a piece of paper, then waited for Tom to continue.

"I was close to Dianne when . . ." Tom paused, remembering the van. If only he had yelled *Don't get in!* "A small van stopped to give Dianne a ride."

"What?" Tom's father looked surprised. "Is that accurate, Tom?"

"Sure, Dad. That's what I saw."

"Excellent, excellent." Tom's father smiled. "That gives us a very important lead. Now, Tom, think carefully. What else can you tell us?"

Tom was delighted by his father's praise. He searched his memory. "Well, the driver said something to Dianne."

"Did you see the driver?" Officer Larson interrupted.

"No, I didn't." Tom hesitated. All this was embarrassing, but he couldn't think of his feelings during an investigation. "I, well, I didn't want Dianne to see me, so I couldn't get any closer."

"A shame," Officer Larson said quietly. "If only you had seen the driver."

"But I do have an important clue," Tom quickly added. "As the van drove away, I noticed two words on the rear doors."

"What were they?" Mr. Stones asked.

"Blind Driver."

Mr. Stones laughed, a sudden sound. "Blind Driver? Come now, Tom, are you certain? Or is this another of your jokes?"

"No, sir," Tom said, looking up at the man. "I'm sure of it."

"But how can a driver be blind? I don't mean to laugh, but surely you've made a mistake? After all, how can a blind person drive a van?"

Mr. Nicholson nodded his head. "I agree." He looked at Mr. Austen. "Tom has quite an imagination for an eleven-year-old. It's very possible that he made a mistake."

"But I didn't!" Tom looked at his father. "I saw the words! They said Blind Driver."

Officer Larson shook his head. "I don't know, Inspector. He's your son, and he's got a detective office in his attic, but does that make him a reliable witness? The words don't make sense."

Mr. Austen glanced at him. "My son is very bright. I trust him."

Officer Larson turned to Tom. "What was the van's licence number?"

"I don't know." Tom looked unhappily at his father. "I'm sorry, Dad, but I didn't notice the license. I didn't think Dianne was being kidnapped."

"I understand, son. Did you hear anything?"

"Just Dianne saying hello to the driver, and accepting a ride. She seemed to know him."

"Describe the driver," Officer Larson said.

"I couldn't see him."

"Then you're making an assumption. The driver could have been a woman."

"I guess you're right."

Officer Larson shook his head disapprovingly but Inspector Austen smiled. "You've given us some valuable evidence, Tom. Well done!"

"As for me," Officer Larson said, glancing at Mr.

Nicholson, "I'd have been happy with a plate number. *That* would have been great."

Tom was suddenly angry. "At least I saw the van! At least I've given you a lead!" He stared at Officer Larson. "Why didn't you protect Dianne? That's your job. Why don't you go and find her, instead of being mean to me? I'm trying to help!"

Tom's father reached forward and patted Tom's knee. "All right, son, all right. Calm down. If you're going to be a detective, you need a tough hide. Lots of adults are stressed out, and they can get sarcastic." Inspector Austen stood up. "This has been very useful. Well done, Tom."

Mr. Nicholson cleared his throat. He picked up a metal letter opener and tapped it against the fingers of his hand. A chill passed over Tom. Whenever a student was in trouble, Mr. Nicholson fiddled with that letter opener.

The principal's black eyebrows wriggled as he cleared his throat again. "I'm concerned about your son, Inspector Austen."

"Yes?" Tom's father said.

"It's not his schoolwork, which is satisfactory." Mr. Nicholson paused. "But Tom and his friend Dietmar Oban are the school comedians. Their practical jokes do not amuse me. Recently, a rumour spread in the schoolground that I'd lost my job. The children cheered and burst into songs of celebration. I was not amused." Mr. Nicholson stared at the others. He wore small glasses with wire rims, and his thin hair was turning grey. Lines marked his eyes and mouth. "Tom has now confessed to breaking the rules for school patrol. He left his post."

"But . . ." Tom protested.

The principal held up his hand. "It is true that you provided valuable evidence, Tom. *But* you also broke the rules."

Tom dropped his eyes to the floor.

"Therefore," Mr. Nicholson said, "I must ask you to resign from the school patrol."

Tom's head snapped up. "No! That's not fair, Mr. Nicholson. I love being on the patrol!"

Mr. Austen put his hand on Tom's shoulder. "You must accept your punishment, son," he said. "Mr. Nicholson is right. I appreciate your evidence. Now, take your medicine like a man."

"Yes, Dad," Tom said quietly.

"Fine, fine." Mr. Nicholson stood up. "Turn in your patrol belt after school, Tom."

He left the principal's office squeezing back tears. The hallway was lined with art projects, a riot of color, but Tom's vision was too blurry to see anything.

"Tom!"

Feet hurried his way, and then Mr. Stones was beside him. "I'm sorry, Tom. I shouldn't have laughed. I can't picture a blind man driving, but perhaps there's an explanation. Do you forgive me?"

"Sure, sir."

"You must have seen those words." Mr. Stones smiled. "Good detectives don't make mistakes."

Tom felt better. "We'll get Dianne back, sir. Trust me on this."

Their classroom was strangely quiet. The kids stared at the floor, or whispered together. All eyes were on Tom and Mr. Stones as they came in the door. As

Tom sat down, he looked at a pencil on Dianne's desk. Only yesterday her fingers had touched it.

"Any news?" Dietmar asked. His eyes were solemn.

"Nothing," Mr. Stones replied, "except for the brown van spotted by Tom." He looked around the room. "We're all thinking about Dianne today." His voice was hoarse and he seemed about to cry. "It's a tragedy for us all."

Art held up his hand. "Do you think she's disappeared forever, sir?"

Mr. Stones shook his head. "I think Dianne's been kidnapped for money. She'll be back safely, once a ransom is paid." He stared out the window. "The only question is: what about the kidnappers? Will they be captured?"

Tom nodded. "You bet, sir. They haven't got a chance."

Mr. Stones nodded solemnly. "Perhaps you're right."

* * *

Soon after, a poster appeared showing Dianne's face under the huge word MISSING. Her face looked at Tom from posters in stores, on lamp-posts, inside car windows, and on classroom doors at Queenston School.

Brittney Hayes raised her hand. "Sir, all this stuff scares me. I hear about Dianne all the time. I'm terrified someone's going to kidnap *me*."

The teacher nodded. "Lots of kids feel that way right now, because of Dianne. It takes courage to admit you're scared. Want my advice? Be cautious, know what you'd do in an emergency, and then enjoy life."

He looked around the classroom. "You should all feel proud that you've been asked to help find Dianne."

"What if we don't find her?" Tom Bennett asked.

"Then you'll have tried, just like everyone else. The whole city is doing its best."

After school that day, Tom felt horrible. He no longer had his patrol belt, he no longer had his duties. Walking home alone, he stopped to talk with Pete Tyler. The school custodian was attaching posters to telephone poles on Kingsway.

"I feel so terrible," Pete said to Tom. "Dianne was the friendliest kid in the school. Her father had better pay a ransom, and fast, but maybe he won't."

"Why?" Tom asked.

"Because he's a cheapskate and a rat and a swindler. I hate him."

"Really?" Tom said. "How come?"

"It's none of your business, sonny. Now go away, and let me work."

5

On Saturday afternoon, Tom declined a shopping trip with his parents and Liz. Instead, he had a piece of chocolate cake and a glass of milk while he read *The Twisted Claw* (the pages dry again), and then he went upstairs to his office.

It was in the attic, under the sloping roof. On the door was a warning: KEEP OUT! THIS MEANS YOU. Tom opened the padlock, then checked a tiny slip of paper wedged in the door frame. It was still in place, so no intruder had attempted to open the door.

The walls were covered with the titles of every Hardy Boys mystery, plus posters showing the Morse code and semaphore symbols. There were also maps of Canada, Manitoba, and Winnipeg, a portrait of Sherlock Holmes and, most prized of all, police posters of the Ten Most Wanted Criminals in Canada.

Tom carefully studied the criminals, refreshing in his memory their scars, the way some noses were bent, and the look of one man who seemed to have a glass eye. Tom knew that eventually he would recognize one of these men, have him arrested, and be a hero. He day-dreamed for a minute, then got to work.

At his desk, Tom thought about the kidnapping. A ransom would be paid, or the kidnappers arrested, and then Dianne would come home. Meanwhile, would she be okay? Tom had always liked Dianne because she stood up for herself at school. No one put her down, and almost everyone liked her. She was kind, and fair, and she believed in herself. These qualities made her strong, so Tom figured she had a good chance of getting through the kidnapping safely.

Who was responsible? Tom made notes on the brown van, and then thought back. Only a week earlier, Red's pickup truck had almost struck Dianne. Could the kidnapping be linked to the mysterious meeting between Red and the man shrouded inside the ski mask? Now Tom was writing fast. Red and the shrouded man had arranged a meeting for four o'clock today "at the Golden Boy." He looked at his watch: *only two hours to go*.

* * *

Outside, winter was battering the city a final time. The snowflakes were big and wet, making branches sag and the streets slippery.

Downtown, the snow made driving difficult. Traffic crawled across a bridge over the Assiniboine River near the huge building where the Manitoba government held its meetings. On a dome far above was a golden statue of a boy holding a bundle of wheat; a torch in his hand glowed through the falling snow.

Not far away were some grim streets. Business was bad here, and the people were unhappy. Some had gathered for coffee at a seedy place called the Golden Boy Café, named for the nearby statue. They sat at the counter, exchanging bad political news while chewing on tough doughnuts and sipping weak coffee.

The door opened, admitting the cold wind. A stranger with a briefcase in hand stood in the doorway. He was short, with slicked-back red hair and bulging cheeks. His eyebrows were as black as shoe polish, and he appeared to have a faint moustache. People might have thought he was a short salesperson taking a break from the cold, but secretly he was Tom Austen.

Removing his parka, Tom revealed a blazer, shirt, and tie. After sitting down in a booth, he allowed his blue eyes to travel around the room, memorizing everything. He turned toward a cracked mirror and critically studied the city slicker he saw reflected. Perhaps a touch too heavy on the shoe polish when disguising the eyes, but not a bad job. No one would suspect he was a kid.

A waitress appeared, holding an order pad. "Yeah, kid? Whattya having?"

"Milk," Tom muttered.

The waitress glanced up from the order pad. "What's the magic word?"

"Please," Tom added.

As she marched away, Tom studied a man at the counter, wondering if he could be Red in disguise. The waitress returned with some milk in an old glass. The cow juice was warm, but Tom decided not to complain. He swallowed some, then almost choked on pieces of cotton batten that washed out of his bulging cheeks.

Spluttering and coughing, Tom slammed down the glass and wiped his mouth. Everyone was staring, but Tom decided not to complain.

The clock above the juke box read 4:01 P.M. when Red came in the door and signalled to the waitress for a coffee. Minutes passed while he sat brooding at the counter, stirring the liquid with a spoon while staring moodily at the snow outside. Then his face brightened. Leaning forward, he watched a brown van stop across the street.

On the back were two words: *Blind Driver*.

Throwing a coin on the counter, Red headed for the door. The moment he was outside, Tom leapt into action. Fumbling for money, he pulled on his parka. Hurrying into the storm, he saw Red getting into the brown van. The driver was hidden from view, so Tom scurried across the street and moved closer to the van in a low crouch.

In the driver's outside mirror, he saw a face hidden inside a ski mask. The window was open.

Tom crept forward.

"I'm terrified," the driver moaned. "I live in agony, awaiting arrest. You forced me into this scheme, and now I'm doomed."

"Relax." Red's voice was thick with scorn. "I've got no sympathy. You're a spineless, crawling coward. In thirty minutes, I'll collect the ransom at the Countess, and you'll never see me again. So just . . ."

"Wait a minute!" The eyes of the shrouded man had spotted Tom. "There's a boy listening. I think I know him! He'll recognize me."

Red laughed. "Not with that ski mask you're wearing. Get out of here, and meet me at the Countess. I'll speak to the boy."

A door slammed, and the van pulled away. Red stood in the street—his eyes were mean. "So!" He stared at Tom. "The same kid from the school patrol. I warned you about being snoopy. *Now you're going to regret it.*"

Making two big fists, the man started walking toward Tom.

* * *

Tom ran, fast. Down the street he went, dodging past buses and slow-moving cars. Over his shoulder, he saw Red following. The man was a strong runner, and was close behind when Tom spotted the Greyhound terminal. With a final burst of energy, he raced inside. The bus station was crowded with travellers and suitcases, and buzzed with conversation. Close to Tom was a man in a peaked cap. On his uniform jacket were the words *Security Guard*.

"Help," Tom gasped, stopping beside the guard. "I've found Dianne Dorchester's kidnappers!"

The man's eyes widened. "*What*?"

"It's true," Tom exclaimed. He pointed at Red, coming into the terminal. "Arrest him!"

Red approached with a big smile on his face. "Is my son causing trouble again? He's such a prankster."

The security guard looked down at Tom. "This boy claims you kidnapped the missing girl."

Red's smile was very charming. "He loves playing detective. Look at that moustache he's penciled on, and the shoepolish in his eyebrows. Always in disguise! Don't you believe he's my son? His red hair's the same color as mine." Red grabbed Tom's arm. "Come on, son. I'm taking you home."

Tom slammed his foot down on Red's toes. The man yelled, and his grip loosened. Tearing free, Tom took off running. People stared as he raced between two buses, darted across an empty loading bay, and reached the street. Dropping into hiding behind a trash container, he looked at the terminal.

Through the windows he saw the men, still talking. Then Red hurried outside, jumped into a taxi, and was gone. Tom looked at his watch. He had ten minutes to reach the Countess.

* * *

The wind howled around Tom as he struggled from street to street until he reached the railway station. It was large, with pillars, and faced a parking lot.

In the middle of the lot was the Countess of Dufferin, one of the steam engines that first pulled trains across the prairies and high mountain passes all the way to Vancouver on the Pacific coast. Now the Countess was retired, and had become a favourite place for kids who liked to climb.

Tom stood by the parking lot, staring at the Countess. Someone was inside the engineer's cab. He could see a man in a dark overcoat and an expensive hat—it was Mr. Dorchester! Tom stared in amazement as Dianne's father climbed down the engine's ladder and dropped to the snow. Then he got into a car and drove away.

Out of a side street came the van with the man in the ski mask at the wheel. Red got out beside the Countess. Climbing the ladder, he disappeared inside the cab of the locomotive.

Tom remembered Mr. Stones saying, *When you need help, look for someone in a uniform, or a taxi driver who can radio the police.* Close by, a woman sat in her taxi in front of the station.

But the shortest route was straight past the Countess.

* * *

Gathering courage, Tom ran. Just as he dashed by the old steam engine, he saw Red above at the cab's door. Under the man's arm was a brown package.

Red spotted Tom. "Hey, you," he shouted. "You're that troublemaking kid. Stop!"

Tom didn't obey. Stumbling forward through the snow, he waved at the taxi driver. She rolled down her window. "What happened to your face? What's all that guck?"

"No time to explain," Tom cried. "Get the police here, please!"

"Will do," the woman cried, grabbing the microphone for her radio.

Tom looked back at the Countess. Red had scrambled down the ladder and now stood beside the locomotive, the package tucked safely under his arm. Somewhere in the distance, a siren wailed.

"The police are coming," Tom cried at the man. "Give up, now!"

Without a word, Red leapt into the van. Slipping and sliding, it left the parking lot. The taxi driver opened the passenger door, waved Tom inside, and they took off in pursuit. "We'll stop them," she smiled, stomping the accelerator, "I'm a champion at the wheel."

Rounding a corner, they raced into an industrial area with small businesses, used car lots, and gas stations. Ahead was the brown van, fighting its way through the storm. As the taxi moved closer, the van went out of control; whirling in a circle, it slammed into a snow bank.

Wheels spinning hopelessly, the van failed to break free. As Red jumped out to push, the taxi driver stopped and got out with Tom. Somewhere nearby, a siren howled closer. "The cops are coming," the driver shouted at Red. "Give up!"

Red grabbed the ransom package and took off running. At the same moment, the van broke free from the snow. Tires skidding, it fishtailed down the street and was gone.

The taxi driver and Tom went after Red. The man ran into an alley, but it was a dead end. Brick buildings loomed above, trapping Red. Clutching the ransom package, he stared at the taxi driver and Tom as they came closer.

"Give us the package," the driver said. "Surrender."

"Forget it, lady."

With a look of shock, Tom pointed over Red's shoulder. "Police dog! Look out!"

With a cry of fear, Red spun around. Tom threw himself against the man's legs, and knocked him down. The ransom package fell to the snow, and was grabbed by the taxi driver. She took off running, with Red in pursuit. As they reached the street, a police car came out of the storm and skidded to a stop.

Red reached inside his jacket. A revolver appeared in his hand. He waved it at Tom. "Back off, kid. Don't make me use this thing." Running to the police car, Red aimed the gun at the officer inside. "Out of this car," he yelled. "I need it more than you."

Red fired shots at the taxi's front tires, taking it out of action. He jumped into the police car and it raced away down the street, leaving Tom alone with the police officer and the taxi driver. People were staring from the doors and windows of nearby businesses.

"I've got the ransom," the taxi driver said excitedly to Tom. "That was great, how you scared him in the alley by pretending to see a dog."

Tom beamed proudly. "I remembered the first time I saw Red. He was really scared of a dog."

The stolen police car was later recovered, but Red escaped into hiding. Police raided his house and found evidence of his involvement in Dianne's kidnapping, but nothing that helped find the missing girl.

Things didn't look good for Dianne.

6

The next day, Tom decided to check out Dianne's house. He'd never seen it before, and was surprised at its size. The stone house stood alone in the middle of an enormous estate beside the river. All around the estate was a brick wall to keep out intruders.

A security guard stood by the wooden gate. With suspicious eyes, he watched Tom's approach. "Yeah, kid, what do you want?"

"Um . . ." Tom hadn't expected this kind of security. "Uh, any chance of a house tour?"

"Not a hope."

"But I'm a friend of Dianne's. We go to Queenston School together."

"Her family's too upset to see anyone."

Tom looked across the vast lawn at the house.

Nothing moved behind the windows. "Any idea who's involved in the kidnapping?" he asked the guard.

"Nope."

The man went inside a small security office and poured himself a coffee. Tom moved closer, memorizing every detail of the small office. Windows faced the gate and looked over the estate; he saw a small desk and two chairs, a filing cabinet and a telephone.

"Hey," Tom suddenly exclaimed, "there's our school newspaper! I'm one of the editors."

The guard picked up the paper. "Yeah, another guard left this here. His kid is Elizabeth Whitman— she took these pictures of the school staff. He's real proud of her."

"Elizabeth's my friend, too."

The man smiled. "Hey, you're doing okay for girl-friends." He pointed at one of the pictures. "See this guy? I met him a few months ago when he tried to get a job here, as a security guard. He claimed to be sick of working at Queenston School, but I kind of wondered why. Guarding this gate can get pretty boring."

Tom didn't reply because his mouth was hanging open in surprise. The man who'd tried for a job at the Dorchester estate was Pete Tyler, the school custodian.

"Yeah," the security guard continued, "he almost got a job, but then Mr. Dorchester found out about his criminal record."

* * *

At school the next day, Tom discussed the case with his friend Stephen Chong as they went into their classroom, where a huge banner proclaimed *Welcome to Kids' Day!* It was strung above the board in Tom's classroom. Mr. Stones had made a big effort, drawing a portrait of each student. These filled the walls, and streamers hung above.

"Life must continue," he said, when everyone was seated. "We all miss Dianne terribly, but I decided to have Kids' Day despite her disappearance. We all need to cheer up." He tried to smile. "Especially me."

Stephen held up his hand. "Sir, I've got a suggestion. When Dianne returns, let's have Kids' Day, Part Two. That'll be a real celebration!"

"Great idea," Dietmar said. "That'll give us an extra holiday."

Other students praised Stephen's suggestion, and then he held up his hand again. "Mr. Stones, here's another idea. When the kidnappers go on trial, let's have a field trip to the courtroom. We can watch the judge sentence them to prison."

Mr. Stones sighed. "I'm sure you're right, Stephen. They will certainly end up behind bars. That makes me sad."

"Why, sir?"

"Not everyone *wants* to be a criminal, you know. Some people get dragged into crime because they have no money, others because they have no hopes or dreams for the future. Our world offers them nothing." His eyes were fierce under the thick brows. "Still others are forced into crime at the point of a gun. Think of a poor man like that, driven into crime. What misery does he feel? Does he think about the prison bars— how cold they will feel to his hands? Does he picture his wife and children, visiting through a wire fence at the prison? What are that poor man's thoughts? What are his regrets?"

The room was silent, all eyes on Mr. Stones.

He forced himself to smile. "That's my thought for the day. A long one, I admit! Now, let's have some fun." After closing the blinds against the sun, he looked at Amardeep Dhaliwal. "Tell us a joke, Amardeep."

The friendly student grinned. "What do you get when you cross an elephant with a horse? A pony with big feet."

As everyone laughed, Mr. Stones pulled some papers from his pocket including some old receipts from *Pizza Perfect* and a few other restaurants. "Ah, here's what I want! I've written an Honour Roll of your accomplishments. Every one of you is a winner, I'm pleased to say. You'll receive a Certificate of Achievement." He looked at Elizabeth Whitman. "You're first, Elizabeth. Recently I boarded a crowded bus, and saw you giving up your seat to someone. Well done!"

Smiling shyly, she received her certificate. As the honours continued for other students, Mr. Nicholson appeared in the doorway. With him was a stranger.

"Tom Austen," the principal said. "This man's from the newspaper. He wants to interview you about the kidnapping."

"Wow!" Tom glowed. "You bet—for sure!"

The man shook hands. "The name's Byron Xavier Lewis. Call me B.X., everyone does." Thin and short, he wore a crumpled shirt and trousers. His collar was open at the neck, showing an Adam's apple that moved when he spoke. "So, you're the hero who almost captured the kidnappers." B.X. had pale grey eyes that flicked from Tom to Mr. Stones to Mr. Nicholson, then back to Tom. "Tell me how you did it."

"Sure," Tom said, "but where's your notebook?"

"Huh?"

"How will you remember what I say for your newspaper article?"

"Oh!" B.X. swallowed. Digging around in his pockets, he pulled out a crumpled restaurant napkin. "This'll do."

"Need a pen?" Mr. Stones asked, offering one.

B.X. gave the teacher a curt nod. "Thanks, fella." He looked at Tom. "So, how many kidnappers were there?"

"Two."

"Did you identify them?"

"One, the guy named Red. The police raided his place, but he's gone into hiding. He lived next door to a deserted house, and they think he used it for secret meetings. I saw a meeting with my own eyes."

B.X. wasn't writing anything down, he was just watching Tom. "What do you mean?"

"The night before the kidnapping, I was hiding in the attic. I saw Red with another man."

"My goodness!" Mr. Stones leaned across his desk. "Tom, is that true? That's important information."

B.X. studied Tom. "Did you recognize the other man?"

"No, because he was wearing a ski mask as disguise." Watching B.X.'s face, he saw the worry lines relax. The man hadn't written a word since the interview began. Tom looked at Mr. Stones. "Okay to leave the room, sir? I'm not feeling well, too much lemon-ade I guess. I'll phone my Mom for a ride home."

Tom hurried down the hallway. At the principal's office, he borrowed a phone book, then called the newspaper. "Hello," he said. "May I please speak to a reporter named Byron Xavier Lewis?" There was a silence, during which the school secretary studied Tom's face. Then he said thanks, and hung up. "The newspaper's never heard of that man," he told her.

B.X. appeared in the doorway with Mr. Nicholson. Both of them looked upset. "You didn't finish the inter-view," B.X. said. "I've got some more questions."

"You're not a reporter," Tom told him. "You're just trying to get information from me. How come?"

B.X. turned to the principal. "Thanks for your help," he said. "I'm on my way." Quickly he went into the pale sunshine of early spring, and walked away.

"Sir," Tom said urgently to the principal. "Arrest that guy! He's a fake reporter."

Crossing his arms, Mr. Nicholson gazed down at Tom. "Another gag, young Mr. Austen? Another not-very-funny prank?"

"Phone the newspaper yourself, sir! It's true!"

"In your classroom, you said you were sick. Weren't you going to phone your mother for a ride?"

"Sure, but . . ."

"You lied, Tom. Go to your classroom, immediately. I'll deal with you later."

Head hanging, Tom walked mournfully along the hallway. Pausing at the school's side door, he looked outside. The fake reporter named Byron Xavier Lewis was waiting at a bus stop.

"Hey, Austen!" Dietmar Oban appeared beside Tom. "What's going on? Mr. Stones wants to know how sick you are. I told him you should be in an institution. He sent me looking for you."

Grabbing Dietmar by the arm, Tom pushed open the door. The air was cool outside. "I need some help, Oban."

"Forget it!"

"You like Elizabeth Whitman, right?"

"Maybe."

"Tell you what, Oban. I'll write you some poetry to give her. She'll fall in love for sure."

"What's the price?"

"A short bus ride." Tom dragged Dietmar across the school yard. "Hurry up, I see a bus coming now."

"This is insanity, Austen! We'll be in deep trouble at the school."

"We've got no choice. Come on, climb aboard."

Tom forced Dietmar into the bus. As it lurched away from the curb, he saw B.X. watching them from the back seat. The other passengers were a mother and her baby, and a white-haired man gripping a cane. "They could be his accomplices," Tom whispered to Dietmar as they sat down at the front. "Act innocent."

"What's going on?" Dietmar demanded.

"That guy isn't a reporter. He was trying to find out if I recognized the second kidnapper. He must be part of their gang. If we follow him, we may find where Dianne's hidden."

The bus swung hard around a corner, pitching the boys forward. Tom stared at the driver, wondering if he was also involved. He began to sweat—maybe they'd blundered into maximum danger.

241

Dietmar looked at him. "I just thought of something. How can we follow that guy when he's already seen us?"

"I'll think of something," Tom promised. "Trust me."

"That poetry better be good, Austen."

Tom got out his notebook. "One thing I've learned today," he told Dietmar as he made notes on the case. "There are at least three guys in the kidnap ring. Red and B.X., plus the man in the ski mask."

"Maybe that was B.X.," Dietmar suggested.

"No, he's far too short."

"Why don't you phone the cops?"

"I will, the minute B.X. leads us to the kidnappers' hiding place. If he gets scared, and escapes, Dianne won't be found."

Slowly, the bus made its way downtown. Outside, yards were brown after the long winter and snow still lingered in shady places. As the bus crossed a bridge over the Assiniboine, the boys gasped. "Look at the river!" Dietmar exclaimed. "It's a raging torrent."

The brown water surged past. Swollen by melting snow, it had climbed the river banks almost to the bridge. High above the flood-threatened city, the Golden Boy held his torch aloft. Tom and Dietmar watched him through the window, then the bus continued downtown past department stores and businesses and churches with onion-shaped domes. Other people left and entered, but B.X. remained on board. His eyes never left the boys.

* * *

Finally, B.X. left the bus in an industrial area. There were warehouses along the street, and equipment yards surrounded by chain-link fences.

As the bus drove away, B.X. gave the boys a dirty look. "You two following me?"

Tom stared at him. "Why'd you question me at the school? You're a kidnapper, not a reporter."

"Rubbish," the man scoffed. "Now beat it, both of you."

"Or you'll call the cops?" Tom said. "I doubt it."

"You're right," the man said, making a fist, "but I'll use this on your front teeth."

Dietmar gulped. "Come on, Austen. Let's go home."

Tom nodded. "Okay, but we'll have to walk. I'm out of bus fare."

As the boys went down the street, Tom used a tiny pocket mirror to watch B.X. The man stared after them, then hurried toward a side street and was gone. "Let's follow him," Tom said urgently, running toward the street. "Come on, Oban!"

"Forget it, Austen."

"I'll write you *five* poems."

"No deal."

"But that guy could lead us to Dianne!"

"Okay, Austen, but I don't like this."

"Nothing will happen, and we've got to learn where Dianne's a prisoner."

Scurrying between parked cars, the boys followed B.X. along a dusty street until he reached a furniture warehouse where large banners read *Closed Due to Bankruptcy*. After glancing up and down the street, B.X. went inside.

"Let's call the cops," Dietmar said.

"First, let's make sure Dianne's in that warehouse. It'll only take a minute."

"This feels like quicksand," Dietmar said. "I keep getting deeper and deeper, and I never wanted to be here anyway."

"You'll be famous, Oban. Isn't that important to you?"

"Not in the slightest."

Tom shook his head. "Sometimes you're so weird, Oban. All I want from life is my picture in the newspaper."

"It'll probably happen, but you'll have a number on your chest and be wearing a striped prison suit."

"Funny, funny." Tom raised a warning hand. "Now, pipe down, Oban. We're going into that warehouse."

The boys raced across a litter-filled yard and tried the door. "It's open," Tom whispered. "Come on." Passing along a short hallway, they entered the furniture warehouse. Pale light came through dirty windows, showing a roof far above. Some furniture was stored on enormous shelves, but most was displayed on the big floor. They could see sofas and tables and beds and several piles of mattresses.

At the far end of the warehouse was a steel staircase, rising to the floor above. Up there was a small office, where a light glowed through an open door.

"Look," Tom said, "there's B.X. Let's get closer."

"Hold it, Austen. My nose is vibrating—I think I'm allergic to something in here. I'd better wait outside."

"You've got an allergy?" Tom said with heavy sarcasm. "Since when?"

"It's true, Austen! I'm going to sneeze, for sure."

"Stick with me," he said, squeezing Dietmar's arm. "We're almost finished."

"That's what I'm afraid of."

Reaching the steel staircase, they crept up. Dust danced in the light from the office, where B.X. stood in the doorway and Red sat behind a desk. "Honest, boss," B.X. whined, "I tried. Everyone at the school believed I was a reporter."

"Except the kid himself," Red snarled. "But at least you learned he didn't recognize my man in the ski mask. That's good news. It was worth taking a risk by sending you as a fake reporter."

"I did a good job, boss."

"Did you use a fake name at the school?"

"No. Was I supposed to?"

"Of course, you fool!"

"Sorry, boss."

"Ah, forget it. Your name isn't in the phone book, so the cops can't track you down."

"Something I can't figure, boss. Why'd you need another person to help us?"

"Like I told you before, nitwit, we needed someone Dianne knew to drive the van. I was pretty sure I could find a helper at that school."

Tom climbed higher up the stairs, pulling Dietmar along. The office looked down at the display floor, far below. The displays could also be watched from a steel catwalk that connected to the office. Trying for a better look at the two men, Tom led Dietmar onto the catwalk.

"I'm terrified of heights," Dietmar moaned. "Get me out of here."

"Don't look down. That's always a mistake."

Tom signalled for quiet. Now he had a clear view of Red, who was smoking a cigar behind the desk. "I've made a decision," the man told B.X. "We're going to leave town. Just for a while, until the pressure lets up. Then we'll try again for a ransom payment."

"Sounds good," B.X. said.

"We're moving to our hideout in Ontario. I'll take 2014 and you drive there in the pickup truck. You know where to meet me."

"What about the Dorchester brat?"

"We can't take a chance on moving her. Not with posters of her face all over town."

"Your man in the ski mask will keep feeding her?"

"He'd better." Red stubbed out the cigar. "Let's get going."

As the man stood up, Tom realized they were now trapped on the catwalk—it was impossible to reach the stairs without being seen. Motioning at Dietmar, he led him farther out the catwalk. Far below, the furniture was only dim shapes in the faint light.

"Don't make a sound, Oban," he whispered.

Dietmar's only response was a moan.

The men's footsteps echoed as they descended the metal stairs. In a corner of the warehouse, Red pulled a tarpaulin to one side. Hidden behind it were two vehicles. "There's Red's pickup truck," Tom whispered to Dietmar, "and there's the brown van. Now I understand why it says *Blind Driver* on the back. It's for delivering blinds and other furniture."

Red rolled open a big outside door, and B.X. drove away in the pickup truck. Then, moments later, Dietmar sneezed. The sound blasted through the warehouse, echoing between the walls. As Tom stared at him, Dietmar gestured with his hands. "Sorry! But I warned you."

Red headed for the stairs, moving fast. "You little meddlers," he shouted. "I'm going to arrange an accident for you. It's a long fall from that catwalk to the display floor."

Tom looked for another escape route, but they were trapped. Dietmar's eyes were huge with fear. "Help," he groaned. "Do something!"

Tom pointed down at the piles of mattresses. "Let's jump. It's our only chance."

"Jump? You've got to be kidding!"

"You want to get thrown off by Red? Come on, move!"

"No more investigations, Austen. Never!" Dietmar climbed on the catwalk railing, groaned once, and jumped.

Tom looked at Red. He had reached the catwalk, moving fast. "I'll get you, kid," he snarled.

Tom's stomach clenched with fear as he jumped. His heart rose into his throat, then he slammed into the mattresses.

"Come on, Dietmar," he yelled, rolling off them, "run!"

The boys dashed into the street. Moments later, the brown van raced away with Red behind the wheel. "Find a phone," Tom told Dietmar. "Call the police!"

"What will you do?"

"I've got a hunch where Red's gone. I'm going to check it out, and call the police if I'm right."

"I can go now?"

"You bet, Oban. Thanks for your help."

"Remember just one thing, Austen. *Never again*."

7

Before long, Tom reached the railway station. He looked at the Countess of Dufferin, remembering the chase after Red and wondering how the man always escaped. He was a slippery character, for sure.

Passing between enormous pillars, Tom entered the station. Sunshine flowed through windows high above, warming the crowds waiting for a train's departure. Some people cried in each other's arms while luggage handlers rushed by with suitcases.

At the *Train Departures* notice board, Tom's eyes lit up. As he'd thought, there was a train with the number 2014 departing now. And Red had spoken of leaving town on the 2014!

Tom looked for a phone booth to call his father at the police station. People stood in every one, talking to friends and relatives. Meanwhile, the station slowly emptied as people boarded 2014 and loudspeakers warned it was about to leave the station.

The people still gabbed on the phones! Tom realized he would have to board the train and alert the conductor to arrest Red. He ran out of the station to the corner, went through an underpass, and reached the railway yards.

The tracks spread out like metal spaghetti in every direction. Yard engines shunted back and forth while freight cars crashed together, creating an exciting scene, but one that Tom had no time to stop and enjoy.

He looked across the yard. Standing quietly in the midst of all the motion was a long string of passenger cars, steam drizzling from couplings and hidden pipes. At the head of the cars was a big diesel engine, ready to take the train on its journey east.

Tom stumbled on the wooden ties as he ran across the yard, anxiously hoping the engine wouldn't move. A woman looked up from her work and stared at Tom as he ran past, his breath heaving in and out. A whistle on the engine shrieked and Tom ran faster.

He rounded the end of the train and pulled his tired body up onto the station platform. Another blast from the whistle. He looked along the train and saw that the porters had already climbed inside and closed the doors; the only person left on the platform was a distant conductor waving his arm toward the engine.

It seemed too late, but Tom found the energy to make his legs carry him toward a sleeping car where the top half of the door was open. A young woman leaned out, watching Tom.

"Please," Tom gasped, looking up at the woman. "Please, open the door."

"What did you say?" she shouted above the hissing of steam from couplings.

"Open the door," Tom yelled, pointing to the handle. "My mother is sick!"

A puzzled frown appeared on the woman's face, and she looked toward the end of the train as if expecting a sick mother to appear in a wheelchair.

"Open the door!" Tom repeated.

This time the woman seemed to understand; she reached for the handle, took a few seconds figuring out how it worked, then pulled the door open. But a steel platform still lay across the steps, preventing Tom from boarding the train.

"The platform!" Tom yelled, pointing at a metal catch that held the steel plate in place. "Push that catch with your foot!"

The woman looked down at the catch, puzzled once again. The train lurched as the big engine started forward.

"KICK THAT CATCH," Tom shrieked, dancing from one foot to the other. He started to run beside the train as it rolled forward, pointing desperately at the catch. The woman kicked feebly at it, then tried again and the steel plate came free, rising up out of Tom's way. He jumped onto the bottom step and grabbed a railing, unable to speak as the train rattled out of the station.

"Are you all right?" the young woman asked anxiously.

Tom nodded, still holding tightly to the railing.

"Where is your mother? Did she miss the train?"

Tom shook his head, more interested in catching his breath than lying to the woman. Besides, in the fight against crime, no one could be trusted. "My mother will be fine," he panted, "just fine."

"Where is she? Does she need help?"

"No, thanks." Climbing up the steps, Tom slammed the steel plate back into place and closed the door. "Thanks for helping me."

Tom gifted the woman with a bright smile as he pushed open the door of the car. He would have to find the conductor and alert him.

The train swayed back and forth as it left the yards and began to pick up speed. Tom looked into the back yards of some old houses, and then was startled by a rumbling sound as the train rolled onto a steel trestle. He looked down at the deep brown waters of the Red River surging past under the trestle and felt suddenly afraid of the rising flood waters.

The clatter of the couplings was loud in Tom's ears as he crossed the shaking metal plates that connected to the next car. Somewhere, behind a closed door, a baby was crying. Tom moved slowly through the train, looking carefully at the passengers, aware that Red could be in disguise. He reached the end of the car, crossed more shaking metal plates, and entered another car.

Faintly, in the distance, the train's whistle sounded. Tom looked out the window as they flashed through a tiny town and roared back onto the open prairie. Green buds showed on trees gathered together near water, and spring sunshine warmed the fields.

No crying baby in this car. Tom hurried along the aisle, receiving some hostile looks from the faces he was examining. One man was hidden behind a newspaper he was reading and Tom hesitated, not wanting to waste time, but not wanting to miss any faces. How to get a look? The problem was solved by the man, who lowered the paper. It was Red.

"Oh!" Tom said, shocked. He could feel the blood draining away from his face as he stared at Red's jacket—he could see the outline of a shoulder holster!

Tom began to back away, almost tripping as his feet tangled together.

"Just a minute," Red said sharply. He put down his newspaper and seemed to reach toward his jacket.

"Don't shoot," Tom cried. "The police have the train surrounded!"

A strange look passed across Red's face. He tried to grab Tom but his hand clutched thin air. People watched in astonishment as Tom dashed to the end of the car, where a door marked *Toilet* stood half open. Fear shaking his body, he rushed inside and slammed the door shut.

Red's feet crashed to a stop outside the door. Tom turned the lock.

"Open up!" Red's voice called.

Tom leaned against the door, his eyes filled with terror as he watched the handle moving back and forth. He looked around the tiny washroom for a means of escape, but there was nothing.

"What's the problem, sir?" a voice outside said.

"Nothing," Red replied. A pause, then he added, "My son has locked himself in the washroom. Can you open the door?"

"I can," the conductor replied, "but why should I?"

"He's got my razor blades. He's a hysterical boy, and I'm afraid he'll cut himself real bad."

Silence. Tom could picture the conductor trying to decide if Red was telling the truth.

"All right," the conductor said, "we'd better get him out of there."

A scraping sound of metal against metal as a key turned in the lock. Reaching inside, Red grabbed Tom.

"Come here, son." Red tried to sound like a friendly father, but his blue eyes were cold and mean as he yanked Tom out of the washroom.

"Where's the razor?" the conductor asked.

"There isn't one," Tom shouted. "This man's a kidnapper!"

Red slammed his hand over Tom's mouth but Tom bit him, hard. With a shout of pain, Red released his grip. But then he pulled a gun from his shoulder holster.

"Don't move, kid." He aimed the gun at a man sitting in one of the seats. "Try anything, and you're a dead turkey."

"I didn't . . ." the man protested.

"Don't interrupt!" Red locked a powerful hand on Tom's arm. "You must have sawdust for brains, kiddo. How can the police surround a moving train?"

"I don't know," Tom muttered. He looked around for help, but the people in the car looked too afraid to move and one man was even crying. Fear had changed their faces, making them look like trapped animals.

"What are you going to do?" Tom asked Red, trying not to sound afraid.

But the man ignored him. Glancing at his watch, he motioned with his gun along the car. "Get going," he said to the conductor, giving Tom's arm a rough tug. "You too, kiddo."

They started forward, the conductor in front with the pistol pointed at his head, Tom at Red's side.

"Anyone moves," Red shouted, "and the conductor qualifies for a nice funeral."

The crying man huddled in his seat as they approached. Red laughed. "Must be a cop."

The words made Tom furious. "You think the police are so stupid? They're going to ambush your gang. The baggage car is full of police, with guns and everything."

Red only laughed harder, and pushed Tom forward with the conductor. Between cars, surrounded by the crashing noise of the couplings, Tom grabbed his stomach.

"Oh," he groaned, "oh, I'm sick."

"Come on, keep moving," Red said angrily.

"I can't," Tom moaned, leaning forward and clutching his stomach tighter.

"What is it?" Red said, stopping to look at Tom.

As the man's grip loosened on his arm, Tom tore himself free. Before Red could move, he grabbed the emergency cord and pulled hard.

"You little fool!" Red shouted.

But it was too late to change anything. Steel wheels screeched against steel tracks as the brakes slammed on. Shuddering and bucking, the train came to a grinding halt in the middle of the prairie.

8

After the immense noise of the moving train, the silence filled Tom's ears. He stared at Red, waiting for the man to do something terrible, but the anger passed quickly from his blue eyes.

"Come here, kiddo." Gripping Tom's arm, Red turned to the conductor. "Open that door, Pops."

"Yes, sir. Don't shoot, sir."

After pulling open the door, the conductor kicked the catch to free the steel plate across the steps.

"Lie down and count to 50," Red barked.

"Yes, sir." The conductor lay down on his stomach. "One, two, three . . ."

"Let's go," Red ordered Tom. They went down the steps and jumped to the gravel beside the tracks.

"What's going on?" a man's voice yelled.

The porter in the next sleeping car had left the train and was looking their way. A cloud of steam hid him for a second, and when he reappeared his eyes were popping as he stared at Red's gun.

"Get back in the train!" Red shouted.

"Sure thing, sure thing," the man said, racing up the steps. The door of his car closed with a slam.

Another porter had climbed out far along at the head of the train, his white coat a distant blur in the sunshine. A few other people leaned out from the doors between the cars, but no one was coming to help Tom.

"This way," Red said, pulling him toward the end of the train. Faces looked down from the windows as they passed, feet grinding on the gravel.

"Faster." Red began to run, his hand holding firmly to Tom. They reached the end of the train and stopped, looking at the emptiness that stretched under billowing clouds to the distant horizon. Dust rose from the wheels of a car coming toward them along a dirt road.

"Flag him down," Red ordered.

Tom waved both arms. The driver, who had been staring at the train stopped in the middle of nowhere, braked beside Tom and Red.

"Hi!" he said, a friendly grin on his chubby face. He had a pimply nose, and wore a hat too small for his head. "What's going on?"

Red pointed the revolver at the man's head. "I don't know what's going on, Jumbo, but this is going off unless you give us a ride."

The grin melted off the chubby face. "I've got a wife and kids," the man said. "Don't shoot me."

"You want them to have a father tomorrow, you do what I say."

"Yes, sir."

Keeping his gun aimed at the driver, Red pulled Tom around the car to the passenger door. They climbed in beside the fat man.

"Let's go," Red said, slamming the door.

"Yes, sir."

The driver's nervous foot jumped off the clutch and the car leapt forward, rocks and dirt shooting from the wheels. "Sorry," the driver shouted above the noise, his hands fighting the steering wheel as they bounced along the road and left the train behind.

"Where to, sir?" the driver asked.

"Ontario."

"What!?"

"You heard me, Jumbo. Ontario, and don't spare the horsepower."

"But I'm a salesman. I've got clients to see today."

Red laughed. "My brother is an undertaker. You want to be his client?"

"No, sir," the fat man said. "No, sir."

"Follow back roads. The cops may set up road-blocks on the highway."

Sitting between the driver and Red, Tom looked at the black revolver and wondered if Red would really use it. He seemed to make a lot of threats, but no one was a dead turkey yet. Still, Tom didn't think it would be good for his health to call Red's bluff. At least, not yet.

A large checkerboard sign appeared ahead. Turning onto a paved road, the car picked up speed as it headed across the flat land. Tom saw horses grazing in a field, their tails lazily twitching, but no other sign of life. As flies and bugs splattered against the windshield, he tried to think of an escape plan. The fuel gauge registered full, meaning there wouldn't be a chance to make a break during a pit stop. He looked up at the driver, wondering if an escape plan was forming in the man's head.

"What do you sell?" Tom asked the driver.

"Ladies' underwear," the fat man muttered.

As Red roared with laughter, the driver's chubby face went red. Tom was silent, unable to think of another question.

"Boy, oh, boy," Red chuckled, "ladies' underwear."

A boy walking along the side of the road with a yellow dog looked at Tom as they passed. Would he alert the police? Not much chance, since he wouldn't know Tom had been kidnapped.

Kidnapped! Tom suddenly realized what had happened—this was just like a Hardy Boys mystery, but he was sure Dianne wouldn't think kidnapping was an adventure. Tom looked up at Red.

"Why did you kidnap Dianne?" he said, watching his face closely.

Red glanced at Tom. "Button your lip, kiddo."

Tom was silent—obviously, Red could stand up to ruthless questioning. He tried to remember how Frank and Joe Hardy grilled criminals, but the books seemed like distant, faded memories.

The car tires hummed against the pavement as they rolled steadily onward, watching the land change from flat fields to bush and rock. After they'd passed a sign welcoming them to Ontario, Tom's stomach began to rumble.

"I'm hungry," he said.

"Aren't we all," Red murmured.

"Can't we stop for a milkshake?"

"Keep your shirt on, kiddo," Red said. "I'll fry up some fish later tonight."

"But I want to eat now," Tom insisted.

"You want a mouthful of lead?"

Tom didn't answer, still not certain if Red was bluffing with his gun. The sky turned scarlet, streaked by black clouds. A single ray of the setting sun lit the earth. Tom saw more horses in a field.

"Are they wild?" he asked.

Jumbo shook his head. "Farmers own them. What a life, eh, out in the open with nothing to do but run wild and free."

Red glanced at him. "Hey, Jumbo, you're a poet, not a salesman. Why aren't you out there, writing?"

He shrugged his sloping shoulders. "I never took a chance in life. It's too late now to start over."

Red snorted. "I figure you only get one turn. Make it count, that's what I say."

Tom held up his hand. "Sorry, but I've *gotta* find a bathroom soon."

Red looked at him suspiciously. "Are you planning an escape? If so, think again. That's the only warning you get."

He motioned at Jumbo with his hand. "I see a campground ahead. Pull off there."

By now, Jumbo had the headlights on. The yellow beams spotted the campground. It had dirt roads, a few

trees, some wooden picnic tables, and a central building with showers and washrooms. To Tom's dismay,
no one was around to help.

Slowly, he got out of the car. As Red pushed him
toward the washroom, Tom stumbled and then fell.

"My ankle," he cried. "You made me twist it!"

Red leaned forward to examine Tom's ankle. As he
did, Tom grabbed some dirt and flung it into Red's
face. Crying out, the man clawed at his eyes with
both hands.

Tom ran toward the car. "Start the engine," he yelled
at Jumbo, "let's get out of here!"

"You bet," the man shouted. The engine turned over,
then died. Jumbo leaned over the wheel, desperately
working the starter while his eyes watched Red wiping
his face. "I've flooded the engine," Jumbo yelled as
Tom reached the car. "It won't start!"

"Come on," Tom cried to the man, "let's use the
horses!" Running toward a nearby field, he climbed to
the top of the fence. It was now getting really dark, but
he could see the horses.

Jumbo reached the fence, panting from the run, and
began to climb. "I'm out of shape," he gasped, "please
help me."

Reaching down, Tom helped the man over the fence
as they hurried across the field. The horses stamped their
feet nervously as Tom approached making soothing
noises. Jumbo was just behind, but there was no sign of
Red in the darkness.

Seizing a bridle, Tom pulled himself onto one of the
bare backs. The horse was warm to his touch. In the
distance Red appeared, climbing over the fence.

"Hurry, mister," Tom urged. "Get on that horse, and let's go!"

"I can't," the man moaned. "That thing's too high. I can't climb on it." Jumbo looked at Red. He was moving slowly, still wiping at his eyes, but he was coming their way. "Go ahead, kid, ride for safety! I'll be okay."

"No, I can't do that," Tom replied, sliding off the horse. "We'll make a break for it together."

As they crossed the field, their eyes got used to the darkness. Tom saw Red following. Reaching a fence, he whistled in astonishment. "Here's a bicycle! It must belong to the farmer's kid."

"Are the tires inflated okay?"

"You bet," Tom said. "Hurry, we can ride double."

Jumbo shook his head. His entire body was trembling with fear. "I've tried that with my kids, and it doesn't work. My stomach's too big. Go ahead, ride out of here and find the police."

"No," Tom said, "you take the bike."

Jumbo stared fearfully at Red, who was coming their way. "I, I . . ."

"Take it," Tom urged. The man's fear made him sad. "Go on, you've got a wife and kids. What if they never see you again? Ride out of here, fast!"

"You're right," Jumbo mumbled, climbing on the bike, "they need me." The bicycle lurched forward under his big feet, then began to gather speed. Jumbo disappeared into the darkness, moving fast.

Tom ran in the opposite direction, following the fence. The ground was uneven for a while, then became smoother. Ahead, Tom saw the dim outline of picnic benches and a small building. Somehow he'd found his way back to the campground, where he'd seen a pay phone.

Tom crept through the darkness toward the building. The phone was attached to the outside wall. As Tom picked it up he looked at the surrounding night. It was absolutely silent, and he couldn't see anything.

"*Operator*," a voice said on the phone. "*What number, please?*"

"Thank goodness," Tom exclaimed. "Listen, operator, I'm in big trouble!"

"*Yes?*"

Tom heard a footstep, somewhere behind. He whirled around, staring at the dark air. Nothing could be seen. Still he stared, then raised the phone to his ear. "Sorry, operator, I thought that . . ." Stopping, Tom stared at the phone in his hand. It had gone dead.

Again he heard a sound, and this time saw Red. The man had pulled out the telephone wire and was twirling it in one hand. In the other, he held the gun. It was pointed straight at Tom.

* * *

"You're some kid."

Red was with Tom in the salesman's car. "You've got a lot of courage, I'll say that, but I'm starting to get upset." He looked at Tom. "We're driving to Lake of the Woods. It's mighty big, and mighty deep. One more trick, and I'll deep-six you in the lake. Know what that means?"

Tom gulped, and nodded.

Without another word, Red headed for the road and they continued their journey into the night. At last, two reflectors appeared ahead in the dark, shining in the headlights like the eyes of a cat. As they came closer, Tom saw the reflectors were on the back of a pickup truck parked beside the highway. B.X. was at the wheel.

Red pulled the salesman's car off the road, left the keys inside and ran with Tom to the pickup.

"Hey," B.X. demanded as they climbed into the front seat. "What happened to you? I waited at the Junction, but 2014 never showed up. So I came here to wait, like we agreed."

"Tell you later, B.X. Let's get going."

Soon the pickup was flying down the highway, much faster than the salesman had managed with his car. Tom watched anxiously as the speedometer needle climbed, afraid a tire would blow and they'd overturn in a ditch.

"Take it easy, B.X.," Red said. "I want to die of old age."

Their speed dropped slightly. The trip continued in silence until the pickup abruptly turned onto a gravel surface. The trees at the side of the road seemed thicker as they followed the road up and around several hills.

"Can you drive a car, kiddo?"

"Not yet," Tom replied.

"What a shame. I could use a new driver. B.X. is too fast."

"Yeah!"

Red laughed, and B.X.'s mouth turned down at the

corners. "What'll we do with this kid?" he asked. "Ransom him for money?"

"Nah. His family's not rich. Maybe I'll just use him for target practice."

Tom didn't let his face show anything. He was sure now that Red was bluffing with that gun, so he wasn't afraid of becoming a target.

"Nerves of steel, huh?" Lifting the gun, Red put the cold muzzle against Tom's temple. The hammer of the gun clicked. Tom closed his eyes and forced himself to pretend that he was back in school, adding up numbers in math. When he opened his eyes, Red had lowered the gun.

"Here we are," B.X. said.

As they got out, he switched on a flashlight. Holding tight to Tom, Red followed B.X. along a dirt path. Tom heard water swishing, and the soft slap of waves, then saw the flashlight beam hit a powerful speedboat.

"Hey," he said, unable to keep his excitement from showing. "Is that your boat?"

Laughing, Red gave B.X. a poke on the arm. "Keep moving."

The flashlight beam stopped on an old rowboat with an outboard motor clamped to the back. Tom stepped down into the boat, staggering as it rocked back and forth. "Give the engine a kick and let's get going," Red ordered B.X.

Tom saw the brilliance of a thousand stars above the lake. The splash of small waves was a peaceful sound, but then was drowned out by the motor roaring into life. The smell of gas and oil stung Tom's nose.

"Throw off the line," B.X. yelled over his shoulder.

The propeller bit in, bubbling the water. As they headed out under the stars, cold lake air swept over the boat. Tom shivered, thinking how upset his family must be. He was cold and tired and hungry, and a sense of terrible loneliness crept into his mind. What if they did kill him, what if he just disappeared like Dianne? The thought made tears come to his eyes.

9

"I say kill him."

Tom knelt under the open window of the cabin, listening to the argument between Red and B.X.

"And I say you're crazy," Red's voice answered. "You think I could put a bullet in that kid's head?"

"I'll do it."

Silence, then the smack of a fist hitting flesh and a crashing sound as someone fell to the floor.

"You aren't killing anyone, B.X.," Red said angrily.

Tom wanted to look through the window, but knew it would be suicide if he was seen. He was supposed to be at the far end of the island, fishing.

"I'm going to check the boat," Red said. "If anything happens to that kid you're a dead man, B.X."

Tom ran to the woods that grew close to the cabin.

Safe among the trees, he heard the cabin door slam, and saw Red walk down the path to the boathouse. Unlocking the door, he went inside.

Tom started toward the place where he had left Red's fishing rod; it was a very small island and he was there in a few minutes. He sat down on the big rock overlooking the deep water.

With a flick of the wrist, Tom cast the line. Sailing gracefully through the air, it fell into the water with a quiet plop. Tom let the line run deep, then reeled it in, watching for the beautiful sight of the spinner flashing up through the cold water.

Since arriving on the island, Tom had not seen a fish, but it was pleasant to sit in the sunshine and watch for signs of the police boat that he knew would be coming to his rescue. By now, the salesman would have told the police about Red, Tom, and the theft of his car, and before long they'd be searching the islands scattered across this huge lake.

When the spinner came dripping out of the water, Tom looked across the water. On the distant shore, a cabin cruiser moved past under the bright sun. Tom had seen many of the big boats go by, but they were always too far away for people to hear a shout for help.

* * *

The next afternoon, Red returned to the island in the boat after being gone all day. He closed the boathouse door and locked it; the key was always on a thong around his neck. He carried two bags of food to the cabin, and the door slammed behind him.

Sneaking forward to an open window, Tom took out his notebook. Red and B.X. often quarrelled; Tom had picked up information, but nothing very useful. Dianne's location hadn't been mentioned.

Tom saw B.X. moodily carving a point on a wooden stick. Red was on the sofa, feet up. "I talked to our man in the ski mask," he said, "to be sure the Dorchester kid is getting fed okay. Then I met with O.L. He's going to send the Dorchester family a new ransom demand. If they don't cooperate this time, the girl will die."

Tom gasped in shock, then quickly scribbled the initials O.L. At last, some important information—another person was involved in the kidnapping!

"We reached an agreement," Red continued. "If any of us gets busted, we admit to nothing. Providing the cops don't arrest all of us, the ransom demands can continue. The money will be shared equally—including anyone in prison."

B.X. stared at Red. "*Prison*?"

"Hey, relax. Nothing can go wrong."

Looking sulky, B.X. said no more. His moods could last for hours, so Tom closed the notebook and crept away. Somehow he must escape!

Following a trail through the trees he soon reached a rocky bluff overlooking the lake. In the distance was an island with a large house; he'd seen lights there at night, but how to alert the people?

There must be some way. Tom walked back and forth on the rocky beach, concentrating on the problem. He felt like Robinson Crusoe, trapped forever on a desert island. He should put a note in a bottle advertising for a

Man Friday. No—they might send Dietmar Oban by mistake.

Wait a minute. Wait a minute!

Tom grinned, pleased he'd thought of a way to escape at last. He hurried along the trail to the cabin. The sound of hammering came from the boathouse, where Red was trying to repair the leaky roof.

Creeping to the back of the cabin, Tom lifted the lid of the garbage can. He rooted around until he found the wine bottle that the two men had emptied during dinner last night, then pushed aside tin cans and sticky coffee grounds to find the cork.

Tom rushed back through the woods to the beach, where he got out his notebook and pen that he had used to play battleships with Red. Carefully, Tom printed: I AM PRISONER ON THE SMALL ISLAND WITH CABIN AND BOATHOUSE—TOM AUSTEN. He stuffed the paper down the neck of the wine bottle and jammed the cork in place.

Tom lifted the bottle and threw it with all his might. It twisted in the air and splashed down, disappearing under the surface. His anxious eyes saw it reappear, bobbing like a cheerful little boat among the waves.

Which way would it go? The bottle seemed to hesitate, then got mixed up with some small waves and disappeared south. Tom crossed all his fingers and wished it luck before walking back to the cabin. He felt good.

Hammering still echoed in the clearing. Not wanting to share the cabin with B.X., Tom went into the boathouse. "Hi," he said to Red, who was standing at the top of a stepladder repairing a support beam.

"Hiya, kiddo," Red said, smiling. "How's the fishing?"

"I caught six pike, but I threw them back. Too small for me."

Red laughed. "That makes 54 imaginary pike you've caught this week. Beats my record for sure."

Sitting on the edge of the wooden planking, Tom dangled his feet above the water. "I'm bored," he said.

Red finished hammering a nail. "What did you say?"

"I'm bored."

"Want a game of checkers? I'm finished work now."

"No, thanks. You always win."

Climbing down the stepladder, Red sat beside Tom. "I get bored too, kiddo, but that's the way it goes."

Tom looked up at the man. "How come you're a criminal?"

Red shrugged. "I don't know."

"But there must be some reason," Tom insisted.

"Yeah, well, I guess it's for the excitement. Like on the train when you appeared and messed up all the plans. It was exciting to get away without being caught."

"But what if something had gone wrong? What if the conductor had started a fight, and you'd had to shoot him?"

Red was silent, looking down into the water that murmured around the boathouse supports.

"Have you ever killed anyone?"

Red smiled. "Sure have, kiddo."

Tom stared at the man, not sure if he was telling the truth. "I don't believe it," he said finally.

"There's a place in Saskatchewan called Moose Jaw," Red replied in a calm voice. "Three years ago,

I held up a bank in Moose Jaw. As I came out the door, a police car stopped and a Mountie got out with a gun in her hand. I shot her right between the eyes."

Tom felt sick. He tried to look away from Red's face, but he couldn't.

"You see, kiddo, it's like a game. You kids play cops and robbers, right? Some of us just keep playing the game when we grow up. Your father decided to be a cop, and I decided to be a robber. It's still fun, just like being a kid."

"But we don't kill each other."

Red shrugged. "That's the way it goes. The Mountie was going to shoot me, so I plugged her first."

"But maybe she had kids!"

"So what? Nobody asked her to be a cop. Getting shot is part of the game."

Tom was silent. Now he realized what lay behind Red's easy smile.

He winked at Tom. "How about some checkers? I'll give you a two-man advantage."

"No, thanks," Tom muttered, looking down at the water.

"Don't be upset, kiddo. Life is tough. Now, come on, let's play some checkers."

"No," Tom said. "I don't like you anymore."

Red stared at him. Slowly, his face turned crimson. "Why? I like you, you're a nice kid. We've played checkers, and everything. I taught you to fish—it's not my fault you didn't catch anything. Why don't you like me?"

Tears rose in Tom's eyes. "You kill people! That's the most horrible thing I can imagine."

"Oh, so that's it." For a moment Red was silent. Then he shook his head, eyes sad. "You're lucky to be eleven years old. You wanna know why? Because you've still got a clean future ahead of you, anything's possible, you haven't made any major mistakes. If I could be young again, I'd do it differently." He waved toward the door. "Go on, beat it. I'm feeling tired."

The bright sunshine outside stung Tom's eyes, making tears run down his cheeks. He ran to the trail and followed it to the big rock, wishing he had never asked Red about being a criminal. Climbing up on the rock, Tom looked at Red's fishing rod lying in the sunshine. Impulsively, he picked it up and threw it into the lake, watching as the rod bubbled down through the water and disappeared.

He sat on the rock until night, going over and over the conversation in the boathouse. He listened for the sound of feet in the woods, hoping that Red would come and say that he was joking, but he had seen the man's eyes when he told Tom about killing the Mountie, and Tom knew the story was true.

At last, feeling tired and hungry, Tom went back to the cabin. The kerosene lamp was burning, throwing warm yellow light on the wooden walls and making the cabin feel comfortable.

B.X., as usual, was carving old sticks with his hunting knife. "Look who it is," he said, his voice sour.

"Hiya, kiddo." Red got up from his chair and went over to the wood stove. "Feel like some grub?"

Tom looked at the man's smiling face. How could he be so cheerful when he was a murderer?

"Ham and eggs and fried potatoes," Red said, "followed by coffee and doughnuts. What do you say, kiddo?"

"Okay, I guess," Tom said quietly. He went to the table and sat down. Butter sizzled in the frying pan, and the door of the stove banged as Red opened it to throw in more wood. Lowering his eyes, Tom slowly ran a finger back and forth on the table. He didn't want to eat but, when Red brought the food, he forced himself to have it all. He wasn't about to anger a killer.

* * *

The next morning, Tom woke up early. He lay in his sleeping bag, feeling sad, then put on his clothes and went outside.

The smell of the early morning air cheered him. Crossing the clearing, he started along the trail, thinking he might get lucky today and catch a pike. When he remembered the fishing rod was at the bottom of the lake, he stopped walking. His unhappiness felt like a lump of rock in his stomach.

He had to get off the island! What about the bottle? Tom started toward the south end of the island, hoping for some sign that help was on its way.

He came out of the woods and stopped. The lake was magnificent, with a soft white mist floating above its surface. The sun was low in the sky, burning huge and red behind the mist, while somewhere in the distance a bird was calling. Tom walked down to the shore. As he stood on the rocky beach, he saw a bottle rolling gently back and forth between tiny waves at the edge of the water.

The cork came loose with a *pfffft*, revealing a piece of paper inside. It was damp, and the ink had smudged, but he was able to read that Tom Austen was a prisoner on the small island with cabin and boathouse.

In sudden anger, Tom flung the bottle out over the lake. It smacked into the water, ruining the calm of the morning. Now Tom knew he was really trapped, alone on the island with two men, one of them a killer and the other probably worse. He decided to swim for it, then realized that was crazy. The lake was too wide, the water colder than cold.

What, then?

There was one possibility. Earlier, it had seemed a dirty trick to play on Red, but now Tom didn't care. He walked back and forth on the beach, thinking about the plan. It was taking a chance, but he had to get off the island.

Tom returned to the cabin. He opened the door cautiously, hoping the two men were still asleep in their bunk beds. He listened for their deep breathing, then tiptoed around collecting the kerosene lamp, matches, and a can with extra kerosene.

Tom followed the trail to the big rock, where the island was narrowest. Pouring some kerosene on the underbrush, he began to make a trail of fuel. Soon the island was cut in half by the smelly kerosene.

Tom looked toward the distant shore, where a big cabin cruiser lay at anchor. There was no sign that anyone was awake on the boat, but Tom couldn't wait. Lighting a match, he tossed it into the kerosene. There was a *poof!* and the flames shot across the fuel, eating into the dead wood of the underbrush.

Tom jumped back, startled by the fury he had released. The fire was everywhere at once, burning the kerosene by the big rock and rushing along the line of fuel that divided the island. The burning wood crackled, and hot flames jumped from branch to branch among the low bushes, reaching up to the bark on the big trees.

The heat made Tom sweat. He wished he could put the fire back inside the match. Climbing quickly onto the big rock, he looked at the white and black smoke twisting thickly into the air.

Nobody had appeared on the cabin cruiser. Idiots! The fire was roaring among the high branches of the trees. How could anything spread so quickly? The island was already cut in half and now the flames were eating in two directions, toward the south, and toward the north, where the cabin waited.

"Red," Tom shouted. "Red and B.X., watch out!"

But his words were carried away among the clouds of smoke. Tom tried again, screaming his warning, but he knew it was hopeless. The heat was unbearable—he jumped from the rock and staggered onto the rocky beach with sweat dripping from his face.

Across the lake, a speedboat was rushing toward him.

Tom wiped the sweat out of his eyes and looked again, sure he had made a mistake. But the boat was still coming fast. Waving his arms, he waded into the lake until it was up to his waist. He looked at the fire crackling through the trees, then turned to wave again. A man in the boat waved back, as the engine noise grew above the roaring of the flames.

"Help," Tom shouted, wading deeper. The waves glowed orange, reflecting the inferno above. The boat slowed as it approached. Two men were inside, one still wearing his pyjamas. As he helped Tom into the speedboat, it veered sharply away from the fire.

"Two men are on the island," Tom cried. "Around the other side, at the cabin. Hurry!"

The man at the wheel opened up the power. He glanced back at Tom. "What happened? What caused the fire?"

"I did," Tom said. "Those guys are criminals—they kidnapped me and Dianne Dorchester."

The man looked amazed. "You're one of the kidnapped kids? You mean, we're going to be heroes?"

"Sure," Tom replied, "but first you've got to capture Red and B.X. They've got a gun."

The men looked at each other.

"It's true," Tom exclaimed. "They've kept me prisoner on that island."

The man in the pyjamas looked at Tom. "You sure about that gun?"

"Yes."

"Okay."

He moved to the bow. Tom felt the wind on his face as the boat skimmed forward across the water; he looked at the terrible fire he had caused, then put his head down. At least he was safe.

"Are those the guys, sonny?"

Red and B.X. were on the tiny pier in front of the cabin, waving their arms and shouting. Tom wondered why they hadn't escaped, then saw the smoking ruins of the boathouse.

When they were close enough to see the fear on the faces of Red and B.X., the man slowed the boat.

"Help," Red yelled. "Come on, help us!"

"Yeah, help," B.X. called, staring fearfully at the flames that jumped toward the pier where he stood with Red.

The man at the steering wheel cupped his hands around his mouth. "Throw us your gun!"

"What gun?" Red held up his empty hands. "Come on, save us!"

"Throw your gun to us," the man repeated.

Flames shone on B.X.'s sweaty face as he said something to Red and pointed at the fire. Red shook his head.

"All right, boys," the man at the wheel shouted, revving the engine. "You can stay and fry!"

"Stop!" B.X. grabbed Red's shirt with both hands. For a second, it looked as if he was going to throw the bigger man into the lake, but then Red knocked B.X.'s hands away and turned toward the speedboat.

"Okay," he shouted, "you win."

There was a pause in which Red stared at Tom, and then he reached inside his shirt to the shoulder holster. The black revolver appeared in his hand and sailed through the air, dropping with a clunk into the bottom of the boat. The man in pyjamas picked it up.

The boat moved in quickly to get Red and B.X. "No tricks now," the man warned, covering Red and B.X. with the gun as they climbed into the boat, "or we'll throw you both overboard."

Red laughed. "Sure thing, Mr. Pyjamas." Turning, he winked at Tom. "Well, kiddo, I take off my hat to you. When it comes to cops and robbers, you're a better player than me."

Tom looked up at the man's blue eyes, but he couldn't smile.

10

Although Red and B.X. were soon under arrest, the
case was not closed. The man in the ski mask remained
at large, Dianne was still missing, and the police had
been unable to locate the mysterious kidnapper known
only as O.L.

The city's two rivers had risen higher and higher,
swollen by heavy rains and runoff water from winter
snows. Now they were close to flooding, despite the
hundreds of sandbags that had been piled on top of the
dikes along the riverbanks. Those areas of Winnipeg
threatened with flooding had been evacuated. No one
was supposed to be there, but Tom had decided he
couldn't miss the excitement.

Heavy rain soaked him as he walked along a street of
empty houses before turning onto a main road that ran

straight to the Assiniboine. At the end of the street was the strange and thrilling sight of a bridge almost covered by the raging waters of the river; sandbags had been heaped across the road, cutting off the flooded bridge.

A terrible grinding sound filled the air. The metal girders of the bridge were heaving under the pressure of the water. If the bridge collapsed it might tear a hole in the dike, flooding everything.

The evacuated neighborhood was an eerie sight. Rain-soaked plywood covered the windows of stores; houses and apartment buildings were entirely dark. The streets were empty of cars, empty of people.

Headlights shone in the distance. Tom crouched behind a garbage can, watching a car approach through the pounding rain. It stopped in front of an old apartment building, and Mr. Stones stepped out.

The teacher walked quickly to the building, carrying a pizza container. Going inside, he was swallowed by the gloom.

More headlights shone in the distance: a police car, moving fast. It swerved to a stop by the curb, then Officer Larson leapt out and ran swiftly inside.

What was going on?

Tom hurried through the cold rain to the building. The door was unlocked; he stepped into a lobby containing some old furniture and a row of mail-boxes on the wall. There was one elevator, but it failed to respond when Tom pressed the button. Pushing open a door, he stepped cautiously into a narrow hallway. Stairs led up.

Tom climbed slowly, his hand on a cold railing. He heard nothing except the beating of rain against the building and the distant grinding of the bridge under the river's pressure.

Then, Tom heard voices.

Creeping higher, Tom cautiously stepped into a dark hallway. Faint light showed under the door of an apartment. He moved closer, hardly daring to breathe. Now he clearly heard the voices of Officer Larson and Mr. Stones.

"Where *is* he?" Mr. Stones said. His voice was ragged, hoarse, horrible. "He's late!"

"Calm down," Officer Larson replied. He sounded grumpier than usual. "In a few more minutes we'll be rich. But don't forget, there's an equal share for Red and B.X."

"I don't want your money," Mr. Stones cried. "I want my sanity! I want to be free of your terrible threats to my family. I want Dianne to go home again. I want my life to be back to normal!"

"That will never happen," said Officer Larson. "You'd better escape into hiding, then change your identity. That's what I plan to do."

"I was blackmailed into helping your scheme! My family was threatened."

"Quit bleating. I've heard it all before."

"Why have you done this? *Why*?"

"For money, what else? I don't make enough as a cop."

"Rubbish!"

"It was a lucky break when my investigation of the kidnapping led me to Red. I demanded to be included in his conspiracy, or I'd bust him. This will make me rich forever."

Tom was desperately scribbling in his notebook. Somehow he must get help, fast. He began moving away from the door, and then suddenly stopped.

Someone was climbing the staircase.

* * *

Tom's eyes darted back and forth in search of hiding. Nothing. He crouched against the wall, listening fearfully to the footsteps on the creaking stairs. A man appeared, wearing an expensive hat and overcoat.

Mr. Dorchester.

Tom was so thrilled to see Dianne's father that he jumped up from hiding, a big smile on his face. But this startled Mr. Dorchester, who yelled in shock.

Immediately the apartment door swung open, revealing the orange glow of candlelight. Officer Larson stood in the doorway, gun in hand.

"Tom Austen—I might have known. Get in here, you little meddler. Dorchester, bring that ransom into the apartment. Move it!"

With a heavy heart, Tom stepped into the apartment. Through a window, he could see the bridge outside swaying back and forth, gripped by the powerful water surging past. Mr. Stones sat on a frayed sofa, tears streaming down his face. Yellow candlelight shone on Dianne, who stood at the kitchen counter with pizza in her hand and a look of utter astonishment on her face.

"Tom," she cried, running to him with open arms. As they hugged she saw her father, and rushed to hold him. Her skin was pale and there were dark smudges under her eyes.

Tom looked at his teacher. "Why'd you do it, sir?"

"They threatened to hurt my family, Tom. Someone Dianne trusted was needed to drive the kidnap van. Red and B.X. were hiding in the back. They put Dianne out with a needle while I drove to this apartment they'd rented."

"Didn't anyone see her being brought in?"

"She was in a wheelchair, wearing a grey wig and a shawl. She looked like someone's grandmother, sound asleep in her chair." He turned to Dianne. "Please forgive me."

She hugged him. "You had no choice, Mr. Stones. Thanks for bringing me pizza."

Mr. Dorchester handed an attaché case to Officer Larson. "Here's your money. It's all there, in cash. Count it if you must, but I'm a man of my word."

Tom walked into the kitchen. "Okay to have some pizza?" he asked Officer Larson.

"I guess so." He checked the contents of the attaché case, then closed it. "Tomorrow I'll be on a tropical beach, enjoying my sudden retirement from the police force. I hated saluting people like Tom's conceited father."

Tom came out of the kitchen, eating pizza. In his hand was a candle. Walking toward Officer Larson, he said, "Want a bite? This tastes great!"

Officer Larson pointed his revolver at Tom. "Don't try anything."

Tom thrust the pizza at Officer Larson. As the man tried to push it away, Tom tilted the candle. Hot wax fell on Officer Larson's hand. Shouting in pain, he dropped the gun.

"Get it, sir," Tom yelled, kicking the revolver toward Mr. Stones.

Officer Larson grabbed the attaché case, broke for the door and disappeared down the stairs. "So long, suckers," he yelled. At the same moment, the building shook as the bridge outside collapsed. Ugly brown water surged through a hole in the dike and rolled down the street toward them.

"Bring the gun," Tom cried to Mr. Stones.

The wood of the old building groaned as it was struck by the river. Reaching the stairs, Tom saw water gushing and roaring below. Officer Larson, clutching the attaché case, stood watching the flood that blocked his escape.

With Mr. Stones pointing his own revolver at him, the disgraced officer slowly climbed the stairs and handed the attaché case to Dianne's father.

"I surrender," Officer Larson said bleakly. "I was a fool."

Tom looked out the window. "The flood's covered your cars! But I see police out in boats—let's signal for help."

Mr. Dorchester hugged Dianne again. "I'm so glad you're safe, sweetheart. Your mother will be thrilled. We've missed you so much."

"Wasn't Tom splendid, saving us all from being shot?" Dianne smiled at him. "Thank you," she said quietly. "You were wonderful."

11

As the flood waters receded, the safe return of Dianne
Dorchester provided citizens with welcome news. The
front page of the newspaper featured a huge picture of
Tom, grinning under a headline that said: HERO OF
THE YEAR!

Dianne was recovering in hospital from her ordeal.
When Tom arrived for his first visit with her, the
room was jammed with people. Reporters from the
media were there, along with doctors and nurses, Dianne's parents, even patients from other wards of the
hospital. As Tom entered the room, he felt all their
eyes staring, waiting to hear what he and Dianne
would say. So they said nothing and just smiled at
each other, knowing they could talk when the world
had gone away.

The newspaper photographer asked Tom to put his arm around Dianne and give her a smile. The next day, the picture was on the front page of the newspaper with a story saying that Dianne would soon be out of hospital. A few days later, Tom was surprised to receive in the mail an envelope marked "Tom Austen, c/o City Police, Winnipeg, Manitoba." A Montreal woman enclosed a picture of Tom and Dianne clipped from *Le Devoir* newspaper, and a letter saying what a wonderful boy Tom must be. A girl wrote from New Orleans to say she wanted to marry Tom as soon as possible.

Each night after dinner, the family filled their scrapbook with newspaper clippings and Tom's fan mail. "This is getting ridiculous," Liz grumbled as she labored over a huge newspaper headline from Scotland. "My brother's not *this* big a hero." She looked at him. "I could do detective work. I bet it's easy."

Tom laughed. "It requires a redhead's superior brainpower."

Liz's dark eyes studied him. "Those are challenging words, dear brother. I think I'll start looking for clients."

* * *

Before life returned to normal at Queenston School, there was a special event. Late in May, Tom and the others decorated their classroom with banners reading *Welcome to Kids' Day, Part Two!!* and *Welcome Back, Dianne*.

It was great to see Dianne back in the classroom, talking happily to Mr. Stones. The teacher had not been charged with kidnapping because of Red's threats against his family. The Dorchester family had urged the authorities to let Mr. Stones continue his work at Queenston School, and the teacher had returned to his classroom.

The second celebration of Kids' Day went well, with large quantities of ice cream and lemonade quickly evaporating. Pete Tyler was there and spent some time talking to Tom. "I've never liked having my picture taken," he explained, "because of my criminal past. Cameras have depressed me ever since I had mug shots taken at the police station when I was arrested."

"Were you ever a kidnapper?" Tom asked. "I thought maybe you were the man in the ski mask."

Pete shook his head. "When I was young, I stole cars for cheap thrills. Then I ended up behind bars. A criminal record makes things tough—I'm lucky to have this job. Mr. Dorchester turned me down for work at his estate, which really upset me, but that's life, I guess."

After talking to everyone else, Tom got a chance to speak to Mr. Stones.

"I should have figured out you were feeding Dianne, sir. In class you had receipts from *Pizza Perfect* but pizza gives you heartburn. The food must have been for someone else, and we all know Dianne loves pizza." Tom smiled. "You made another mistake, sir. Remember in the principal's office, when I first described Dianne being kidnapped? I didn't say the van was brown, but afterwards in the classroom you mentioned its color. As Red would say, you're not very good at the game of cops and robbers."

"It's not a game, Tom, I've learned that. I'm just glad everyone's safe."

Next, Tom talked to Dietmar Oban. "I've got the

poems I promised you. They're excellent, real heart-breakers. I should charge you money."

"Forget it, Austen." Dietmar snatched the poems from his hand. "Jumping from the catwalk at that warehouse was the worst experience of my life. I deserve these poems."

Dietmar crossed the room to Elizabeth Whitman, who stood by herself near the windows, sipping lemonade. Sunlight glowed in her dark hair as she read the poems. Tom wished he'd given them to her himself but it was too late now.

Mr. Nicholson came into the classroom and called Tom forward. "I'm pleased to announce you're the new captain of the school patrol." As everyone applauded, he presented Tom with a patrol belt. "I predict a brilliant future for you as a detective. Perhaps one day you'll write about your adventures."

"If I do," Tom grinned, "I'll call this one the Case of the Golden Boy."

When the principal was gone, Dianne came over to Tom. Up close, her eyes were very blue. "Congratulations, Tom. I never told you before, but you look handsome in your patrol belt."

He blushed. "Really?"

"Yes." Dianne smiled. "I'm looking forward to passing your corner after school today. Maybe you could read me one of your poems."

She brushed his cheek with a kiss. "You're my hero, Tom."

It was the best moment of his life—so far.